T0279194

The Art of Us

The Art of Us

Julie Wright

SHADOW
MOUNTAIN
PUBLISHING

This is a work of fiction. Characters and events in this book are products of the author's imagination or are represented fictitiously.

Visit us at shadowmountain.com

Library of Congress Cataloging-in-Publication Data
(CIP data on file)

ISBN 978-1-63993-325-9

Printed in the United States of America
Publishers Printing

10   9   8   7   6   5   4   3   2   1

To Cindy, Ginger, Julie, and Lynn
In alphabetical order.

For the houses we toilet papered,
the statue we decorated,
the late-night laughs,
and the later-night deep discussions
where we tried to puzzle out
our places in the universe.

Thank you
for making high school not just bearable,
but something worth looking back on,
and for proving that the best friendships
really can last forever.

CHAPTER ONE
Ireland

Being a homeless teenager wasn't the worst thing that could happen.

"Totally one of your top-ten lies," Ireland Raine muttered to herself. She scowled into the dark and tugged the sleeping bag she'd bought from the thrift store more tightly around her. The cold of the public bathroom seeped from the poorly painted cement floor beneath her and the cinder block walls around her and into her bones. She chuckled darkly. So many metaphors applied to her situation. The one that made her laugh was "my life is in the toilet." It shouldn't have been funny, but . . .

The bathroom floor was big enough for her to stretch out on while lying down—which was good because even though at five feet, eight and a half inches she wasn't exactly the tallest human alive, she wasn't the shortest either. And she had never been able to sleep while curled up. The bathroom allowed her that space even if it didn't offer much more. It sat at the edge of the woods located on the outskirts of the town of Arcata, California. The bathroom was practically forgotten since it wasn't on the primary trails. Ireland had been sleeping there for the past several weeks,

and, so far, no one had bothered trying to use it—at least, she
didn't think so. So she kept going back, finding a routine in her
circumstances that were not exactly ideal but not as bad as she
had first thought.

Sure, the dirty walls and spiderwebs in the corners by the
small windows near the roofline were not fantastic. And, sure,
if the devil showed up with his horned head and fanged mouth
offering her a deal to trade her soul for a comfortable bed, a hot
meal, and a hotter bath, she'd consider it a bargain. "At least I'm
safe," she whispered to herself. Safe-ish, anyway.

Not everyone in the world could say that.

The first day after Ireland's dad left her had passed in a blind
panic. The opened letter on the counter next to the bowl of cold,
congealed ramen noodles gave her all the information she needed:
the landlord was done with her dad's excuses. A couple of guys
would be coming that night to remove them from the apartment. By force, if necessary. The landlord was the criminal sort
of greasy, weaselly guy who would consider busting out kneecaps
and breaking fingers "necessary" if anyone was still found within
the walls of the apartment when they showed up.

So her dad had done what he did best. He skipped town.

He just forgot to take Ireland with him this time. Her chest
tightened at the betrayal she felt when she thought about it too
long. *He'd left her.* Just left. Like it was nothing.

She knew he was gone for good because his stuff—meager
and insignificant as it all was—had also disappeared. Some of
her stuff had turned up missing too. She was sure he'd scavenged
through her belongings in the hope of finding a few bucks or
something valuable enough to sell.

Joke's on him, she thought for the millionth time. He hadn't
found her money before he'd left. She'd kept her extra cash in
a jar outside behind a rock that was almost invisible due to the

overgrown weeds. Experience had taught her that her dad couldn't be trusted around her money. He'd used it to buy cigarettes, alcohol, or both when she'd left enough lying around.

So what if he'd left? He hadn't gotten his hands on that last bit of cash. Her chest swelled with satisfaction.

Of course, there would be more satisfaction if she'd managed to squirrel away more in her jar.

Eighteen bucks and a handful of pennies that didn't even add up to a quarter.

Ireland had remembered the jar after the first wave of panic over her father leaving had passed and she was able to think rationally. Her current school was a good one. She was doing well, the teachers liked her, and her dad had done her the favor of applying for the free lunch program, so she was guaranteed one meal every weekday until she graduated in June. That was six months of food. Staying and finishing school would go a long way toward securing her independence. She would turn eighteen in a couple of months, so at least no one could put her in the system if her situation were discovered. Being a homeless legal adult was better than being a homeless child.

Lie?

Maybe.

Ireland had found the sleeping bag at Goodwill for six dollars and forty-seven cents. When she'd first seen it, the slightly suspicious stains, the zipper that didn't work so it could never be unzipped, and the fact that it would take a third of her available finances made her turn up her nose at it.

She went back for it the next day, praying it was still available and almost weeping at the many degrees of gorgeousness that it still sat unclaimed on the shelf. A night of shivering without it and waking up so cold it took half of the next day to thaw out had also drastically thawed her frosty opinion. Of course, that had also been before she'd found her outhouse apartment, complete with electricity, running water—albeit cold—and a flushing toilet.

Ireland looked around in the dark and counted her lucky stars. At least she had shelter when it rained or got too windy—which, since it was January, was half of the time. At least she had a locking door.

As if to remind her that the lock wasn't exactly substantial, something scratched around outside the bathroom door. She gritted her teeth and squeezed her eyes shut.

There is no such thing as vampires, she thought to herself. There was no werewolf wanting to chew on her jugular. There was no public-restroom poltergeist rattling chains of eternal toilet torment.

And, okay, there *were* serial killers and rapists and people who were the worst, but she'd decided not to think about them either. She was as safe from those societal monsters in this locked bathroom as she'd been in her locked apartment. So what if this door led directly to the outdoors? Didn't all houses have doors that led to the outside? This was no different.

Total lie. Maybe not on the top-ten list, but it was up there. Top twenty. Maybe twenty-five.

The scratching sound, which was probably just a raccoon, finally stopped. Ireland let out the shaky breath she'd been holding despite telling herself there was nothing to be afraid of.

"I need a job," she whispered to the dark. She whispered in case there was someone outside her door. Just in case a vampire, werewolf, specter, or serial killer decided to answer that they were hiring.

She needed a job that would allow her to save enough money to live somewhere near the college campus, where rentals were slightly cheaper and her being on her own would be just like everyone else instead of something strange.

She would rise above this situation. Her last name, Raine, was French for "queen." At least, that's what her dad had always told her. Whenever she felt like she was drowning in her situation, she reminded herself that she would rise above it, the way a queen was meant to do.

Of course, her dad was probably lying about what their name meant. And then there was the chance that Raine wasn't really her last name but something he'd made up one day and then decided to make official by changing the paperwork. He was the kind of guy who changed the world around him to suit whatever mood he was in.

She hated that about him.

Ireland finally closed her eyes and imagined summertime flowers and sunshine soaking into her skin, all while playing the tune of one of her favorite songs, "Daylight from a Single Candle," in her head. The indie band Cosmic Cloak had a soulful poignancy that tended to calm her. She finally relaxed enough that she was able to sleep.

The sound of the melodic birdcall alarm from her phone made her pop an eye open to see that the new day had indeed come.

"See?" she asked herself. No werewolves after all. It was always easier to believe herself in the daylight. Ireland had no desire to leave the warmth of the sleeping bag to face the icy air, but the birdcall alarm was still going, reminding her that she had to get to school. She'd specifically chosen the nature sound to keep any nearby hiker or jogger from hearing a typical phone alarm and getting curious. She was grateful for the phone and the link it gave her to the outside world, but her father had only covered service to the end of the month. She'd have to figure out how to pay for an extension on that service or do without. Frowning at that thought, she turned off her alarm and forced herself up.

If getting out of the sleeping bag could be considered a mouse-sized effort, the task of washing her face could be considered an elephant-sized one.

Ireland braced herself against the ice-cold water from the sink and rinsed the sleep from her eyes and the grime of the floor from her face and hair. She huffed out several breaths, as if she could expel the shock of the cold water, before she pulled out a tooth-brush and looked at her warped image in the metal front of the empty towel dispenser. "You look seriously sick," she told herself. Not sick as in cool or awesome, but sick as in "grab your plague mask." Next to her dark hair, her fair skin always looked pale, but it seemed worse lately. "Get a pillow," she added out loud to her reflection, since her normally clear blue eyes were bloodshot due to the lack of quality sleep. She frowned at the military-grade duffel bag her father had deemed too worthless to take with him. She would have to find a really *small* pillow, or it wouldn't fit in the pack without popping out of the zippered confines.

Ireland sighed and spit in the sink. Small it would be, then.

She looked in the mirror again and noticed a stain in the shirt she wore—an accident from eating lunch yesterday. There wasn't anything she could do about it since her other few shirts smelled like death due to her lack of deodorant, and her frigid sink-baths made it hard to properly clean herself. Maybe no one would no-tice the stain, in the same way she hoped they wouldn't notice the fact that she wore the same clothes over and over. But they would for sure notice her if they could smell her.

She needed a shower. A real shower with hot water. It seemed she couldn't get the acrid smell of body and street and bathroom out of her clothes and off of her person. "You stink," she told the mirror.

With a grunt of irritation, Ireland pulled her shirt down to the sink and began scratching at it under the water. A few tears leaked from her eyes as a few curse words leaked from her mouth. She finished and glared back at the mirror, daring it to give her a bad review. Better? Maybe. The shirt would dry on her walk to school. She would use the last bit of bar soap she had to wash her clothes in the sink as soon as school was out. Hopefully, it would all dry during the night. If she had to pack it away wet in the duffel, it would mildew, which would be a different problem.

After twisting her hair into a sloppy bun that she tied off with a ponytail holder, she turned to gather her things and carefully pack them away.

Her phone chirped again. Ireland cursed under her breath. She had to hurry, or she wouldn't make it to school on time. She lugged the duffel to a tree behind the bathroom, looped the rope she'd previously set up through the straps, and tugged until the duffel disappeared into the foliage. She tied off the rope, picked up her backpack with the things she needed for school, and hurried to the animal trail that led into town.

When she finally approached the front doors of the school, she had to weave through pockets of students gathered to socialize. Some wore jackets, but several sported cargo shorts and T-shirts with beanies as their only protection against the cold.

I do not understand you people.

Ireland hoped she hadn't said that out loud but really didn't know if she had or hadn't. Not that it mattered in relation to the truthfulness of her thought. The fashion trend of a beanie and shorts made no sense to her when she was doing everything she could to stay warm. She tugged on the door handle and heaved a sigh of relief when the warm air from the heated building hit her skin.

Better. So much better.

Ireland threaded through the student body mosaic of her school as she made her way to her first class.

"Hey, girl!" An overly ecstatic female voice called out, but Ireland didn't bother to turn and see who it was. No one would be talking to her. And she wasn't stupid enough to feel sad or slighted by that fact. She didn't try to strike up conversations with anyone, so why would they try with her?

It wasn't that she didn't want friends, but with a dad who could decide to make a hasty exit at any moment due to not paying rent or due to people hunting him down to try to collect money he owed them for one weird venture or another, she didn't think attachments were a good idea. They never had been in the past.

If she'd known her dad was going to ditch her, she would have tried for friendships. Maybe a friend would have let her crash on their couch until she could figure something out.

"Never too late to start," she muttered to herself. Maybe if she made friends now, she could still get a couch-crash invite.

She smiled as she passed a group of girls in the hall. One of them, the tall, thin Black girl with red-rimmed glasses, smiled back. Sure, it wasn't like the girl had stopped to talk or anything, but a smile felt promising—promising enough to empower her to try speaking to someone else. Someone in particular. Someone she had wanted to talk to ever since he'd transferred to their school five months ago: Kal Ellis.

He'd moved from Arizona. He'd said as much during an oral report he'd given on his personal history. The personal history report she'd given had been total fiction. She had no idea about her family history, and her personal story was just messed up. Not like Kal's at all.

Ireland had liked listening to his story. He came from a good family and had moved to California to be closer to his grandpa.

He was a nice-looking guy. She wasn't such a total mutant that she didn't notice things like that. He kept his dark hair short but long enough to style it with hair product of some sort. He had deep dimples when he smiled. And his olive complexion made him look the part of a California surfer.

But it wasn't because of his looks, sigh worthy as they were, that she liked him. He was the quiet, studious type who kept his serious brown eyes focused up front where the teacher was lecturing rather than on the leggy cheerleader in the seat on the other side of him. His above-average intelligence meant he was the one who screwed up the curve for everyone else in class. He also had an artistic side to him that appealed to her.

And he was nice to people. Genuinely nice. She had once watched as he stopped in a crowded hallway to help a kid, who had tripped and fallen, to pick up the myriad fantasy paperback books, papers, and cell phone fragments (the kid's phone had splintered into a few pieces). Helping a stranger pick up scattered debris in the hall was the classic high school good deed. Classic even though she'd never seen it happen in real life before that moment.

She liked that Kal Ellis didn't mind being classic.

"Hi," Ireland said to him as soon as she arrived in her first-hour class—history. He seemed startled that she addressed him.

"Hi?"

She tried at a grin, knowing her social skills to be less than polished but determined to forge ahead regardless. "Is that a question?"

He gave her a sort of smirk that proved he had a good sense of humor. "Probably. You just distorted my whole belief system regarding you."

"Wow. A belief system, huh? I don't know that I deserve a whole belief system."

"It's nothing complicated. You've been sitting next to me since September. That's what? Five months? I just wasn't aware you had a voice box until right now."

Direct hit. Ten points for honesty. "Yeah. Sorry. I'm not talkative."

Kal shifted in his seat so he was facing her more. "You aren't talkative in the way a tree isn't talkative."

Oof. He was not pulling his punches. "Maybe you just hang out with the wrong sorts of trees?"

He laughed at that, a sound that vibrated deeply and melodically. Could a guy's voice be called melodic? Ireland decided that it could. Why not? Kal lifted a shoulder in a half shrug. "You'll have to introduce me to some of your trees sometime. I'll bring my phone because talking trees? Might be worth something. It's Ireland, right?"

"Right. And you're Kal?" She said it like she was asking, but she wasn't. She'd thought about talking to him since the first day he chose the seat next to her and smiled at her. She hadn't smiled back at the time, which now seemed like a shrew kind of move. But she hadn't thought she'd be in school with him for as long as she had been. Once she'd started off being a little prickly, she hadn't been sure how to do a course correction even as the weeks of sitting next to him turned to actual months. Now she knew she was in the school until the summer break. She couldn't keep up her solitude; she needed to talk to someone besides the spiders in her bathroom. And she *wanted* the someone to be Kal.

There are two types of new students in high school: the ones who gain immediate popularity because they ooze charismatic vibes and the ones who are completely overlooked. She definitely belonged in the camp of the uncelebrated, while Kal basked in the glow of effortless acceptance. A guy like him could have easily let that acceptance go to his head, but Kal didn't. Again, he was a genuinely nice guy.

"So why now?" he asked.

She shrugged, her fingernails nervously scraping up the side of the raised letters on the Bic pen she'd found on the ground near her gym locker. It was a glide gel type that wrote smoothly and made even hurried, sloppy handwriting look a little tidier. "I wasn't sure if I'd be sticking around long enough to get to know people."

The excuse sounded weak, but sometimes the truth *was* weak.

His smirk widened into a grin. "It took you half the year to decide you were sticking around?"

"Yep."

"Huh. Well, good. Your art rocks."

Her face warmed. He'd seen her art?

Though she hadn't asked the question, he answered as if she had. "Whenever Mr. Nichols is droning, you sketch in your sketchbook. You've got some mad skills."

He'd noticed her sketching. The warmth that someone was paying attention to her trickled from her head and down her spine until she felt entirely filled with the sensation. She'd always assumed she was basically invisible, but he'd seen her. "Mr. Wasden gave me the sketchbook. We turn it in every few weeks for a grade."

Kal laughed. "Wasden's all right. But don't shred what you do by saying you only do it for a grade. That kind of skill comes from doing it more often than you'd need to for homework."

"Maybe," Ireland said and then decided that if he could be so forward, so could she. Because the truth was that she paid attention to his comings and goings in more than just the history class they shared. "I guess it's the same with you and music? Your band is really good."

Had she thought his smile was wide enough to be a grin before? Because now that smile split his face into two separate sections. And the dimples dug their way into the deepest regions of
his cheeks. "You've heard us play?"

"It's why I crave pizza on Friday nights." Was she flirting? She
thought that maybe she was and hoped she was doing it right.
And she wasn't even lying. She craved pizza even if she never actually *bought* any from the local pizza joint, Geppetto's, where they
played. Who had money for that sort of thing?

But she stopped in sometimes to hear them play. Since becoming homeless a few weeks prior, she'd gone into scavenger
mode. She remembered from her few times of going out to eat
that sometimes people left slices of untouched, uneaten food on
their tables. She figured pizza would be the easiest to grab-and-go
since the crust was like an edible plate and she didn't need silver-
ware. She'd scouted out a few pizza places and decided Geppetto's
was her best option because of its door locations and lighting.
She'd gone there three times to forage for food. If she went in
through the side door and made her way to their public restroom
and waited a while, she just looked like a regular customer returning to her table. She chose the tables in back because it was darker
there and around the corner from the main part of the restaurant.

She'd listen to Kal's band, then sneak a few slices before leaving the same way she'd come in. She knew she couldn't do that all
the time because if she became too familiar to the workers, they
might catch on to what she was doing. But on the nights she went
to bed hungry, she could close her eyes and daydream about what
it had been like to sleep on a full stomach.

Ireland hadn't eaten since yesterday afternoon. She had
three hours and twenty-two minutes left until lunch. Her eyes
must have glazed over as she imagined the food because Kal was

looking at her as if he expected her to respond to something he had said.

"Sorry," she said. "I must have wandered off a little."

"Hazards of being an artist. I was wondering if you'd want to come listen tonight. It's Friday, after all. Maybe hang around until our break. Joe, the owner, gives us free pizza for playing. So you can get dinner out of the deal."

Did he know that she needed dinner? Had he seen her stealing slices of pizza from empty tables? But no. He couldn't have. She'd been careful. She instantly felt defensive. Her immediate reaction was to say she was busy. But as she opened her mouth to decline his invitation, she remembered that she was trying to make friends for the first time in a long time. It was hard to do that if she was rejecting the hand of friendship when it was offered. Since the weekend was coming up, she had no solid plans for getting food. Kal's generous offer filled more than the need for friends; it filled survival needs too. "Sounds great. Thanks."

He only had time to smile in response because Mr. Nichols had finally stood to start class. Mr. Nichols grinned at them all, making his beard hair look bristled as he shoved the sleeves of his sweater past his elbows. He puffed out his pale cheeks and shoved his glasses higher on the bridge of his nose. This stance meant he intended to lecture.

Ireland was self-conscious as she pulled out her sketchbook, knowing that Kal had been watching her draw. But she honestly had a hard time paying attention and focusing unless she was sketching at the same time. She didn't know how else to learn.

Her art teacher, Mr. Wasden, had given her the book at the beginning of the year. He said everyone, artist or not, needed a sketchbook, a place where they could jot down their ideas, their worries, their thoughts, things that made them laugh, things they were grateful for. He didn't care if the art students drew pictures or wrote words. He just wanted to see them fill the books with their own ideas.

She had to admit it had been pretty therapeutic, and it had taught her to focus in a way she'd never been able to do before. She was getting good grades for the first time ever.

She felt Kal's stare on her as she filled in the lines of the sketch she'd made of the bathroom she now lived in. Did he always stare like that?

What did he think of her sketch?

She sucked in a hard breath and quickly flipped to the next blank page where she began doodling a spiral design. She didn't want him to have clues about her circumstances. The longer the teacher went on and on and the more intently Kal stared, the more she worried.

Because there was a chance he *had* seen her stealing pizza. And there was a chance he understood her sketch of the bathroom was *really* a sketch of her new home. She suddenly regretted that today was the day she had decided to open up and make friends. She should have stayed silent and continued ghosting through the school.

Because now there was a chance Kal knew her secret, which was the absolute last thing she wanted.

CHAPTER TWO

Kal

Staring was rude. Especially when Ireland was trying to pay attention to Mr. Nichols as he pontificated on the highlights of World War II. But Kal couldn't help it. Ireland Raine just looked so much like his friend Brell. Not from the front so much. When he looked at her straight on, the differences were enough to spoil the illusion. But from the side?

They could be twins from the side. Their espresso-brown hair was the same. The slight, barely noticeable upturn of their noses was the same. The pale, oval-shaped face. The glacial blue eyes. He'd stared at her for the first several days after transferring schools and sitting next to her in the history class they had together.

He couldn't help it.

It was like seeing a ghost.

He'd expected her to turn to him and ask to borrow a pen or paper or some other random object that she'd forgotten because the thing about Brell was that she was never prepared. If they were going out in cooler weather, she would need to borrow a jacket. If they were going out when it was too sunny, she would need a hat or sunglasses or sunscreen.

Ireland never turned to him to ask for anything because she wasn't Brell.

Brell was gone.

He'd moved to California. The distance had been too much for her to deal with and their only contact had been the occasional likes, hearts, and smiley faces online.

She moved on to new friends. Friends who sucked the life out of everything they touched.

When he'd got the news that Brell had been in a shooting accident while she was out drinking with those new friends, he'd felt destroyed. He hadn't been there for her. And now she was gone. He could logically say it wasn't his fault. He hadn't chosen those friends for her. But even though he didn't believe in ghosts, he was pretty sure Brell was haunting him.

He sucked in a hard breath and tried to focus on what Mr. Nichols was saying.

Ireland was not Brell. He'd told himself that in the beginning when Ireland had rather pointedly ignored him, indicating she wasn't interested in getting to know him. So he'd moved on.

Except he apparently hadn't moved on because he'd noticed Ireland again a couple of weeks back. He'd seen her slip through the shadows of Geppetto's while he had been in the middle of a set. He'd seen her, thought it was Brell, and almost forgotten the lines to the cover he was singing.

She wasn't Brell. He had to remember that. It wasn't fair to impose his emotional baggage for one girl on the other. He'd forced himself to look away so he could finish the song. Once done, he looked back in time to see Ireland tucking a piece of pizza into her bag from off a table that hadn't yet been cleared by the busser.

He suddenly wasn't as worried about how she looked like a blast from the past. He was curious why she would need to steal someone else's abandoned food. He'd watched her slip out of the restaurant through the side door, and then he'd spent the rest of the night wondering what that had all been about.

Kal liked having a mystery to solve.

When he saw her again in school, he'd gone back to surveying her, trying to figure her out. He felt okay about the staring because he was pretty sure she didn't notice him at all.

Now that she was talking to him, he found he wanted her to keep talking. And he also figured she noticed the staring.

She had a look in her eyes he didn't really understand. Wariness. Fear. Worry. Anxiety. He knew the names of those emotions—had spent years working to perfect capturing them in ink and paint—but he didn't understand them on her. Ireland Raine was haunted. He just didn't know what was haunting her. Basic high school drama, like friends or no friends? Trying to figure out college? Maybe she had an actual ghost floating along behind her every step. Or maybe she was haunted by an old boyfriend like he was haunted by an old girlfriend? Memories of people were sometimes painful specters.

Brell had said she understood when his parents had moved him out of Phoenix, Arizona, to Arcata, California. She had held his hand when he told her that his grandma died. She'd made it seem like no big deal when he'd told her that his family was moving so they could help take care of his grandpa. His grandpa was becoming far frailer and struggling to do basic things for himself, and with Grandma gone, there was no one to help him. She had been the one who'd held Grandpa's life together in any organized kind of way.

Moving had made sense to Kal logically. But emotionally? Emotionally, he was wrecked. He had thought he and Brell could make a go of the long-distance thing. But, apparently, that wasn't going to happen. Brell dropped him and didn't look back. She'd gone off to a different life. And that life had killed her.

That loss cut into his heart.

Which meant he was haunted too. He knew he needed to move forward in his life, but moving forward was not the same thing as getting over it.

He hadn't gotten over anything.

But he was trying to move forward.

Moving forward was psychological first aid.

That's what his dad said, anyway.

His dad felt sympathy for his broken heart, but his mom was the one who felt the empathy. They encouraged him in his painting. They encouraged him to join the band, Shadow Dimension, when the band was looking for someone who could really sing. His parents had all but demanded he try out for the gig at Geppetto's when they were holding tryouts for Friday night entertainment, even if it only paid in pizza and a bit of pocket change for each band member.

His dad liked the way that particular extracurricular looked on a college application.

His mom liked that it fed his soul.

It didn't at first. No talent can make up for the terror of stage fright. When he first got up on the little stage at the side of the old-fashioned pizza parlor, his first instinct was to duck and hide. He was too out in the open, too visible. His vision narrowed and he almost fell off the stage and passed out. But he saw his mom looking panicked and his dad nodding his head and mouthing the first few words to the cover he was doing, and he was able to sing. The music took the edge off the fear and almost made him forget that he was in front of a crowd.

He sent the video clip his mom had taken of him onstage

with his new band to Brell. She didn't respond, and it felt like she'd stomped on his heart all over again. He even got mad at her. But then he got the news that she was gone. Gone because of one of her so-called new friends because they were young and drunk and stupid.

Could he have stopped it if he hadn't left Arizona? Could he have stopped it if he had called every day in the beginning after he'd moved? Maybe. Maybe not.

Since he'd first noticed Ireland Raine stealing remnants of other people's dinners, it had taken his mind off of everything in a way that even his music or art hadn't. She had given him a new focus, one that helped him to forget that the person he'd thought was *his* person didn't think he was worth even a text message.

He supposed that was why he invited Ireland to dinner. She clearly needed food for some reason, and it was within his power to feed her as much as she could handle eating—at least on Fridays.

Brell had loved pizza. She didn't care what toppings were on it. She didn't care if it had been left out all night or even if it smelled a little off. How many times had he warned her that she was going to die of food poisoning?

Ireland is not Brell.

And Brell didn't die from being poisoned.

I'm spiraling.

Kal needed to pull himself out of the whirlpool of his thoughts. He reminded himself several more times that Ireland was not Brell before class was over. He expected Ireland to talk to him after class. Maybe they'd walk out together, hang out in the halls for a minute. But she ditched fast, with nothing more than a strained smile and a nod.

Weird.

Or "oddball," as Brell would say.

Stop it.

He shook his head and went to his next class.

Art.

He was a little sad that he didn't have this class with Ireland. He really did like her style. She was good—really good. She deserved to be in the advanced art class. He couldn't figure out why someone with as much raw talent as she had was taking a beginners' course.

It didn't make sense.

"Hey, Wasden."

The art instructor looked up from where he had been tacking up blank white posters at the front of the room.

"What's up, Kal?" Mr. Wasden replied.

"Just living the dream, man." *Or living the nightmare. Over and over and over and over and over—stop.*

I'm spiraling.

Kal took a deep breath. Then he took a second one because the first hadn't done what it was supposed to. Then a third.

"You okay, kid?"

The third one worked. "Yeah. 'S all good. You're looking extra tanned today."

Wasden didn't really look tanned so much as burned. His skin had apparently taken a beating.

"Should've worn sunscreen," Wasden said. "Did some fishing with my daughters after school yesterday."

"It's still winter, man."

"With my girls, the sun is always shining. And, okay, though the sun was out, it was seriously cold, but no regrets. I'm stealing every minute I can before they grow up on me. You know what I mean?"

"Yeah. Gotta take moments while you've got 'em."

Mr. Wasden placed a hand on Kal's shoulder and gave a quick squeeze of solidarity before Kal made his way to his seat.

"Okay, class." Mr. Wasden clapped his hands together, and everyone stopped what they were doing to listen. "We're doing monster races today." He reached into a bowl of the large artist trophy he kept on a pedestal at the front of the room. "Mara Washington?" He glanced around the room until he made eye contact with Mara, who was twirling the end of one of her ebony box braids and staring out the window. "Come on up."

Mr. Wasden reached in again, his burned fingers crinkling the slips of paper together until they found one. "Kal Ellis." Mr. Wasden looked at Kal and flourished a hand toward the front. "You're up."

Once both he and Mara had placed themselves in front of one of the posters, Mr. Wasden handed them each a compressed charcoal stick and told them the rules of his game. "It's monster races. What that means is that you are all going to create a monster by shouting out characteristics. Mara and Kal here are going to sketch out what they hear you say. It's totally up to their interpretation. And don't limit yourselves to just physical characteristics. Talk about what these monsters are like on the inside. The things that go on inside our heads and souls affect us physically and can be drawn by a skilled artist. Everyone in this room is skilled enough to be capable of portraying internal characteristics. Okay!" He clapped his hands together again. "Let the races begin! Don't be shy. Start shouting out characteristics."

"Huge," someone yelled.

"Horns," someone else called.

"Fangs."

"Claws."

"Cruel."

Kal let the bit of charcoal in his hand glide over the surface of the poster.

"Growling."

"Hairy."

"Striped."

"Late for dinner." That one brought laughter from everyone.

"Tail."

"Scary and breathes fire."

At this, without thinking, Kal drew a gun in the claws of his creature. He stopped so abruptly, the charcoal in his hand dropped to the floor with a clatter.

Breathe.

He took a deep breath. Another one. A third. People were still calling out words that sounded fuzzy and far away. They weren't traumatized by what he'd drawn the way he had been. They didn't know his past. They weren't psychoanalyzing him, but simply playing the game.

Breathe.

He bent and picked up the charcoal.

I should go home, he thought even as he added a hunch to the shoulders of his monster and a menacing stare in the eyes.

"Scales."

"Spikes."

Kal stopped when Mr. Wasden called out, "Time! Take a step back, Mara and Kal, and let the class get a good view of your monsters."

Doing as he was told, Kal stepped back so the class could view the finished product.

His monster was definitely more frightening and monsterlike than Mara's. Hers could almost be called cute, like something that would be lurking in the woods of the book *Where the Wild Things Are*. Kal's was menacing—dark in a visceral way that could leave people with nightmares if they were the sort of people who had nightmares.

Kal was the sort of person who had nightmares.

He wasn't always, but that was before he'd started imagining Brell's final moments.

The class was applauding the two efforts. They were both good. Mara's was better, but Kal wasn't surprised by that. Mara was an excellent artist. He felt certain she'd be working for Disney, or at least giving Disney some competition, once she graduated college.

Mr. Wasden's voice brought Kal back to attention. "So let's consider the concept of ideas. It's my belief that ideas are all around us just waiting to be picked out of the air and put to good use. And just because one person pulls an idea out of the ether doesn't mean it's not still available to the next person who reaches for it.

"Ideas are not on a first-come, first-served basis. The most interesting thing isn't the idea, but the creator who puts the idea to use. We are all unique individuals with our own quirky viewpoints and interests. It makes the work we do and the lives we live unrepeated and unrepeatable. Mara and Kal were given the exact same material and information to work from and yet returned to us two wholly different results."

Mr. Wasden took the class through the style, tone, and voice of each piece. He didn't call attention to the gun in the monster's hand. Mr. Wasden then invited the class to participate in the discussion so they could talk about the things they noticed.

Charisma, who sat in front and was enrolled in an art school in Japan to learn anime after she graduated, said, "I like that Kal included the gun as his way of describing 'scary' and 'fire.' It is not at all what I was thinking when I said it." She pushed her red-rimmed glasses up higher on her nose as she squinted

thoughtfully at the images in front of her, and said, "I was thinking of a fire-breathing dragon, but that was definitely a different
way of illustrating it."

Kal tensed. He shouldn't have drawn that, shouldn't have
called attention to the monster of his nightmares. Mr. Wasden
only agreed with Charisma and moved on to the next comment
from Julianna, a blond who lived a few houses down from Kal.
She didn't get out much, so he only saw her in art class and at the
occasional art club meeting even though they lived so close to
each other. Julianna discussed the various levels of scary for different audiences. Kal's shoulders relaxed, and he managed to make it
through the rest of the class period without the internal chanting
telling him that he should go home.

As Kal gathered up his stuff at the end of class, Mr. Wasden
said, "Hey, Kal. Do you have a minute to talk?"

He tensed again because Wasden knew about Brell. Kal had
told him everything one evening when they'd been making flyers
for the school's art show, but even so, he might not be chill about
Kal's visual of a gun. He nodded and shuffled to Mr. Wasden's
desk.

"You okay?"

Kal shifted and gave another nod. "Sure."

"I get what happened there, but maybe let's leave firearms out
of our classroom art, huh?"

"Yeah. Sorry."

"It's okay. This time. Take a seat. Let's chat."

Kal sat in the beat-up, azure-blue armchair. The upholstery
could have used a makeover, but the chair had become the art
room's icon of chill, which meant no one would ever do anything
to change it.

"You know," Mr. Wasden said, "art is an excellent way to
work through all the stuff in our heads. Our worries, our hopes,

our fears, everything. I have a little daughter. She's four. And I often help my wife do her hair. At first, that was my least favorite thing to do for her because her hair was always so tangled in the morning. But my wife bought this detangler spray, and now I can brush through her hair without her crying and telling me how much she wishes Mommy would help her instead."

Wasden tapped his reddened fingers on the desk. "Art is a detangler for the knots that happen in our minds. I know this is probably kind of a crappy metaphor, but I'm an art teacher, not an English teacher. So there's that. Anyway, I know you've been dealing with some ridiculously hard things, and probably have enough going on to keep you busy without new things, but would you be willing to help me assemble a school-wide art project? I want something that unifies us, something that gives hope. I like your level of creativity. What are your thoughts on that?"

"Yeah, I could do that." Kal wasn't sure why he agreed. Maybe because he was sitting in the chill chair.

"Perfect! So come up with some ideas, something that can spread some positivity—a little detangler for everyone. I think we can all use that, don't you?"

"Yeah. Definitely." Stupid chill chair. Yet Kal liked the idea of unifying the students. Even without the chair, he would have said yes.

"Good. Then we agree. You have great ideas, and I think we have the potential to do some good in the school. By Monday, bring me at least three concepts for a school-wide project that anyone can participate in—not just the art students. Okay?"

Kal felt like a bobblehead with all the nodding he was doing. "Okay."

"Are you okay? Do you want to talk?"

Kal shook his head. "I'm fine. Actually doing better. Thanks." He really did feel like he was doing better, but that might have been the chill chair's influence as well.

"If you say so, but Kal? I'm here, you know. I know I just sat here doing all the talking, but if *you* ever need to talk or vent or even just sit in silence with someone else who won't judge, you can. Anytime."

"Right. Thanks, Wasden. I appreciate it."

"You bet. Also, I heard you were playing at Geppetto's. That's cool, man. I'll have to come in sometime and hear you. What instrument are you on?"

"Guitar and vocals. How 'bout you? You play?" Kal asked.

"Not unless you count Spotify."

Kal laughed and reluctantly relinquished his time in the chill chair as he stood. "Nice. I say it counts."

He then turned to leave at the same time Ireland was coming in for her class. "Hey!" He smiled wide as if letting her see all his teeth would prove to her that he was glad to see her. He would have rolled his eyes at himself but didn't want her thinking he was rolling his eyes at her.

They weren't exactly friends—not yet, anyway, but Ireland had a fragility to her that made him want to help her.

She looked from him to Mr. Wasden. "Hey." Her wary tone made Mr. Wasden look in her direction. The guy was a perceptive person. Did he see how something was . . . off with Ireland Raine? Did he see how she seemed to need someone?

If he did see it, he didn't say anything.

So Kal waved. "Catch you later, Bre—Ireland." He felt his face flush hot and hurried out. Had she noticed how he'd almost called her a different name? Maybe she hadn't.

But he noticed.

And he hated that he kept comparing her to his friend from Arizona.

She's not Brell.

She couldn't be.

Brell was dead.

CHAPTER THREE
Ireland

After classes, Ireland frowned at her reflection in the school bathroom mirror. She tried to stay clean and tidy, but without the luxury of an actual shower and the fact that her makeshift home was a filthy public restroom at the edge of the woods, she couldn't ever actually be clean. She wished she went to a school where a shower room was adjacent to the gym's locker room, but the locker room just had lockers. She knew because she'd once stayed late and toured the school, even the boys' locker rooms. Her school simply didn't have showers.

What kind of school made gym class mandatory but then didn't give kids the chance to wash up after? Didn't they know that teenage boys perpetually gave off nose-stinging fumes even without ever working up a sweat? Of course, with the number of creepers in the world, she could see why high school showers could be a bad idea.

A loud clang and bang at the door made Ireland startle and pull back from the mirror.

"Sorry. Didn't know anyone was here." Janice, the custodian, looked surprised to see anyone standing in the bathroom at this time. She angled her supply cart so that it wasn't blocking Ireland's exit.

Janice's cheeks flushed red with the exertion, making Ireland believe the cart had to be pretty heavy since Janice wasn't a light-weight. The woman might have been older, but no one would have accused her of having mom arms. She stopped to rest for a moment and placed a trembling hand to where her graying hair had been pulled up into a sloppy bun.

"You need help?" Ireland asked, feeling a little concerned at how pale and yet red the custodian looked all at the same time.

"Oh no. I'm good. Just tired. Long week." Janice panted be-tween each of her short responses and offered a smile that looked as tired as she'd declared herself to be.

"You look like you don't feel very good. Maybe call a sick day?" Ireland had never really spoken to Janice before. The cus-todian did a good job of being around all the time but also being invisible.

Like me, Ireland thought.

"No sick days left." The custodian laughed as if that were funny somehow. She slumped against the wall like she was using it to hold herself up.

The woman was definitely not okay. "I don't have anywhere to be. Tell me what to do, and I can help."

"I'm fine. Just this bathroom left." Janice glanced around to see what needed cleaning.

Ireland pulled a spray bottle from the cart along with a fresh rag. "Okay. So what you're saying is I'm not committing to any-thing hard. Great. Point and direct."

Janice's eyebrows came together as an incredulous smile crossed her features. "Why?"

It was a valid question. Ireland wasn't exactly certain why she wanted to help. She shrugged. Janice accepted that as answer

enough and began giving directions. Granted, she didn't go into
detail about anything. Each instruction seemed to be only three
words: Spray the mirrors. Wipe the sinks. Sweep the stalls. Mop
the floors. Janice didn't give in to long, drawn-out conversations.
Ireland was glad about that.

Ireland found she was grateful for the work. It took her mind
off her situation, and there was some sort of satisfaction in taking
a messy space and making it new again.

"Should pay you," Janice said.

"Actually . . ." Ireland glanced at the spray bottle of all-
purpose cleaner in her hand. "Would it be okay if I borrowed
your cleaning supplies? Just until tomorrow morning. I swear I'll
bring it all back before school." She added the last when Janice
looked concerned about her supplies leaving her care.

"Why?" Janice asked.

"Honestly? I'm kinda on my own and don't have a way to
clean up my space. I could help you again to pay for what I use."
She didn't know why she'd told Janice the truth. Even if it seemed
unlikely that the less-than-talkative woman would tell anyone,
Ireland had surprised herself by speaking up. But somehow she
felt safe with Janice.

"Which ones?" Janice asked.

Ireland pointed to a few of the cleaning items, and Janice
nodded. "You'll have it all back tomorrow?"

"Absolutely."

Ireland must have looked trustworthy because Janice agreed.

Ireland put the broom and mop together and then bundled
the other items into a towel that she tied to the ends of the poles,
which she put over her shoulder like she'd once seen in an old
comic strip of a kid running away from home.

Janice chuckled at the effect. Maybe she'd seen the same
comic strip.

They both thanked each other again and parted ways. Ireland pushed through the doors to the back parking lot, which was mostly empty since school had been out for a while.

But not nearly empty enough, Ireland decided, as she noticed the group of three girls gathered at a small gray FIAT 500x. The car belonged to Mara Washington. Ireland recognized the car because Mara's was the only one with big eyelashes attached to the headlights. Mara's dad owned the bakery-café chain On the Rise. And her mom helped him run things. They had four restaurants in California and one in Oregon. Her dad had been given the Black Business Award for his entrepreneurial efforts. He also got the Best of State Award and deserved both. His bakery chain made some great food. Ireland knew because she'd pulled some remnants out of their dumpster a few weeks back. Mara complained about the family business all the time, but Ireland didn't understand why. Mara's family was definitely on the wealthier side of things, and her dad had probably bought her the car as a gift for simply existing.

Everything about Mara was a sign flashing, "Look at me. Look at me. I'm wealthy." Her designer clothing fit her as if someone had sewn each outfit specifically for her. Her long black hair was done in multiple perfect braids that could only have been achieved in a salon, and her warm brown face glowed like she'd just come from having a facial.

At that moment, Mara's friends, or the hag and the harpy as Ireland thought of them, were looking at Mara as if she were declaring some eternal truth. Red-headed Tinsley with the creamy complexion of the over-moisturized, and Emily with a blond ponytail and eyes so blue Ireland felt sure they were contacts. Ireland had some pretty intensely blue eyes, and she considered them her best feature, but even her eyes weren't as intense as Emily's. The three girls lounged against the car in a way that made it seem they owned the whole parking lot. Ireland felt like she was intruding somehow as she heard Tinsley say, "So? Spill the tea."

Mara squealed. "It's true! Rowan wants to date only me. He said he'd make it official at the clambake tonight!"

"You know what this means, right?" Emily asked. She didn't give time for Mara to answer. "It means he's off the market forever 'cause no way is he going to ever break up with you after spending all this time with you."

"Absolutely true, darling." Mara struck a pose with her hand under her chin and batted her eyelashes in a way that made her look like her car for a moment.

Tinsley twisted her red hair up off her neck. She giggled along with the other two, but she actually looked like she'd eaten something that tasted like day-old broccoli left sitting on the counter. Rumor had it that Tinsley had been in love with Rowan since the second grade. It had to be killing her that she had to look happy about her friend having him.

"Do you think it's weird he hasn't asked me to the Heartbeat formal yet?"

"Oh, you know Rowan," Tinsley said. "That guy is last minute on everything. Do you have a dress already?"

"But of course. What kind of amateur do you take me for? It's perfect." Mara fluttered her eyelashes, again looking like the human version of her car.

Ireland hated to admit it, but she thought the eyelashes on Mara's car headlights were kind of adorable, and they made her feel like the car was smiling at her every time she passed it in the parking lot.

Unfortunately, none of the girls standing next to the cheery vehicle were smiling as they finally noticed her approaching. No one asked anything more about Mara's dress for the Valentine's dance. They were now all staring at Ireland. Mara's expression was one of open curiosity as she took in the poles of the broom and mop over Ireland's shoulder and the little bundle of cleaning supplies swinging behind her. Emily curled her lip as if she was now the one smelling the day-old broccoli—maybe that was just the natural expression of her face and Ireland had never noticed before. Tinsley's look was one of pure annoyance, as if Ireland had purposely interrupted them and was actively eavesdropping—which she was, but it wasn't as if she could help it. They were talking so loudly that Ireland wondered if they wanted to be overheard.

Ireland tried to smile in their direction as she walked by, but Tinsley made a noise that seemed like an outright rejection of Ireland's smile. "No offense, but did you just get out of hobo class?" She turned to her friends. "I didn't know they taught hobo class here."

"They don't," Ireland said. *No offense* always meant that someone was about to insult you and they just expected you to suck it up.

"Oh, don't be so extra," Tinsley said with an eye roll. "We're only joking."

Ireland didn't know how confirming that no such class was taught counted as her being extra. And everyone knew that if you had to say the words "I'm only joking," then whatever you were saying wasn't a joke. Seriously. These people.

Mara looked uncomfortable about her friends being the absolute worst and opened her mouth like she was going to say something, but she said nothing. Her eyes dropped to the ground, and she didn't call her friends out for being horrible. In Ireland's mind, not speaking up in those situations was just as bad as being the verbal abusers.

"Hobo class sounds like it could be fun, though," Emily said with a smirk.

Ireland narrowed her eyes at the girls. "Not as much fun as the hags and harpies class though, right? I heard you guys are both getting an A in that class. So you're probably better off where you are."

Emily and Tinsley exhaled puffs of indignation as Ireland shook her head and kept walking. Who were these girls to her? No one.

Knowing that didn't stop a hot tear from escaping her eye. She didn't reach up to swipe it away until after she'd rounded the corner and was out of their line of sight, however. She would not give them the satisfaction of knowing that their verbal arrows had struck their mark. She had to pass a few other people on her way to the old animal trail that led to the edge of the woods where she now lived. She tried not to feel self-conscious as those people eyed her pack. *Maybe they're not thinking I look weird,* she thought. *Maybe they're thinking I look cool in a quirky kind of way.*

Ireland snorted at herself. She was carrying cleaning supplies while wearing rumpled clothes and needing a shower. She didn't look cool in any kind of way, quirky or otherwise. When she arrived at her restroom, Ireland checked the surrounding area to make sure she was alone. There was no one around except the birds and insects, chirping and chirring cheerily.

She opened the door and surveyed the small space of cobwebs and dirt. Ireland wrinkled her nose in disgust. "If this is home, then it's time to make it livable." Determination fueled her words as she spoke out loud to the bathroom. With that, she unbundled the cleaning supplies, stopped up the drain with the rubber plug Janice had loaned her, and filled the sink with water and soap. She started at the top of the bathroom where both dead and alive insects gathered at the window. "Sorry," she said to the ones that were still moving. I guess it's time for you to be evicted. But really, you'll be fine and figure out new accommodations somewhere else." *After all, I did,* she finished in her head.

Ireland swept the soap-soaked rag over the area, then shook it outside of the bathroom so the bugs didn't clog her sink. Unclogging drains had been an activity she'd had to do in the past, but she wasn't exactly good at it. It would have been so many degrees of glorious to play music on her phone from where it was plugged into the wall by the door, but she didn't want to draw the attention of anyone who might come along. Anyway, the buzzing from the few flies she'd upset after wiping down where they'd been by the window added a soundtrack of sorts to her work.

Dunking the rag again and again in the soapy water, Ireland scrubbed each surface. With every swipe of the rag, she felt the accumulated dirt give way to her unflinching resolve. Like with cleaning the restroom in the school, it felt good to do the work and see the results of that work. Sweat soaked her neck behind her hair.

Minutes stretched into what felt like hours as Ireland methodically worked her way through the task. The repetitive motions of cleaning soothed away even the discomfort she'd felt when Mara's gang had made fun of her.

Once she was done scrubbing the walls, she tightened her grip on the worn handle of the broom and swept everything out the door, then mopped the floor. Finally, she allowed herself to stretch out the kinks in her back and shoulders from being bent over for so long. Then Ireland stood back and gazed over the freshly clean space. It was brighter now that the light could shine in unhindered by the grime and dust that had been on the windows. She felt better about her situation, better than she had since before her dad left. Maybe better than she'd ever felt before.

The chirping bird alarm went off on her phone, reminding her it was time to get ready to meet Kal. It also reminded her that she was going to have to figure out how to pay the coming phone bill, or she would lose that bit of access to the world. Letting out an exasperated growl at that recollection, Ireland washed her hair in the sink and then braided the wet strands so that they were tidy. She wanted to look nice for this dinner. He hadn't said it was a date, but . . . well, she didn't want to think too hard about why she worried over her image in the mirror.

She gathered all the cleaning supplies together and put them in the corner, then unplugged and pocketed her phone and opened the door. With a satisfied smile tugging at the corners of her mouth, Ireland glanced over the bathroom once more. It wouldn't be so bad to sleep here anymore. She wouldn't have to think about the spiders and bugs. She wouldn't have to try to *not* think about the yellowed stains on the wall near the toilet. Everything had been sanitized and scrubbed clean. She was almost excited to come back to go to sleep. *My home,* she thought and let out laugh of triumph. "Take that, Dad." She could survive without him. Her chest tightened, but she refused to try to quantify the thought as a lie or not.

Ireland stepped out of the restroom and closed it up before turning to the path that led back into town, where she would meet up with Kal. She would get dinner tonight, free and clear, with no sneaking necessary. And she would get to listen to a cool guy sing and play the guitar—a thing she'd found she really enjoyed.

By the time Ireland showed up at Geppetto's, she felt almost euphoric. She entered through the front door rather than the one at the side. She made eye contact with people rather than skulking around trying to hide her presence. She smiled at Kal, who grinned at her from the stage.

The smell of baking pizza came from the brick oven proudly displayed behind the glass partition separating the kitchen from the dining area. The warm stone tiles and red-checked tablecloths that made up the ambience of Geppetto's added to her euphoria, but the bigger joy was knowing she wouldn't have to steal her dinner. She might even be able to take home leftovers to get her through the weekend. She hated how it felt like she was always being bossed around by food. It seemed her every choice was determined by where and how she would be getting her next meal. Staying warm at night was a close second. She was glad the weather would eventually be warming up.

Not that food and shelter hadn't always been central concerns, but before, she worked through them with her dad, whereas now, the worry belonged to her alone.

"Stop thinking about it," she whispered to herself and then felt dumb for vocalizing her thoughts out loud. She spent so much time alone that she was starting to pick up some bad habits. People who talked to themselves weren't exactly mentally stable, were they? She didn't know.

She stood to the right side of the restaurant near the stone fountain surrounded by indoor plants while she waited for Kal to finish his song—whether it was an original or a cover, she couldn't tell. She didn't really know all that much about music. She had a few favorites and listened to them almost exclusively.

The stage was tucked into the far-left corner, likely so the people seated around the opposite corner away from the main dining area could still catch a glimpse of the local musicians if they wanted. Kal's eyes kept turning to her, and his smile seemed to widen each time until she wasn't sure how he could sing so clearly through such a wide grin. His voice felt strangely soothing all mingled together with the burbling fountain water and the hum of conversations punctuated by the occasional burst of laughter.

The soft glow from the vintage-style pendant lights gave a

cheery, warm sort of glow—the kind that felt welcoming and comfortable all at the same time.

That was how she felt. Welcomed and comfortable.

Yep. That decided it. She had never been so many degrees of gloriously happy as she was at that moment.

Kal sang the last few words of his song with confident, raw emotion. People clapped and cheered. "Thanks, everyone," he said into the antique-looking mic. "We're going to take a quick dinner break. We appreciate your support."

He set his guitar on the stand and then came down the two wooden steps to the stone floor of the main room before making his way straight to Ireland. "Hey! You made it! Come meet the band."

He took her to a table near the front where the other three members of his band were just getting seated. Two large pans of pizza were already on the metal stands at the center of the shiny wood table. The three people she recognized from school but had never talked to looked up at him.

"This is Asha. Our lead guitarist." Kal pointed to a girl with rosy pink cheeks, flushed from being up on stage. Her entire vibe was like an advertisement for bright and cheerful feelings. Her long blue-green hair, bright blue eyes, and cute, slightly upturned nose made Ireland think of a mermaid.

"And this is Bailey. She's our drummer." The girl with short cropped brown hair was also flushed, but she didn't give off the same kind of happy vibes as Asha. She was more like a neon sign flashing, "Go away."

"And this is Cooper, on bass." Cooper gave a wave-sort-of-salute and flashed a smile before he scrubbed his hands through his red hair. He looked like he'd had to fold himself up to sit on the chair. Ireland imagined that he was ridiculously tall. She tried to remember how tall he was compared to Kal, but when she'd come in, she hadn't really noticed the others on the stage. She'd only seen Kal.

"And everyone, this is Ireland."

"Like the country?" Bailey asked.

Ireland smiled. "Yeah. Like that, only with fewer shamrocks." It was her standard answer when people reacted to her name.

Kal pulled out a chair for her and indicated for her to sit. She did so, her previous euphoria giving way to the awkward in this social situation that she wasn't sure how to navigate. She'd only just barely decided to start talking to people. And now here she was talking to four all at the same time. And she was definitely the interloper of the evening. Recognizing these people from school didn't mean she could call them friends. She shifted uncomfortably, suddenly wishing she could leave, but was compelled by the hunger gnawing at her insides to stay and eat first.

Except they weren't eating. The food was on the pans with steam rising up, but no one was taking a slice. Would they think she was rude if she helped herself? Why weren't they eating?

Bailey was on her phone. Asha had a pen and was writing on a napkin. Cooper was smiling at the waitress, who kept tossing little smiles back at him. And Kal was looking at her. Her stomach growled, and Kal smirked. He pulled a slice of pizza off the pan, *finally*. The cheese stretched from the slice to the pie still on the pan as he moved it to a plate and then pushed that plate in her direction.

"Here," he said. He watched her momentarily, as if expecting her just to eat even though no one else was. He must have seen her hesitation because only then did he pull a piece off for himself.

When he took a bite, she did as well. Relief flooded her at the knowledge that she would go to sleep on a full stomach.

"Is no one else eating?" she finally asked quietly.

Kal looked at his bandmates. "They always wait a few minutes to cool off after performing."

It made sense, even if she hated eating without them. But now that she'd taken a bite, she planned to keep going with or without them. "I liked the song you guys played."

Asha glanced up, beaming. "Thanks. I wrote it."

"*Just you?*" Bailey tilted her head and scowled.

With a blush, Asha hurried to clarify. "Well, we all had a hand in writing that one. But the first few lines were mine."

"It was great." Ireland took another bite, chewed, and swallowed before realizing the conversation had come to a full stop. Were they expecting her to do all the talking? Or did they expect that they would all eat—or not eat, as the case was—in silence? "Do you guys always write your own songs?"

"Not always," Kal said. "Half the time, we do covers. People like music they're familiar with."

"Hey, guys?" Cooper glanced at the door with a look of longing. "We still have three songs to do before we can wrap. Can we get to it? I really do have to leave."

"You don't want to eat first?" Kal asked.

"They're doing a clambake." Cooper cast a furtive glance at Bailey, who was rolling her eyes.

Bailey pushed back her chair with a scrape over the stone floor. "Let's get this done so pretty boy here can stop slumming with us and get back to his bougie friends."

Cooper looked like he wanted to defend himself to her but said nothing. Kal dropped his pizza to his plate, downed half a glass of water, and wiped his mouth and hands on his napkin before dropping it to the table. "Let's get you on the road, then."

They all went back to the stage, took their places, and did three more songs. The first two were the happy, bouncy, good-vibes sort. The last was a soulful number about loss and missing people. As Kal sang, Ireland's vision blurred with tears. *I miss my dad.* It was the first time she'd had that thought since he'd left her. She hadn't been aware she could miss him. She was so mad at him, so . . . *betrayed*, that to consider missing him felt like she was killing any self-respect she might have had.

Kal sang the lyrics:

> *The way we used to talk to the beat of the pouring rain,*
> *I'm haunted by the echoes, memories I can't explain.*
> *I'm standing right here, holding out my hand.*
> *Didn't you know I was a safe place to land?*

Ireland suddenly didn't feel like she was abandoning her dignity to miss the man who had been a constant part of her life since she could remember. And really, she had to give him some credit. Her mom bailed on her when Ireland was a toddler. Her dad stuck it out for a lot longer. That meant something, didn't it?

And she couldn't help but miss him. He might have had issues with his addictions and might not have been trustworthy around her cash, but he was quick to see the humor in things and had an arsenal of dad jokes at the ready.

For the first time in weeks, Ireland let herself feel her feelings.

It was okay to miss him.

It was okay to hope he was okay.

It was okay to be mad at him.

It was okay to feel betrayed.

It was all okay.

And maybe it was all *going to be* okay.

She looked down at her pizza plate and tried to wipe at her eyes without being noticeable about it. Her first time out with people her age and she was getting all crybaby on them? How embarrassing. She didn't want to look ridiculous in front of these guys—especially not Bailey, who was a little terrifying.

The band finished their set and Cooper grabbed his jacket and hurried off without returning to the table. Asha and Bailey came back with Kal, but they didn't bother to sit down again.

"We've got to get going," Bailey said. "Asha's taking me home and apparently has relatives in town she wants to see." She made a face as if seeing relatives was the worst thing she could imagine.

Asha kissed her fingers and tapped them to Kal's cheek. "Be good, Superman. See you in school."

Bailey gave a half-hearted wave and followed Asha out of the restaurant.

"Looks like it's just us," Kal said.

Maybe Ireland should have been nervous to be alone with a guy who was heart-stutteringly good-looking, but she was too mesmerized by the fact that the group had left nearly two full pizzas. She wondered what was going to happen to all that pizza. Would Kal take it with him? Would he let her take some of it? She swallowed and forced her attention back to him. He'd asked her a question. She had to consider a moment before she remembered what it was. Right—he'd asked her how she liked the songs.

"They were really great. Did Asha write those as well?"

"The first two were covers. I wrote the last one."

Ireland felt like one of those animated characters with her eyes bulging out of her head and her jaw hitting the table. "You? Seriously?"

"Yeah. I was going through some stuff this last year, and writing it out helped me." He watched her a moment longer before picking his pizza up off its plate. He looked at her and then her pizza as if indicating she should pick hers up too, which she did. "Cheers," he said and tapped his pizza to hers. He took a bite while continuing to look at her.

She didn't need any more encouragement than that. After finishing that piece she ate a second and a third. Kal didn't make a big deal about the fact that she was packing away calories like a bear going into hibernation. She was glad about that since she felt a kinship with any creature who had to figure out how to make meals last.

"So you and Asha . . ." She trailed off, not really sure how to finish her thought out loud without being more awkward than she already was.

He waited, but when it became apparent that she had decided not to continue, he said, "We're just friends. She was the one who put up flyers for a lead vocalist in the band and she was the one who heard my audition. She's got a gift with lyrics and the guitar but has trouble finding pitch with her voice. She was the first friend I made in Arcata."

Ireland felt like an idiot for acting like some jealous shrew and hurried with a follow-up question to (she hoped) make him forget her first. "Why does she call you Superman?"

Kal smirked. "Well, it's kinda my name. My dad wanted to name me Kal-El, but my mom said no."

"Wait. I don't get it. But your name is—"

"Kalvin Ellis, which was as close as my mom would let my dad get to naming me after an alien from Krypton. My dad actually calls me Kal-El. Honestly, sometimes my mom does too. When Asha found out, she just started calling me Superman. She thinks it's funny."

Ireland smiled. It was funny. And sweet, too.

Kal's parents and life sounded so normal. Not like hers. As if reading her thoughts, he asked, "What about you?"

"Me?"

"Why are you named Ireland?"

She shrugged. She had no idea. "My mom just liked it, I guess."

"You never asked her?"

Her shoulders, which had been relaxed, suddenly tightened. "Never had the chance. She bailed even before I was walking. I haven't seen her since. Wouldn't even know how to find her."

Kal's brown eyes filled with compassion. "Oh. I'm sorry."

She shrugged again. "No big deal. I don't remember her enough to miss her."

"And your dad?"

His question sent a wave of panic through her. Did he have to be prying into her world like it was any of his business? But he looked at her like he really cared. Like he wasn't intruding on her life—just trying to understand it. "Dad and I were on our own— just the two of us after Mom left." It was the truth. Not the whole truth. But enough.

"So you can ask him why you're named Ireland."

"Right." Ireland forced a smile. "I'll ask him next time I see him." All these questions . . . no one told her there would be questions. She glanced at the Coca-Cola clock on the wall. "It's getting late. I should get going. Thanks for inviting me. I loved hearing you play. And thanks for dinner."

She stood to go, but Kal stopped her by placing his hand gently over hers. Her heart stuttered to a brief but abrupt stop as she stared at his hand warm on hers, tethering her in the smallest way to him. She wondered if this was what a heart attack felt like. It wasn't exactly a bad sensation. No. Definitely not bad. But it made her feel like her skin was suddenly too tight and that the room had become too warm.

"Why don't you take the pizza home for you and your dad?" he said.

"You don't want any?" She hated how her heart not only started beating again but that it was now jackhammering against her ribs with the hope of taking back such a haul.

"I eat a lot of pizza. I'm kinda over it."

She glanced at the practically untouched pizzas and hoped the need wasn't visible in her eyes. "If you're sure . . ."

"Yep. Lemme get you some to-go boxes." He left and returned a few minutes later with two boxes and a plastic bag with something heavy-ish in it. "The guys in back said these two take-out salads were paid for but never picked up. He asked if I'd take them, but I'm not really a salad guy. Do you want them?"

"Sure." She tried to make it sound like it wasn't a big deal, but vegetation? Something healthy? The good luck was dizzying.

They boxed up the pizza, and then Kal loaded her arms with the food while he asked, "Did you drive here?"

"No, I walked."

"Oh, well, lemme drive you home then."

"No!"

His eyes widened in surprise at her abrupt response.

"I mean that I like walking. And it isn't far."

"But . . ." He glanced meaningfully at the boxes and the bag.

She laughed. "It's not like it's heavy or even awkward."

He opened his mouth, likely to protest, except at that moment a guy who looked like the manager called his name and waved him over. Kal made a noise that sounded like a low growl of frustration but said, "I'll be right back."

Once his back was turned, Ireland inched toward the door. When she reached it, she tugged on the handle and fled the restaurant.

"I'm stupid to have run away," she said out loud when she made it to the edge of the woods. But what else could she do? It wasn't like she could let him drive her to a public bathroom in the woods. And Kal Ellis didn't seem like the type of guy to let her walk. Fleeing had been her only legitimate option.

As she moved down the trail, she considered the amount of food she had and wondered how to keep it from attracting animals, specifically the bears. She'd never returned with enough to last beyond the next meal. This was an entire weekend's worth. How did she keep it from going bad even if the animals stayed out of it?

She wished she could afford a small cooler, but even if she had the money, she had nowhere to store it. She'd have to eat what she could and throw the rest out. She should have considered this dilemma before she loaded up the boxes. Kal was likely just being nice when he'd said he was over pizza.

"Who is ever over pizza?" she asked out loud. He would have taken it if she hadn't. She was a greedy, grubby-handed *taker*.

She sighed at that. She had never wanted to be a taker. She had never wanted to be like her dad.

She made it to the bathroom, set the food on the sink, and went to retrieve her duffel. Once she had the duffel in the bathroom, she locked the door. When she turned to set up her bed, she jolted at what she saw out of the corner of her eye. It was splotches of red writing on the far wall. Blood?

Alarmed, Ireland froze. Had someone come and scrawled some warning in blood on her wall?

"You should leave," she told herself. It would have been the smart thing to do. But she didn't. Instead, she stepped closer to the wall to inspect the writing.

"This is how every episode of *Supernatural* starts," she muttered to herself. But she stepped even closer. No. Not blood. It was hot pink.

That gave her the courage to step closer and read the message.

My every heartbeat is now a wracking sob, wrapped in a cloak of betrayal. I'm a hideous beast now—scarred, repulsive, and howling at the uncaring moon.

"Definitely the start to a *Supernatural* episode." She'd watched the entire series one summer when her dad had gotten them into an apartment with paid streaming for several different services.

"What the stupid kind of message is this?" Ireland asked. Now that she was close enough to really see what she was looking at, and now that she wasn't panicking and jumping to paranoid conclusions, she could tell the message was written in a playful pink lipstick. So likely a woman wrote it, which meant some woman had been there in her bathroom while she was gone. It wasn't as abandoned as she'd allowed herself to believe. This meant she had to stay extra careful.

Not that she wasn't careful, but just that morning, she'd considered not putting her stuff into the duffel and hoisting it into the trees. It was just so much work. Now she was glad she hadn't given in to that impulse.

She glanced around at the rest of her clean bathroom and then back to the wall with the writing. She scowled. "Seriously?" she asked. "What kind of meth-head harpy writes on a wall in lipstick?"

With a grunt of frustration, she pulled out the cleaning supplies and went to work to scrub away the mess. "Lipstick is the worst!" she whisper-yelled. It was all grease and smear and smudge and mess. "And who does this?" she asked. "Who runs around vandalizing other people's bathrooms like this? Don't they know? Don't they know how hard it is to clean? Does it not occur to them that *someone* has to clean it up? Entitled pieces of shrewish dumpster trash." The grumbling didn't make the cleaning any easier, but it made her feel better about it.

When she was done, she felt tired and furious, and she cursed the anonymous vandal all over again. Then she prepared her bed, wishing she'd taken the time to get a pillow, and turned out the light.

But once the light was out, it felt like the words were seared

in her mind. *Scarred, hideous, beast, betrayal.* Her fear rose on the
tide of those words washing into her head. She wished they didn't
leave her feeling vulnerable and paralyzed.

They were like some ominous omen, and, just as she had finally admitted to herself that she missed her father, she also finally
admitted that she was terrified to be so completely alone as the
uncaring moon shone in through her window.

CHAPTER FOUR

Kal

Kal scrubbed his hands over his head and stared up at the ceiling of Geppetto's. Ireland had left without saying goodbye. Dude. Not cool. Also intriguing. Why didn't she want him to take her home? Was she living in a crap neighborhood and so felt ashamed of her situation? She couldn't think he was that shallow, could she?

Maybe she thought he was some sort of skeeze and she didn't want him to know where she lived.

He dismissed the thought with a laugh as soon as it came to him. Not likely. Nothing about him could have been called skeezy. Average, maybe . . . sometimes he felt like he wallowed in average.

He turned his head to look at the door. How long could she have been gone? Taking the heavy cans off the shelves in the storeroom took fewer than two minutes. She had the pizza boxes, which would slow her down. Kal lifted his chin in the manager's direction to get his attention. "Hey, Chaz. I gotta get." When Chaz acknowledged him back with a raise of his own chin, Kal hurried out.

At the sidewalk, he inspected both directions. Nothing. She

was nowhere to be seen. He chose right and started jogging. When he reached the next block, he spied her lithe frame and long, dark braids. She balanced the pizza boxes and turned left when she reached the next street, away from the direction he would have assumed. She was heading to the outskirts of town. There weren't any houses in that direction.

Kal stayed low and used cars, trees, and shrubbery to block him from her view so she wouldn't know she was being followed.

"Okay," he said to himself. "Maybe I am a skeezer."

He was surprised when she entered the almost invisible animal trail by the dumpsters behind a Lutheran church and disappeared into the tree line. "What are you doing, Ireland?" he whispered to himself. Maybe her family lived in a trailer in the woods?

Maybe.

He found it was harder to track her once they were in the trees because the trail had small twigs and branches that could snap with any step. But she stayed on the trail, keeping her footsteps one in front of the other as if she was purposely keeping her path as small as possible. He did the same, figuring he could respect whatever it was she was doing. It was getting dark, and with the sun's exit from the sky, the temperature was dropping. Kal considered that he should have noticed the cold more, but the adrenaline pumped hot through him.

Adrenaline was weird—how it could boil blood and sharpen and dull senses at the same time.

Kal worked to be as silent as possible, but it felt like his breathing rasped loudly in the air around them. There was no way she couldn't hear him. And maybe that was the appropriate thing. Maybe he should just call attention to the fact that he was following her rather than stalk her from behind like some axe murderer. Maybe he should call out, "Hey, Ireland, where are you going? Do you need a hand with those pizza boxes?"

But how did he explain the fact that he'd already been following her for as long as he had? She'd yank out her cell phone and call the police faster than he could say, "I'm sorry for being your local stalker." Or worse, she could pull out a can of mace and spray him in the eyes. She could tell him he was the idiot that he knew himself to be and never talk to him again.

That would definitely be the worst. Because he liked her. And now that she was talking to him, he really wanted her to keep talking.

Because he'd stopped paying attention to the trail due to the attention he was giving to his internal battle, he caught a branch wrong, and it scratched the side of his face and across his ear. He bit back a yelp. If he was smart, he would go back. But how could he possibly go back now when Ireland was wandering through the woods by herself? She was doing something. And he needed to know what.

Blood trickled from the new wound in his cheek. He pulled the collar of his shirt up higher to apply pressure so the bleeding would stop. Stupid branch had got him good. He'd be lucky if it didn't scar. But maybe the scar would make him look more adventurous? He scoffed at that. A musician with a scar. How much more clichéd could he get?

Kal finally came to a place where the trail seemed to open, not a lot, but enough that he didn't feel like he was battling trees. And suddenly there was a building.

Well, "building" might have been an exaggeration. It was more of a cinder block shed. Careful not to snap any branches or twigs, he ducked behind some shrubbery and watched because Ireland had stopped. She glanced around and licked her lips and then rubbed them together. She disappeared inside the shed with the pizza boxes but came right back out without them.

She glanced around again and then went to a nearby tree and

untied a rope he hadn't noticed was there until she called attention to it by tugging on the knot. She balanced herself against a rock and started to lower whatever had been tied up in the tree. For the first time, it occurred to Kal to worry that maybe, of the two of them, *she* was the serial killer. Maybe she was the one hiding bodies out in the woods, and he had suddenly come across an evil plot he didn't really want to be involved in. Especially when the thing that lowered from the tree line was a large duffel bag. It was big enough to hold a body, easy.

Stop that, he chided himself. Because really, what could a girl have out here in a duffel bag in the woods that she'd be willing to carry a bunch of pizza boxes to? If there was a dead body in that duffel, she wouldn't have taken a picnic to it. Even so, Ireland clearly was up to something, or she wouldn't look so nervous. So guilty.

Ireland untied the duffel bag from the rope and hefted it to the door of the shed. It was then that Kal noticed the door had a worn-out, sun-faded sign indicating a male and female. A bathroom?

She opened the door and went inside with her duffel bag. She closed the door behind her, and he heard the distinct sound of a lock clicking into place. What? A light flicked on through the small windows at the top of the bathroom. He waited for several moments, thinking she was just using the restroom before she continued on with wherever she was going. But she never came back out.

He crept closer, being careful not to step on anything that could snap or crack and give him away.

He could hear muttering from inside, a voice bouncing off the cinder blocks. She sounded like she was cussing someone out. Then he could hear water running. Still, she didn't come back out. Was she going to stay there all night?

And then realization hit him like getting punched in the face. This is where she was sleeping. This is where Ireland Raine was *living*. Alone. In the woods. Totally vulnerable. This was why she sneaked pizza off of plates. This was why she ghosted through the school.

Ireland Raine was homeless. And he was pretty sure nobody but him knew it.

He stood there for a long time, unsure of what to do. Did he knock on the door and say, "Hey. I know your secret. Do you want to crash at my place for a night or two or three while we figure this out?" He couldn't leave her there, could he? How safe was it for a teenage girl to be out on her own in the woods? And it's not like he watched the news, but he heard enough about what was going on in the world to know that human trafficking was real, and for someone looking to exploit the vulnerable, Ireland had definitely put herself in a position to be of interest. He didn't know what to do.

Kal pulled his phone out several times, intending to call someone, but he could never figure out who he was supposed to call. The police? His mom? One of Ireland's friends? But as far as he was aware, she didn't have any friends. It wasn't just that she didn't talk to him, but that Ireland didn't talk to *anybody*.

He now felt like he understood why. She didn't make those connections because she didn't want anyone to know her secret.

He could respect that, which was why he put his phone back in his pocket. At the very beginning of this new friendship with her, he was not in a position to betray her secret. After all, she *had* locked the door. She was probably safe for now. Obviously, she'd been doing this for a while, so she could probably make it through the weekend. That would give him time to think of what he should do. There had to be something.

He carefully picked his way back to the trail that had brought

him to Ireland's little shed. As soon as he'd moved away far enough
to be sure Ireland wouldn't see it, Kal pulled out his phone and
switched on his flashlight app so that he could see his way back
to the Lutheran church where they had started. The last thing he
wanted was to get lost in the woods. Ireland might know where
she was at, but he really didn't. He was new enough to the town
that becoming disoriented in a maze of redwood and shrubbery
sent a visceral shiver through him. Coming from the desert meant
that there hadn't been a lot of woods for him to get lost in growing up.

His brain worked furiously on the situation that was Ireland.
He wanted to tell an adult. Hadn't he always been taught that
when something happened, you tell an adult? But did that count
for when it was something that happened to someone else?
Probably. But maybe not. He desperately wanted to do the right
thing.

Helping Ireland doesn't bring her *back*, he thought to himself.
Until that thought came to him, Kal hadn't realized what he'd
been thinking: that maybe by saving one girl, he could save the
other. But the other girl was far out of his reach. Out of anyone's
reach. She was buried under a headstone with horses carved into
the granite. And there was nothing he could do about it. But
maybe he could keep *this* girl from being lost in the same way his
friend was lost. Couldn't he?

Kal tripped over a branch that had been just barely sticking
up out of the soft earth. He landed on his hands and knees and
cursed. His mom and dad would have no idea what had happened to him when he showed up bleeding and scratched with
dirty clothes. What would he say to them? How could he explain it without revealing the secret? The following Ireland into
the forest part of the secret was his. Surely it was okay to tell that
part. But wait; he couldn't, right? How could he tell one part

without revealing all of it? He picked himself up off the ground and rubbed his hands together to remove the dirt, small rocks, and leaves that had tried to embed themselves into his palms.

He worked to pay better attention to the trail even as he placed one foot in front of the other in a way that kept his trail as small and unnoticeable as possible. Kal didn't want to lead some sleaze to Ireland's shed and put her in danger.

Scary people existed in the world. No one knew that better than Kal. And he was not about to lose another friend to the scary people of the world. At the very least, he could make sure she had food. That was something in his power. He could figure out a way to get her shelf-stable groceries. Protein bars, cereal, apples, carrots. Stuff that would provide her good nutrition without her needing a fridge.

Of course, maybe she had a fridge. Maybe she had a full luxury studio apartment going on in there. How was he to know?

But then, that duffel bag didn't look big enough to hold a fridge. No. She was trying to hide her presence. She wouldn't have that place tricked out like it was her living space during the day while she was away. Why else would she hide the duffel in the tree?

He had to give her credit. The entire idea of her living situation was sort of ingenious in a *Boxcar Children* kind of way. Kal's grandma had read him those books when he was a kid.

There was a part of him that wanted to say Ireland was living the dream. She had no parents to tell her what to do. No adults giving her rules and regulations. But the logical part of him understood it wasn't a dream but more of a nightmare. There was also no security. No protection. No one to talk to. No love. No reminders to brush your teeth. No mom to insist on hugs and to scowl at you as you pretended you didn't want them.

He felt a burn at the back of his throat and in his eyelids.

Ridiculous. He was ridiculous. Crying over imagined hugs? Who did that?

At least there were no witnesses.

Kal released a noisy sigh of relief when the cross that topped the church came into view. He wasn't going to get lost in the woods today after all. If he was in some sort of old-school Scouting program, they'd give him a merit badge for . . . something. He didn't know the merit badges well enough to know what he would get. Explorer? Adventurer?

More likely he would get a merit badge for Stalker.

He broke into a run when his feet left the path and were on solid pavement again. Kal ran all the way back to Geppetto's, where he gathered up his things, loaded his beat-up, half-rust and half-red Dodge Ram truck and headed for home.

When he got inside, Kal felt a ping in his chest at seeing his dad absently scratching the top of his thick, dark hair. His dad had a laptop propped up on his long legs that rested on the gray footstool in front of the couch. His mom always said Kal was lucky that he got his father's height and thick hair and dark eyelashes. Kal had never really wanted to look like his dad, but now seeing him after having been tromping around the woods made Kal rethink his disdain toward anything about his parents. His dad looked up. "Hey, kid, what kept you so late?"

Kal checked the time on his phone. Dang. It really was late. He was surprised his parents hadn't called him to find out if he was dead in a gutter. They worried a lot more now than they used to, ever since the whole incident with Brell.

"Friends and I stayed after and had some pizza. We got to talking, and I guess we lost track of time. Sorry, Dad." Kal hoped he looked contrite and not guilty. Honestly, he was surprised his dad hadn't called. He was more surprised that his mother hadn't called.

He found comfort in the fact that they worried. It took off some of the burden of worry he was carrying himself.

"Make sure you call when you're going to be late. The kitchen is extra clean because your mom needed something to do instead of hovering. She's now working on my office. Go interrupt her so that she can stop. I can never find anything when she cleans up after me."

Kal grinned and shook his head. Gratitude surged in him, threatening to overwhelm him and make him break down and bawl like a baby right then and there. The fact that his mom had dared brave his dad's office and the avalanche of bizarre receipts and paperwork that he kept in there meant she really was trying to give Kal the space that he had told her he needed.

He clenched and unclenched his fist as his smile slipped and he had to force it back up. "I'll put a stop to that."

In his dad's office, his mom shoved back a strand of loose dark hair that had escaped her short ponytail as she stood and muttered over the desk covered in lopsided stacks of books and papers. Kal only caught every few words, but it was enough for him to get the idea. "What . . . thinking? How . . . find anything . . . infuriating."

"Hey, Mom."

She whirled around as if she was doing a tryout for a horror film and needed to pretend to be more terrified than she'd ever been in her life. Her hand went to her chest in a clear attempt to put an end to the heart attack that had surely begun. "Oh, you're home. Oh good. I really didn't want to clean your dad's office. Look at this." She gestured to the desk and the piles on top of it. "It's like he's trying to do a reenactment of Everest. I'm almost certain that there's climbing equipment in here somewhere."

"Not that anybody would notice," Kal said. "I really am sorry I was late. I should've called. I will next time." Then he did something uncharacteristic of him lately. He stepped forward, opened up his arms, and folded his mom up into them. He'd grown a lot over the last year. He was a good foot taller and could easily rest his chin on top of her head.

"What's all this?" she mumbled against his shirt sleeve.

"It's just nice to have parents who care. I appreciate that you didn't call to check in on me. That you trusted I was okay." There was so much more he wanted to say. He was glad he was safe. He was glad he had a roof over his head and a bed to sleep in. He was glad he had food to eat. And he really wanted to figure out how to help Ireland get the same things.

CHAPTER FIVE
Ireland

Ireland woke up grouchier than she'd been when she'd gone to sleep. After a night of deranged dreams brought on by a deranged poem, she wanted to throttle whoever it was that had invaded her personal space—her sanctuary—and scribbled absurdity all over her wall after she'd spent an entire afternoon cleaning. What kind of abscess on the human population does such a thing? And sure, calling a bathroom a personal sanctuary might seem like a little much, but still.

Ireland growled her way through her morning routine of washing her face, brushing her teeth, and pulling her hair back into a ponytail. She used a washcloth to hopefully remove some of the body odor, but wasn't sure it worked. Then she looked in the mirror and considered.

Kal Ellis.

He had asked her to dinner. And, sure, it wasn't like a date or anything. But it *almost* felt like one, certainly the closest thing she'd ever had to one. The way she moved around all the time with her dad meant that she didn't have a lot of time for forming those types of relationships.

Now? Now she had opportunities. Her father wasn't going to move her anywhere in the next few days, weeks, or months. She was guaranteed to stay put. For a little while, anyway. That meant it was okay if she made some friends. It was okay if she talked to people. It was okay for her to take up space in a real way.

Ireland tugged out the ponytail. It was a basic sort of style that kept her hair out of her face, but it certainly didn't make her more appealing visually. She took a pencil out of her bag and used the tip to part her hair like she'd done the night before. She braided one side and then the other. She didn't need to tie off the braids with any kind of hair tie. Her hair had enough natural curl to pretty much stay where she'd put it. At least when it was in braids.

She didn't know where the curl came from. Without ever meeting grandparents and having only a hazy memory of a mother, it could have come from anywhere. Ireland only knew that if she washed it and then used her fingers to fluff it up while it was still wet, the ringlets appeared. And if she didn't comb through them, they usually stay put. Curls or braids weren't things she did very often. The rushed ponytail was more her speed. But now, after her date with Kal and the way she felt today, she needed to figure out a different sort of pace for herself.

Her life wasn't going to be all about the flight. Not anymore. Her life could have a few roots planted in soil of her choosing. And, honestly, she really liked where she was at now. She'd traveled up and down the coastline, moving into one unfortunate apartment after another. Most of them were crumbling to the ground, and several of them were probably used to cook meth. And the neighborhoods usually matched the apartment. But this time the school was decent. Arcata felt, in the strangest way possible, like home.

Ireland had to admit her dad had done better this time.

Even the apartment in this town hadn't been that bad. It hadn't been great, but at least it wasn't infested with vermin or bugs or tweaked-out addicts. Sure, there had been a few of all of the above. But they weren't leaking out of the cracked plasters of the walls.

She took a deep breath that filled her lungs and let it out. She looked her reflection in the eye. "I can be someone different."

With that declaration, she began to pack up her little home for the day. Now and again, she cast her gaze in the direction of the wall that had been smeared in lipstick the night before. Ireland wanted to keep her eye on it just in case she was the victim of a poltergeist. Did poltergeists use lipstick? How would she know? It's not like she was a medium with a crystal ball.

She ate a salad and several pieces of pizza, figuring eating cold pizza was a stereotype of teenagers everywhere. She'd never read that any of them had died from it, so the food still had to be pretty good. But she wasn't sure how long the rule of cold pizza being just fine to eat could hold out before her pizza actually went bad and gave her food poisoning and some future hiker found her dead in the bathroom. So she ate as much as possible. Better to be a little sick from being full than to be starving or to have food poisoning.

Besides, food that could be attractive to raccoons could end up being a problem for her later on.

For that reason, she stayed close to the bathroom the entire day. It's not like she had anywhere to go. Plus, she had a ton of homework to do. So she worked on that, listened to her music, and ate pizza. Toward evening, Ireland started to feel vaguely stupid that she'd taken the time to do her hair. It's not like anyone was going to see her on the weekend, especially since she had no intention of going into town.

Fixing herself up felt good though. Maybe that was the point.

Instead of looking nice for other people, maybe you fixed yourself up to look good for you. It was an idea she could get behind.

In spite of the day having been productive and her feeling good about it, by the time evening rolled around, her anxiety spiked all over again. She could still see that message scrawled on her wall as if it had been seared into her brain—as if it were still there on the wall, which was entirely more distressing. She locked herself in her bathroom but then wondered if the moment it would take to unlock the door would be her undoing when the poltergeist decided to come after her.

Stop that! she admonished herself. "No poltergeist is coming to get you." But the statement took several hours of repeating over and over to herself along with all sorts of breathing exercises to calm her heart enough for her to go to sleep. And even then, her dreams were fitful and brimming with things chasing her, catching her, clawing at her curly hair; and when she saw the creatures who were after her, there was bright pink lipstick smeared over their faces as if a child had tried to make them look pretty and failed.

Ireland had never been more grateful for school than she had after a weekend of being in her own head. She needed the company of others. So when she slid into her seat and saw Kal smiling at her, her heart rate leveled off for the first time in days.

"Hey there," he said.

"Hey." There were a lot of things Ireland could have said. She could have asked after his weekend. She could have thanked him again for letting her watch him and his band play and sharing their dinner with her. She could have asked if he got the homework assignment done. But all she managed was that one word. She felt all the stupidity of wanting desperately to talk to someone all weekend and then not knowing how when the opportunity finally showed up.

Luckily, Kal was not as tongue-tied as she was.

"It was really great having you there to see us play. Thanks for coming and supporting us. It's good business if it looks like we have friends who can bring customers to the restaurant."

"I didn't exactly bring customers."

He waved away her protest. "It always looks good for the restaurant to look full. It makes it seem like a hot spot and encourages people to come back. It's totally a FOMO thing."

"Glad I could help?" Ireland hated that it sounded like a question. But she wasn't entirely sure that he wasn't just making stuff up about her helping the restaurant. She didn't want to be anybody's charity case. But she also didn't want to look too deeply at the possibility that she *was* a charity case. Because what she really wanted was a friend, and she didn't want to sabotage that by overanalyzing.

Kal was tapping an art pencil on his desk before he blurted out, "I have a favor to ask. So I'm in charge of this art project for Wasden's class. And I'm thinking I could use some help. It's pretty intense, and it's going to require a lot of support from students. And I could use somebody who loves art the way I think you love it. What do you say? Want to be on my art team?" He waited expectantly as if she would be excited about whatever this project was, but he hadn't said *what* it was.

The image that came to her mind was the lipstick on her bathroom wall. Maybe the art project had already started, and she was a victim of it. *Stop that,* she thought. Kal was not running around sabotaging her life in the woods. In the first place, he had no idea where she was living. In the second place, he was not a villain. She was a pretty good judge of people, so she was sure of that. She smiled at him.

"So? Why are you smiling at me like that?"

This time, the smile felt like it went all the way down to her toes. "You haven't actually told me what this art project is. So how am I supposed to know if I want to be involved or not?"

Kal's olive complexion took on a much rosier hue. Blushing. Ireland hadn't been aware that men could blush, since she'd never seen it. His blush warmed her up inside.

"Right. Sorry about that," he said. "So, Wasden put me in charge of doing something that would bring the student body together, whether they were artistically inclined or not. And it seems a mural would be an amazing way for all of us to kind of get to know one another better. A chance to be creative. I want to create a mural that anyone can add their creative flair to. What do you think?"

"Sounds pretty straightforward. What would you need me to do? Hang the butcher paper?" She couldn't see how she could help with this at all.

"Not paper. We're doing this on the actual wall. It's going to be a semipermanent part of our school. At least, it will be if I can get permission. What you will do is help me get the wall ready. Then you and I will put the very first art projects on the wall. That way we can kind of show students what to expect."

It was hard not to be suspicious. Why would he pick her? It's not like she was in the advanced art classes. Wasn't Kal in the art club? Didn't he have people in the art club with him who would expect to be part of a project like that? Ireland wasn't sure if it was because she looked skeptical and probably more than a little suspicious, but Kal interrupted her wandering thoughts.

"I chose you for this because I've seen what you can do. You have an incredible amount of talent. I don't know why you're not in the advanced art classes. But I think it's okay for the world to see that you've got a lot going on. Artistically speaking."

He added that last part in a rush. His complexion went rosy again. It struck her that maybe he liked her. Like *like*-liked her.

Why else would he be blushing? That was new. But she was probably reading more into things than she needed to. Maybe he just was incredibly shy and didn't like talking to people. But if he was shy, how could he get up on a stage and play a guitar and sing?

She did an inner eye roll. She was overthinking things. Maybe he just had a fever or a flu or had eaten some chili peppers before class or whatever.

Kal was looking at her expectantly. That's right. She hadn't answered him yet. She did another inward eye roll. "Yeah. Sure. I can help with that."

"Great! I think we should get started right after school. Sorry if you have plans or if that's too soon or something. If it is, we can totally rework it, but I think the sooner the better, right?"

Ireland thought about the fact that some girls played weird games where they made themselves unavailable so that it looked like they were aloof. Maybe she should have said, "Yeah, sorry. I do have plans. How about three days from now." But she didn't really see the point in that sort of thing. If you were available, you should say you're available. And if you're not, then say you're not. It was something she hated about her dad. The man never said what he meant. He only ever said the things that got him what he wanted. He was a master manipulator. Ireland was never going to be that person. "I'm totally available after school. Let's get this started."

Kal seemed pleased and, for whatever reason, that pleased her as well.

After school, Ireland was making her way to the front hall when she overheard female voices from around the corner. "So? Details! Spill the tea, girl. How was he at the clambake?"

Ireland recognized the voice. It was Emily, the hag in Mara's "shrew, hag, and harpy" group.

The voice that answered was also one she recognized, Mara Washington's. "He was . . . fine."

Mara's friends didn't seem to notice Mara's hesitation when she answered. How could they not see that "fine" was hardly what anyone called a glowing endorsement? But the others seemed to take the word "fine" and apply to it all sorts of innuendos and meanings besides the one Ireland felt sure it actually had.

"I bet it was *fine*." That voice was Tinsley's. "To get cozy in that sweet ride with his hot breath all over you!" She squealed as if living out an actual fantasy. "He did kiss you, right? Please tell me he kissed you. What's the point if he didn't?"

"Come on, guys. I don't really want to talk about it."

"Don't be so extra, Mara," Tinsley said. "It's not like kissing Rowan is some sacred event that must be kept to yourself. We're your friends. We have the right to know."

Ireland wanted to snort at that. They had a right to know? If being friends with someone gave them a right to know every detail about your private life, Ireland was glad she'd never really had friends.

"I bet he was a good kisser," Tinsley continued.

Ugh and blech! Were the shrew, hag, and harpy going to talk forever? Ireland knew she should just turn the corner and walk on past them. But after they'd been ten kinds of horrible to her when she'd carried the cleaning supplies home, she wasn't up to dealing with their ridicule. As it was, she'd had to go to school early the day she'd returned the supplies so they wouldn't see her. She looked down the hall. The only other way she could go was out the back door and all the way around the school to come in through the front. But maybe that would be worth it? She didn't budge though. Something felt weird about the whole conversation she was overhearing. She didn't know why; something was just *off*.

Mara gave a shaky laugh. "Well, of course he was. How could he be anything but?"

Ireland heard the lie. Sometimes she felt like a human lie detector—the hazard of growing up with a father who ate dishonesty for breakfast, lunch, and dinner—at least on those days when he got three meals.

Not that being a lie detector had ever really done her any good. It's not like anybody handed out awards or cash prizes for such a thing. It never got her a better place to sleep. It never gave her more nutritious food. And in her current situation, it was certainly not going to get these girls to be her friends.

That decided it. She turned to go out the back door. Even though Ireland felt pretty certain Mara wasn't *like* her friends, exactly, she also wasn't strong enough to stand *up* to her friends. The whole hierarchy of that friend group confused Ireland. Mara was the queen bee of the group. She was the pretty one. Well. Okay. They were all gorgeous in their own ways. But Mara was definitely the most beautiful of them. However, Mara didn't gravitate toward them; they gravitated toward her—which practically required others to see them when they were with her. Mara welcomed them into her circle but never seemed to notice if others were watching or not. Ireland suspected that, had Mara been left to her own devices and welcomed nicer people into her circle, she'd probably qualify as a nice human too.

"But the world will never know." Ireland said this out loud and then looked around to make sure nobody had caught her talking to herself and was glad she'd moved far enough from the corner where the girls were to avoid them overhearing her. She really had to stop doing that. Just because she spent a lot of time on her own didn't mean she could act like an eccentric hermit person when she was in public.

She exited the school and walked around the entire building.

She hoped Kal was still waiting for her. She'd taken enough time to get to him that he might have thought she'd bailed on him. If the shrew, hag, and harpy made her miss a chance to spend time with Kal, she was going to . . . well, she didn't know what. She wondered: if she'd had the same opportunities that Mara and her friends had been privileged with, would she be shallow, vapid, and offhandedly savage like them?

"The world will never know," she repeated. And for the first time ever, she felt grateful to have had her own experiences because she suspected that savagery lurked in her as well.

CHAPTER SIX

Kal

Mr. Wasden loved the idea of the student mural when Kal ran it past him. He had all sorts of ideas for it and had spent the afternoon talking to the principal to get approval. Now Mr. Wasden and the principal, Mrs. Parker, stood in the front hall with Kal debating the use of the wall Wasden wanted.

Kal saw Ireland pulling the door open and hurried over to meet her. "Where are you coming from? Cutting class?"

"What?" She blinked, clearly confused, until she looked behind her and said, "Oh. You mean because I'm coming from outside. Right. I . . ." Her eyebrows furrowed together as if trying to come up with a reason, but instead of explaining anything, she just shrugged and pointed to Wasden and Mrs. Parker. "What's going on here?"

Since the art teacher and the principal seemed to be in a hot debate, it was no wonder she felt curious. "Eh. There are concerns."

"Like what?"

"Like, can we trust the student body with art supplies like paints and not expect them to graffiti the whole school? Can we trust the student body to not be hateful, crude, or vulgar if we give them free run of a wall and art supplies? Do we really want that to be the first thing people see when they enter the school, and isn't there a wall better suited to such things, like the one in the art hall instead?"

Ireland laughed. "She's got a point. I wouldn't trust any of us with unsupervised access to all this."

Kal hadn't expected Ireland to be on the principal's side. He'd thought the woman was overreacting, but Ireland shrugging off his mockery made him rethink his stance. Kal had once called Mrs. Parker a handwringer since she seemed chronically worried, but both of his parents had chastised him and said he had no idea the amount of pressure that was placed on a principal.

They were right. He didn't have any idea, which helped keep him from being *too* critical. Even so, he thought she was being overly dramatic about the mural. It's not like he was asking if they could play with fireworks and matches in the front hall.

He surveyed Ireland a moment before saying, "Let's go do some peace talks between those two. Maybe you can help me broker a deal." He almost reached out to take her hand when he pulled back, feeling dumb for not thinking that through. She barely knew him and had ditched him at Geppetto's. Why would she want him to take her hand?

Kal tucked his hands into his pockets and led the way back to the adults disagreeing loudly enough to be fighting.

"I was thinking that maybe giving this a framework would solve most of your concerns," Kal said.

Both adults went quiet and turned to him to listen. He had to hand it to them for being cool enough to care what the teenager had to say.

"Yeah. Framework," he continued. "Like maybe we do a large outline of the school's mountain lion mascot lying under our local defining feature, a redwood tree, while staring out at our other local defining feature, the ocean. It ties in a lot of things that feel important to our area while also showing school pride. It helps us incorporate a lot of colors, too, so we can paint the outline in the sorts of colors each area requires, and maybe one of the rules is that students can only use those colors that tie into the outlined area. Like various shades of greens for the treetop, earth tones for the trunk, and blues for the ocean. It'll keep it from being an eyesore."

Eyesore was one of his dad's favorite words. He used it to describe his clothes when they became too dated or worn, his bicycle when it had been wrecked on one of his rides, or even his desk, which he acknowledged was a special kind of disaster.

Wasden practically glowed with approval at Kal's suggestion, so Kal continued. "And we'll have other very specific rules. If anyone puts anything up that's hateful, hurtful, or crude, we will paint over the top of it."

"Right," Wasden agreed. "And we put a time limit for when they can make contributions. So say we only have the supplies available for a week or two. When the time's up, the art club can use their skills to clean it up and make each section flow into the next so it's one cohesive piece."

Kal had learned the word *cohesive* from Wasden in his first-ever art class. He liked the word and used it more often than was probably normal.

Mrs. Parker had her chin resting on her hand. She was definitely thinking it through. "You know what? I like what you're saying, but it still needs to be monitored better than you could do out here in the hall. Even if you paint over something hateful as soon as you see it, it won't change the fact that someone might have seen it before you. We don't need that kind of negativity. The mural being monitored will help people follow their own better judgment. But I don't want the headaches of before- and after-school monitoring. That just seems like a storm of trouble." Mrs. Parker was wringing her hands as if imagining the mischief of kids in her building during nonschool hours.

"We could give access to the mural only during lunch," Ireland said.

Kal loved that Ireland joined in the discussion. Loved that she was supporting his idea enough to help find solutions. Loved that she'd used the word "we" like they were in this together.

"I approve your project," Mrs. Parker said, "but it has to be in the art room on the back wall there. It's the only way it can be monitored at all times and then locked up when you're not in the room."

Kal then added, "Maybe we tell everyone it'll only be up a few months so we can paint over it if it doesn't feel like a good fit to keep long-term. That way, if we do decide to keep it, it'll be a big surprise instead of a letdown."

"Who is responsible for keeping that space clean and not interfering with normal classes?" Mrs. Parker asked.

"I will be," Ireland said. "I can set it up and take it down for lunch every day."

Kal felt his mouth go slack as he stared at Ireland in disbelief.

Mrs. Parker nodded her head several times. "Okay. You've convinced me. Honestly, Mr. Ellis, you should have joined the debate team, not the art club. And Miss Raine, it's nice to see you getting involved. Let's do this." Mrs. Parker waved in the direction of the art hall and hurried off toward her office.

"Excellent!" Kal said.

"Good work, you two," Wasden said. "I liked that you gave solutions that appealed to her. Compromise in situations like this shows good character. Why don't you both come up with some thumbnail sketches to show how you envision the wall looking?

It would be good if you involved the art club in the early stages, so Ireland, if you can, it would be great to see you at the art club meeting. The point of a project like this is to be inclusive, so let's make that happen. Invite anyone else to art club who might want to come. Let's get thumbnails from everyone and then vote on the options given. I'd like to see those thumbnails by the end of the week. We have school pride week coming up, and this would be a great way to kick it off."

With all his instructions given, Wasden excused himself and left Ireland and Kal alone in the front hall. Kal suddenly felt nervous. He wanted to say something . . . anything, but the words seemed to evaporate from his mind before they could fully form, and his tongue felt like it had been sealed to the roof of his mouth.

He had originally been fascinated with Ireland because of the way she reminded him of Brell, but the more he learned about her, the more he liked her because she was someone legitimately worth liking. The way she'd jumped in to volunteer to help every day was huge. It was a major time commitment most people would never have signed up for, and she didn't seem to think it was that big a deal at all.

"You're kind of extraordinary, you know that?" he blurted.

She blinked at him and her mouth fell open, but she didn't say anything. Kal wished *he* hadn't said anything. What was she thinking? *Probably that I'm cracked in the head.*

"Why would you say that?" she asked, interrupting his mental scolding.

"About you? Why wouldn't I? How many people would volunteer to set up and clean up every day for a mural they got roped into helping with?"

She shifted her weight on her feet. "Why wouldn't I? You asked for help. I don't really see how else I can be useful here."

"I didn't ask you so you could be the project janitor. I asked you to help because you're talented—specifically at drawing the redwoods. I've seen you sketch them in your sketchbooks, and they're pretty amazing. It's what gave me this idea."

"Anyone can draw trees," Ireland said. Her ear tips had turned pink with embarrassment at him calling attention to her work.

He shook his head. "I'm gonna have to disagree." He frowned. "I mean, okay, I guess technically you're right, since most pre-schoolers manage to pull it off. But I am going to say that not everyone can draw a *good* tree. You can."

Ireland crossed her arms and leaned up against the wall. "Maybe. But ink on paper is different from painting. The last time I used oils, it looked like a tornado had happened in a paint factory. Not even Bob Ross could claim my work as a happy accident."

Kal laughed. Ireland probably wasn't trying to be funny, but she grinned at him. As he held her gaze, the one word that kept coming to his mind was *cerulean*. Her eyes were the deep blue of a clear sky on a bright summer day. "I Icy," he said. "Want to come get a burger with me and come up with some thumbnails?"

The grin was gone, replaced with something else. "Oh. Actually . . ." she checked the clock on the wall. "I didn't bring my wallet, and anyway, I should get home."

She was going to try to ditch him again. "Wallet schmallet," he said, reaching out his hand and hoping she'd take it. "I actually forgot mine too. Let's go to my house instead. I don't live too far from here. I can make us some sandwiches, and we can work. You heard Wasden. He wants those thumbnails by the end of the week." She looked at his hand as if his fingers were spider legs. "We don't want to disappoint him."

Wasden was the kind of guy who expected the best in people. No one wanted to disappoint him.

Apparently, Ireland wasn't any different because bringing Wasden up decided it for her. "Okay." She slipped her hand in his, and Kal's breath caught at the immediate warmth and comfort that came from having his fingers wrapped around hers. In a way, it felt like she was trusting him with the rough calluses of her palm that came from hoisting a duffel bag into the air every day. Even though he knew she wasn't really trusting him with anything because she didn't know that he knew.

"Okay, then." He walked with her to his truck and pressed the key fob. He regretted having to drop her hand, but he had to so he could open her door and clear away the debris enough to fit another human in his truck. "Ignore the mess," he said as he shoved aside a bunch of various papers and empty food wrappers so that Ireland wouldn't have to sit on them when she got in. Why did he never keep his truck clean? He didn't want Ireland to think he was a slob, but as he cast a critical eye over the front seat, the debris on the floormats and the dust on the dashboard were silent witnesses to the fact that he hadn't spent a lot of time keeping his space clean. To be fair to him, it was too cold to deep clean the car, not that the weather excused the lack of basic upkeep. He peeked in Ireland's direction as she slid in on the passenger's side.

She didn't look repulsed or even slightly bothered by the hygienic negligence. But then . . . she was living in a bathroom, so maybe he should count his blessings that her standards had been reduced by her situation.

Count his blessings that she lived in a bathroom? Where had that thought come from? He peeked at her again, glad she couldn't hear his thoughts. If she could, she would think he was the kind of heartless guy who tripped puppies and yelled obscenities at old ladies.

He hoped his need to feed her wasn't too obvious. Looking casual about the whole thing was harder than he'd imagined. He'd spent the weekend trying to come up with ways to help her or get her to open up to him, but seriously, what could he say? "Hey, so that bathroom thing . . . it sucks, *amirite*? Let's talk about it." And although he'd almost told his parents about her situation, he'd managed to keep her secret from them too—a thing he felt he should get an award for doing because that was harder than he'd imagined as well.

They drove to his house in relative silence. But it wasn't awkward like he felt like silence should probably be. Ireland seemed comfortable with the silence and, oddly, he felt comfortable too.

At Kal's house, they both got out and went inside. He looked around the living room—white, clean, spacious—as if seeing it for the first time. They hadn't lived there long. Not even a whole year yet. They'd bought it because they were moving his grandfather in with them and needed to make sure the space fit everyone comfortably. His mom was a hobbyist interior decorator, so the bookshelves were curated with a mix of classy, leather-bound books, Grandpa's personal mementos, and comfortable knickknacks that Kal and his siblings had made his mom and dad growing up. His mom managed to make all of this come together in a way that looked like it belonged on the homepage of *Good Housekeeping's* website.

If anyone had ever asked him if bits of childish art and actual art could live in harmony next to each other, he probably would have said, "Not a chance." But his mom had proved otherwise.

The perfectly structured shelves, along with the plush area rugs, the oversized sofa with the perfectly matching throw pillows, and the perfectly oversized fireplace made him suddenly feel like a *perfect* snob.

He sketched another glance at Ireland, wishing that he could read thoughts. It wasn't too much to ask to be able to read thoughts, was it? The scene before him was nothing like a bathroom in the woods. He decided then and there to *not* take her on a tour to show off the library or the theater room.

"It's a really nice house," Ireland said. There was a quiet reverence to the comment, which probably wouldn't have bothered Kal, except he knew the circumstances she came from. Guilt saturated every cell in his body. He'd never really thought of himself as rich before. Comfortable, maybe, but not rich. Not before this moment. And, okay, he had friends and even some family who lived in less-than-ideal circumstances, so it wasn't like he had no understanding of people being poor. But Ireland's situation seemed different to him somehow. His friends and family who were not as well off as he was had community and family around them to support them. They weren't alone. Ireland was by herself in the woods.

Kal shook himself out of his thoughts and tried to smile at her. But could she see the conflict in him? Probably. He had to stop being such so ridiculous. They had needed the larger space so that Grandpa would feel okay with moving out of his old house. And his mom had wanted space for his brothers to stay when they came to visit.

"Is this your work?" Ireland pointed to the painting on the far wall. It was of a woman in a white ball gown holding a fistful of balloon strings, but instead of balloons on the other ends of the strings, there were puffy owls and one bumblebee. The background was a starry twilight sky. He'd always liked it.

"No. That's my grandfather's. He's an artist. He sold most of his work over time to pay bills, but we managed to hang on to a few pieces before he could sell everything. He calls this one *Twilight Flyers*. Do you want something to drink, maybe eat?"

She tilted her head back so she could see up into the vaulted ceiling and the windows that let in the warm afternoon light. "Sure." She turned away from him and wandered over to the bookshelves, inspecting the books that were there. Her brow was furrowed in what might have been confusion.

Though he wasn't sure why she would be confused.

"These your siblings?" She pointed to a family portrait showing off the five kids in their family.

"Yeah. I'm the youngest. They're all moved out—either in college or married."

"All boys?"

"Yep. My parents say they wouldn't trade any of us for a girl, but I know they both wanted a daughter. They were glad when they started getting daughters-in-law." Kal wished that Ireland would turn and look at him so that he could know how she felt at that moment. Which was stupid because how was he supposed to know how she felt just because they locked eyes? And yet he did feel that if he could actually see into her eyes, he would be able to know where she was at emotionally.

His mom sometimes called Kal an empath. She said that his feelings were bigger than his body, which was why she thought he fell so hard for Brell and fell so hard again when Brell dropped him. And then he seemed to never stop falling when Brell was suddenly gone. Big emotions. They weren't exactly manly, but he was what he was. And he'd decided to embrace it a long time ago. It was fine to be both a man and be hyperemotional—though his mom said he was still her little boy and not exactly a man yet. She thought she was funny when she said things like that. He thought it was more annoying than endearing.

Ireland finally did look at him then, as if her confusion was greater than it had been when she was looking at the books.

"Right," he said. "Sorry. I'm supposed to go get food now. You want to come with me, or do you want to hang out here?"

"I'll come with you." She followed him through the living room, down the short hallway, and into the kitchen.

He watched Ireland take everything in. Her head kept swiveling, from the leaded glass in the white decorator cabinets to the art on the wall to the single stained-glass window in its octagonal frame in the breakfast nook.

Yes. Guilt had settled uncomfortably over Kal's shoulders. His life really was fire. And he'd never bothered to be grateful for it.

Kal opened the fridge and pulled out the various deli meats and cheeses that had already been sliced by their local butcher. He then pulled out the mustard, mayo, pickles, and romaine lettuce.

Ireland's eyes had shifted from confusion to curiosity to hunger. Kal wasn't going to lie. Having a girl look at him with that ravenous need would have been totally awesome if it had been *him* that she needed. But she wasn't looking at him; she was looking at the foods placed on the island in the center of his kitchen.

"What can I help with?" she asked.

"You can cut the tomato." He pointed to the various vegetables and fruits in the bowl on the center of the island.

He handed her a cutting board and a knife.

"Wow," she murmured.

"What?"

"Even your knives are fancy."

Kal glanced at the knife in her hand. It was a Cutco. His mom insisted on that particular brand. She sent them in once every year to get them sharpened.

He didn't know how to respond to her comment, so he instead asked what kind of cheese she wanted. They busied themselves with sandwich making before taking their food to the breakfast nook to eat and start the thumbnails Mr. Wasden wanted.

They had a dozen good ones before he realized she was staring at him.

"I've got mustard on my face, don't I?" He swiped at his cheeks and around his mouth.

She laughed. "No. I'm just impressed. You came up with those sketches fast. And they're good. Really good."

"Thanks."

"You really love art, don't you? I mean, I sketch because it feels like cheap therapy, but you are on a whole different level."

"Asking if I love art is like asking if I love cheeseburgers."

"Is this where you tell me you're vegan?" Her lips turned up at the corners so slightly that he could only describe it as a Mona Lisa smile.

He laughed at her joke and felt warmth flood his insides at this new connection with her—this connection of just talking and joking and eating and art.

"Yep. Vegan. That's me. The sandwiches we just ate were made of vegan meats and cheeses."

She nodded. "Nice. Quality replicas are hard to find. So, vegan, huh?"

"Yeah. Don't even get me started on the evils of ice cream or, worse, pepperoni."

When she looked pretend shocked at him, he laughed and held up his hands. "I kid. I kid. I love all of that, including the art. Don't tell anyone, but I actually applied for an art scholarship."

"That's awesome. Why would it matter if anyone knew?"

"Eh, my dad. He would think it was awesome times zero."

Ireland leaned back in her chair and puffed out her cheeks in a huge sigh. "You are evil."

"What? Why?" She didn't really think he was evil, did she?

"You turned the word awesome into a math problem. You've completely ruined awesome for me."

Ah. She was joking. Funny. Ireland's sense of humor surprised

Kal. Her circumstances led him to believe that she would be all mopey and sad and scared. All. The. Time. But she thrummed with strength and humor and, sure, hunger too, but she wasn't some helpless girl who needed him to save her. Even so, he couldn't stop himself from trying.

"Why would your dad not want you to have an art scholarship?" she asked, her fingers playing with the cloth napkin by her now empty plate. "Isn't every parent hoping their kid gets a scholarship so they get out of paying for college and buy themselves boats or expensive . . ." She looked around as if trying to think of something expensive enough. "Rocks," she finally finished.

"Rocks?"

"Landscaping is expensive . . . I hear."

"But rocks?"

She shrugged. "Diamonds are rocks."

He laughed at that, then stood and picked up their dishes to rinse off and put in the dishwasher.

"We've got the whole thumbnail thing figured out," she said. "I should get going."

"Right. Let me drive you home." It was a jerk suggestion since he knew what her living situation was like, but he hoped she would decide to trust him enough on her own to tell the truth.

"I actually really like walking." Her words came out too fast.

"I do too. Want me to walk with you?"

"No. No, thank you. I'm good. I'll see you tomorrow in school." She all but fled to the front door to make her escape.

He followed her and waved goodbye from the open door. Then he closed it and hung his head in his hands, letting his fingers drum the top of his head while he considered all the different things he could do.

"I should tell someone," he said to his now empty house. But who could he tell and not have her resent him forever?

He couldn't think of anyone. And worse, he was sure she would do more than just resent him if he told anyone. The independent girl who'd just fled from his house would hate him.

CHAPTER SEVEN
Ireland

He'd held her hand. Kalvin Ellis had held her hand. Hers! Not somebody else's, but *hers*. It had been four days, and it was all she could think about. He had held her hand like it was no big deal, like he wasn't touching some sort of pariah. He had held it like it was something natural and normal, but when his fingers made contact with hers, she'd felt anything but normal and all sorts of wonderfully absurd. Absurd in that she felt like breaking into song like one of those over-the-top actors from a musical.

It had been days, but she still wanted to grab people by the shoulders and shout, "Kalvin Ellis held my hand!" She was sure she hadn't stopped grinning since the moment she'd left his house after they'd created the thumbnails. In spite of the fact that they'd spent a lot of time together since then, he hadn't done it again. She kept waiting for him to extend his fingers in her direction, but so far, no luck.

Not that they'd had tons of time to be doing any handholding. They'd been working pretty much nonstop to get the murals project up and running smoothly. The art club meetings were not worth the amped-up anxiety Ireland had felt before the first one. Since someone as high in the social pecking order as Mara Washington was in the club, how likely would it be that the rest of the club would accept someone like Ireland?

But then . . . Kal had accepted her, so why wouldn't they?

She'd also worried about being used as Mara's punching bag, but Mara had been completely civil. Ireland figured it was because the hag and harpy weren't around. She was sure that if those two had been present, Ireland would've been a target.

The nice thing was that the other people in the art club didn't seem too perplexed when Ireland showed up. They made space for her within their group. Literally. As in, the first day, when Ireland showed up late, people scooted aside their chairs to make room for her at the table. The table was a little extra cozy with her and the six actual art club members, but they hadn't minded smooshing together for her. Of the six, three of them were part of Kal's band—Asha, Cooper, and, of course, Kal. The other three were Mara and two other girls: blue-eyed Sophie and red-bespectacled Charisma. Charisma was the girl who had smiled at her on that first day she'd decided to start trying to make friends, and Ireland still loved her for it.

Ireland felt a sense of belonging for the first time in her life. And she had Kal to thank for it.

Beyond the emotional boost he'd become in her life, Ireland hadn't felt hungry since they'd started hanging out. It seemed like food was a big deal to Kal. Whenever Kal was with her outside of class, they were eating. He'd show up with a fancy cooler bag filled with meat-and-cheese sandwiches similar to those they'd had that first time at his house, or he'd have his backpack half-full of snacks, and he'd dump them unceremoniously on the table where they were working. She would have wondered what his ulterior motives were, except for the fact that he always ate with her and declared himself to be completely starving. It didn't feel as if he was treating her like some sort of charity case. How could he? It's not like he knew what was going on in her life. He was just a nice person who didn't enjoy eating in front of others without sharing. He always brought enough to share with several people. He wasn't just feeding her but everyone who came to the meetings on the mural. It took a lot of the weirdness factor out of the situation for her.

It was as he dropped the cooler bag on the table where the group of art club kids had gathered to do the final vote for the mural that Asha from Kal's band flipped back her long blue-green hair and said, "You really need to tell your mom how much I love her. Maybe ask if she'll adopt me. My mom's idea of fixing me lunch is buying me a gift card to fast-food."

Several chuckles and murmurs of agreement followed.

"*Your* family can adopt me too," Asha continued as she pointed toward Mara. "Your dad's triple-chocolate croissant is a thing of legend."

Mara scoffed. "You'd rethink that whole adoption concept if you were the one waking up at three o'clock in the morning on Saturdays to help him make dough."

Asha was undeterred. She shrugged. "Maybe. But you get to eat what you make, and that would absolutely make it worth it. Plus, I'm guessing he shares his secret recipes with you."

"The secret is hard work and getting up at three in the morning on Saturdays." Mara grumbled this while she peered into Kal's cooler and pulled out carrot sticks and a tub of some sort of dip.

Asha tilted her head and inspected Mara. "You think he does that to keep you from staying out too late on Friday night?"

"No idea," Mara said. "I only know I get tomorrow off because of the Heartbeat dance."

"Are you going with Rowan?" Sophie asked.

"No!" The sharp answer all but sliced the air, but no one

except Ireland seemed to be shocked by it. Or maybe they just weren't commenting on it, like Ireland wasn't. The Heartbeat formal had been the topic of a good many conversations between the club members. Ireland had hung on to every word to see if Kal was going to the dance, but it seemed he hadn't asked anyone and had no intention of going on his own.

Mara sucked in a deep breath and smiled as if she hadn't done a snapping turtle impression when responding about going to the formal with Rowan. She continued her conversation with Asha. "Your best bet is to have Superman's family adopt you. That way you'd get your mommy to pack you snacks and lunch every day." She squinted into the cooler again. "I'll bet if we look hard enough in here, we'll find his blankie and stuffed animal as well. I bet he has a stuffed elephant." Mara put down the bag and stared at Kal with a smirk.

Kal swiped away the tub of dip at the same time that Mara reached for it.

"Hey!"

Kal held it out of her reach. "You mean to say, 'Hey, I'm sorry I was being a cranky head.'"

Mara stood up and lunged for the tub until she'd all but tackled Kal in her effort to get it. "Using words like 'cranky head' proves you *do* have a blankie on your person somewhere," she said with a laugh.

A weird twinge of discomfort twisted in Ireland's stomach. She looked down at her hands instead of at Mara with Kal. It's not like she had anything against Mara, exactly, but she didn't love watching Kal flirt with the prettiest girl in school when that same girl hadn't done anything to prove herself worthy of a guy like Kal.

There. That explained it. Ireland wasn't jealous. She was simply trying to protect Kal's interests.

How would that particular lie rank? Top one hundred? Top fifty? Maybe higher. Oh well. She was sticking to it. Honesty to oneself could be overrated sometimes. That was another lie that was easily in the top twenty. She really had to stop lying to herself.

Ireland forced herself to look up and smile at the antics. Mara was gloating over the hummus dip that she'd wrangled from Kal's grip and settling herself back on her chair as if she were a queen and had won a scepter instead of a tub of mashed-up chickpeas.

Kal's grin, which normally fluttered Ireland's insides like a monarch migration, instead irritated her and made her kind of want to throw a carrot stick at his head.

"Are you two done flirting, or can we vote now?" Charisma asked, not even looking at the food in the center of the table because she had her phone out and was likely texting her boyfriend. She'd already declared she had plans with him that afternoon and had been antsy to get going.

Ireland really liked Charisma, even if the girl had confirmed Ireland's fears that maybe Mara and Kal *had* been flirting with each other.

"Sorry," Kal said. "We're voting now." Mara had handed out slips of paper to each of the club members when they'd come in. They all bent their heads to write the number of their favorite of the design finalists. The designs were based on the thumbnails that Wasden had already selected.

Mara stood and put her own slip of paper in a tulip-dotted white handbag. "Give it to Kate," she sang.

"Kate?" Sophie whispered over to Cooper, echoing Ireland's thought.

"Spade," Cooper said with a smirk.

He said it like it meant something significant, which meant the rather trite-looking bag was expensive.

Mara shook the bag up and dumped it on the table in front

of Kal. He tallied the votes and then declared, "Okay, we have a winner! It looks like Julianna Kessler's design is pretty much everybody's choice." Everyone nodded as if there had been no question. It was the one Ireland had voted for. The use of different colors and open spaces within the tree, mountain lion, and ocean gave creative opportunities for the student body and made it feel like it would accomplish the unification that Mr. Wasden had wanted.

"With the exception of Charisma, who has a date, let's get started." All of the prep work had already been done. Mr. Wasden wanted them to get the outlines done that afternoon so the mural could dry and be ready for the rest of the student body on Monday morning. The back wall had already been cleared and was ready for them. Mara, as art club vice president, assigned each person the space they would be working on so they weren't tripping over each other, and they got to work.

Ireland had been assigned the tree trunk while Kal had been assigned the treetop. Part of her wondered if Mara had assigned her the less complicated part of the sketch on purpose because she didn't trust Ireland with anything else, but she decided she didn't care because the way things were, she got to work alongside Kal while Mara was clear on the opposite end of the wall.

"Who is the most memorable stranger you've ever met?" Kal asked after he'd pulled himself up on the small scaffolding they'd set up and had begun working. He had a tendency to ask those sorts of questions a lot—the kind that led to sharing full stories. "And I mean in a good way. I don't feel like talking about skeezy strangers."

"Good thing you clarified. There were tons of skeezy strangers. Um . . . well, my dad and I moved around a lot, and there was this one time when we'd just barely moved into a new apartment, and, apparently, the next-door neighbor lady had a key to our place.

She let herself in that first morning and started making breakfast. I woke up to the smell of pancakes, eggs, and bacon for, like, the first time ever in my life." Ireland didn't add that it was the *only* time ever in her life because that was just pathetic.

Ireland penciled in the outline of the tree trunk. Unlike Kal, who had started his outlines in paint, she wanted to make sure the lines were the way she liked before she committed to them with the permanence of paint. "Anyway, I get up—thinking it was my dad—and walked into the kitchen and screamed when I saw her. She was this really grandma-looking old lady with a full-on bun and little half glasses, so my screaming was completely . . . well, ten degrees of stupid. She could have been Mrs. Claus with her sweet, round red cheeks and soft eyes. Baby bunnies are more terrifying than that woman. When I screamed, she did too. It took a while to get both of us to calm down."

Ireland finally traded her pencil for the paintbrush, carefully painting over her pencil marks in brushstrokes. "Turns out, the previous tenant had been her friend, and she was moving, so she wanted to cook her friend breakfast as a sort of goodbye. She didn't realize her friend had already moved because she'd been out of town visiting her son. She was sad to have her friend gone, and her genuine concern for that other person was sweet. We ended up eating breakfast together." Ireland paused, her paintbrush hovering over the mural. "I think about that lady with the bun sometimes and wonder where she is and how she's doing, and who she's making breakfast for now."

"How old were you?" Kal had stopped working too and was looking down at her through the scaffolding brackets.

"Seven? Maybe eight." At the time, Ireland had wanted this woman to adopt her and make her breakfast all the time, but they had only been in the apartment a week before her dad had to pack up and flee in the middle of the night. He'd grifted the wrong person—a guy with mob connections—and had to run for his life, and hers too.

"That's amazing that you were this little kid eating breakfast with a random lady." Kal was laughing. "Where was your dad in all this? Did he freak out to see you at the table with some strange woman?"

"He tends to sleep like the dead. He slept right through it." Ireland didn't mention that her dad was likely hungover or possibly just not home from being out all night. She didn't really remember, but either scenario was likely. "I guess between zombie dad and the breaking-and-entering breakfast lady, it was a pretty eventful day. What about you? Who's your most memorable stranger?"

Kal grinned and dropped his paintbrush in a water can, then sat on the scaffolding, probably realizing he wasn't going to paint and talk at the same time. "So there I was, shopping with my mom and dad, and they sent me to the freezer section to get some ice cream. I was like nine at the time. So there I am, carefully reviewing the choices because ice cream is a big deal, and I wanted to make sure I got the right flavor, when this older guy comes up, and he's looking at all the choices too. He shifted in a way that felt familiar—from one foot to the next and back again, just like I do, so I stopped looking at the ice cream and looked at him instead. He was old, like fifty maybe, but seriously, the guy looked just like me when I do one of those age-up filters online."

Kal's eyes lit up as he told his story, getting warm and soft as he seemed to be searching back through his memories. "So we started talking, and it turns out his name is Ellis, like mine. We both picked the same ice cream, and, as he left, he said, 'Live the good life, kid.' And then he walked away and whistled a tune from my favorite video game. And then it hit me: I had probably been talking to my future self, which means I'm gonna get to time travel someday, which is pretty cool."

Ireland burst out laughing. "You think he was you?"

"I don't think. I'm pretty sure it *was* me. And don't be laughing, or maybe I won't come visit you when I'm time traveling."

She poked the tip of her paintbrush up at his nose, leaving a green dot. "If you time travel to visit me, make sure you bring me some future stats on companies I should invest in."

Kal put his hand on his heart. "You wound me! The mockery!" Then he scrubbed at his nose to wipe off the paint and said, "You're lucky I'm a gentleman, or you would be covered from head to toe in paint." He pulled his brush out of the can and tapped out the excess water before dipping it back into the paint.

Ireland smiled to herself. He was such a good guy. She'd gotten to a point where when she wasn't with him, she was thinking about him. Thoughts of him kept her company when she was alone in the woods. They made her feel less afraid—less lonely. She knew it was seriously stupid wishful thinking, but Ireland hoped if he did invent a time-traveling machine and went cruising through the years of history, he wouldn't need to come visit her in the past. She hoped she would still be in his life in that future and that he'd take her to time travel the world with him.

CHAPTER EIGHT

Kal

Kal swirled a few paints together, pulling the emerald down into the forest green before using the results to outline the flat, needlelike leaves of the redwood tree. The faint odor of ammonia in the paint bothered some people, but Kal liked it. He also liked the dried-clay smell of chalk and the turpentine smell when he was working with oils. Simply put, he loved the smell and sound and sight and feel of creativity. He'd have gone so far as to say he loved the taste of it, too, but he'd never taken a lick of his paintings before, so the jury was out on that.

The mural outline was done, aside from a few finishing touches he was currently adding. He'd done some branches in shadow and some in full light. The outlines of the sections left plenty of room for students to fill in with their own art.

"I'd better get going," Ireland said from below him as she stretched out the kinks in her back and neck.

He glanced outside to find that not only was there a sunset in their mural but there was also one in the real-life sky. That meant if Ireland wouldn't let him drive her back to her bathroom, she'd end up having to walk. In the dark. By herself. He didn't dare follow her again in case she caught him, but Kal hated her going alone.

He looked down from his scaffolding and said, "Let me drive you tonight. You don't want to be walking home." *In the dark. By yourself.* He finished the thought in his head.

"I'm fine. But I should really get going now."

"Why?" That question came from a different voice. Mara's.

Ireland seemed confused that Mara was talking to her directly. "Why what?"

"Why leave now? We're not done yet."

"We're done with my part." As if to prove her point, Ireland dropped her brushes into the can of water at her feet and swirled it around.

"I thought you wanted to be part of the club."

"It's okay, Mara." Kal felt like he'd better interject because the two girls below him seemed like they were hovering on the edge of arguing, and he wasn't emotionally prepared to deal with that kind of situation. "Her part is done, so she doesn't need to stay if she doesn't want to." The sooner Ireland left, the less walking in the dark she'd have to do.

"I don't see why any of us should get to go home before the others," Mara insisted.

"Charisma left before we even started," Ireland said, definite irritation in her voice.

"Charisma cleared that with everyone first. You're being low-key selfish right now since you know none of the rest of us can go home until this is done." Mara had her arms crossed over her chest and a scowl so deep that she could have given lessons to the Grand Canyon.

"I have to get home, or I'll get in trouble. Sorry if that's a problem for you, princess. See you later, Kal." Ireland turned on her heel and pretty much stomped off before Kal could scramble off the scaffold to give a decent goodbye.

Rowan, one of the seriously rich kids in school, had apparently been staying late for track practice because he had been in the art room to talk to Cooper when the altercation between Mara and Ireland happened.

Kal had never liked Rowan. The guy used too much product in his dark brown hair and he had a habit of standing straight as if to prove he was taller than everyone else—not to mention his hooded brown eyes tended to trail after girls in the school in a way that made Kal feel queasy. But he liked him even less as the guy watched Ireland storm off. The way Rowan's mouth pursed and his eyes tracked Ireland's every step made his skin crawl. He held his breath to see if Rowan would follow Ireland, but he didn't. Instead, he sauntered over to where Mara and Kal were working.

It appeared as if he were about to greet Mara, which would make sense since they hung out in the same circles, but instead he twisted his face as if he smelled something rotting and said, "Nice paint in your hair, Mara. You do know it's supposed to go on the wall, not on you, right?" Then he went off the way Ireland had gone, making Kal's anxiety spike for reasons that didn't make sense. Rowan wouldn't hurt her, would he?

"What's going on, Mara?" Kal asked, baffled that Mara would lash out at anyone, least of all Ireland, and completely weirded out by Rowan insulting Mara, who was one of the most popular girls in school.

"Nothing." Mara stomped off too, leaving Kal to wonder what had just happened. The thing with Ireland seemed like a power play, but what kind of power? And the thing with Rowan was just plain next-level oddball. Kal frowned while he finished up the leaves and climbed down from the scaffold.

He wanted to tell Mara to go easy on Ireland, but he couldn't think of any way to phrase it that wouldn't make things worse. He worried about Ireland making it home okay. Rowan wouldn't have followed her. That was too paranoid to consider. Yet he couldn't stop considering it. Kal had hoped that by making friends with the art club members, Ireland would find someone in that group to confide in to help her so she wasn't alone and vulnerable.

But if the situation with Mara offered any evidence, she wasn't any closer to those sorts of friendships than she was to being involved in a lunar landing.

Kal hated how the worry was living in his head like some malignant, snarling growth. He couldn't check on her at her bathroom because he was afraid she'd catch him, and then she'd know he knew, and then it would be awkward, and he couldn't deal with that.

But he didn't like the way Rowan had watched her. He didn't like knowing she was alone. And now it was Friday, and he was stuck with another weekend without knowing if she was okay or not.

He felt a tightness in his chest that he didn't know what to do with. He finished up his portion of the mural, adding in the dark- and light-leaf outlines, and when he felt like he'd made it as perfect as he was able, he cleaned up his brushes and paints and climbed off the scaffolding. Cooper was already folding up the scaffolding on his side and took care of Kal's as well while Kal took the paints and brushes to the supply closet to clean them all up in the sink there. On the short walk, Kal made a decision. No more. He couldn't keep Ireland's secret for another minute. Someone else needed to know. He couldn't keep worrying about whether she was fed or cold or safe. He wanted an adult to worry with him. But he didn't want to tell his parents because they didn't know Ireland. They wouldn't know how to help her.

But Mr. Wasden knew her. He was one of those incredibly levelheaded sorts of people who could find solutions without creating more chaos. Kal walked into an adjoining gallery room in search of his teacher.

Once inside, Kal glanced around to see if he could find his teacher. "Hey, Wasden." He walked farther into the room. "Where are you, man?" His eyes filtered over the various framed pictures on the wall done by students past. There was some really great work up there. Every time Kal looked at it, he had the distinct impression he was really in an art gallery. Mr. Wasden had managed to get really beautiful frames from various thrift stores to highlight the beauty of the art. No crummy plastic frames for his students. Wasden wasn't that kind of guy. Everything he did was intentional. Kal wondered if Wasden would ever consider any of Kal's work good enough to place on the wall of greatness.

Kal was just about to go check the supply room when Wasden came in behind him, entering from the art room.

"There you are!" Kal said.

"Here I am. Just checking the mural. It looks great, Kal. Seriously. Great. It's something to be proud of. And the spaces you created for the student body to work within are big enough and provide the color variety we're looking for to be accessible to everyone. For the up-high stuff, we'll need to do a separate sign-out sheet from the lower scaffold. We don't want more than two people on the upper scaffold at a time, so if you'd make those and get them pinned to a couple of clipboards outside the classroom, that would be great." Mr. Wasden stopped talking and really looked at Kal. "Hey, you okay?"

"No. Not really."

"What's up?"

Kal sucked in a deep breath. *Here goes nothing*, he thought before he let it all tumble out from him, from the first time he saw Ireland stealing leftover pizza to the moment he discovered her living conditions in the woods to all the reasons he worried she was so vulnerable to every nightmare villain in every horror film he'd seen.

Wasden didn't interrupt. He listened until Kal finally fell silent, having exhausted his every panicked prediction of Ireland's potential fate. The teacher finally scrubbed the back of his hand under his bristled chin. "And you're sure that's where she's living?"

"Positive."

Wasden nodded. "Let me do some checking into her file and background and come up with some things that we can do to help."

Kal nodded. He was still gripping the paintbrushes and paints tightly in his fists. "Okay."

"Let me take those. You deserve to go home and rest. You've done a lot to make this project work, and I appreciate it. So go home and relax. I promise I'll help Miss Raine, okay?"

"Yeah. Okay." Kal released the brushes and cans to Mr. Wasden and then left, feeling lighter than he'd been in days, maybe months. Having someone else who knew what troubled him didn't seem like it should have helped him so dramatically, but it did.

He'd told someone, which was more than he'd done for Brell when she'd become so distant and he knew she was hanging out with the cesspool crowd of their high school. If he'd told someone on her—no, not *on* her but *for* her—maybe she would still be breathing.

No spiraling, he told himself.

And, for once, he was able to listen to himself because he wasn't in this alone. If anyone could help, it was Wasden. Maybe he wouldn't have to make sandwiches every day. Kal's dad had asked why they were already out of meats and cheeses and then muttered that maybe he'd forgotten to add them to the grocery list. And when his brother came to visit from college in Arizona and found the pantry empty of all the snack foods, his dad had frowned and said that he was slipping in his old age because he was sure he'd stocked it the week before.

He wouldn't be able to sustain his pantry pilfering for too much longer. But if Wasden got Ireland help, maybe he wouldn't have to.

CHAPTER NINE
Ireland

Ireland showed up early to school Monday morning so she could put out the art supplies on the table in the back of the art room. She'd go in during lunch hour to set everything up and then she'd put them away at the end of the day.

Janice, the school custodian, had unlocked the art room door for her and then helped her get out the supplies. It was strange that the older, quiet woman was there so early in the morning when Ireland knew she had to stay late too. Did she ever go home? *Maybe she's like me. Maybe she doesn't have a home.* Ireland scowled.

"You okay?" Janice asked her as they put water in the squat, heavy cans. Ireland had chosen those particular ones so they wouldn't be as easy to accidentally knock over.

"Sure. I actually feel pretty good lately."

"Finally settled somewhere?"

"Settled enough for right now." That was the truth. Ireland had never felt so settled. As she stepped back and took in the mural that she had helped create, a sense of belonging snuggled down into her soul. Yes. She was finally settled.

The morning announcement several days before about the mural had caused a general buzz in the halls. There were already pieces of student art painted directly on the wall, filling in the spaces that had been framed for them by the tree, the mascot, and the ocean. Ireland had never taken part in a school-wide activity before and was surprised at how energizing it had been. If someone could see her aura at that moment, they would describe it as a glow of pride and a feeling of inclusion.

More than that, she couldn't stop thinking about Kalvin Ellis and felt like her cheeks were going to fall off from smiling so much. She liked the boy who believed he'd time traveled to pick out some ice cream with the younger version of himself. Like *really* liked him.

She went through the week saying hi to people, smiling at them in the halls, and feeling like she belonged simply because the tree trunk outline that she'd painted stood tall and proud on the art room wall. On Monday, Kal was abnormally quiet in the first class, but she'd felt too buzzed with satisfaction to let his evasive mood get her down. Something must have happened over the weekend to kill his usual good humor. When she saw him again as his art class ended and hers began, he avoided looking her in the eye. "Are you okay?" she asked.

"Yeah. Just a little sick. I think I'm coming down with something."

"Oh. Okay. Let me know if you need anything."

"Absolutely. You would be the first to know." He hurried out then like he was embarrassed.

The first to know?

She grinned all over again. If he thought of her enough that she would be the first to know if something was wrong, then surely he liked her as much as she liked him. She rubbed her cheek. Who knew smile muscles could hurt?

And the next few days continued like that. Whatever funk Kal had been in must have righted itself because by Friday, he'd seemed to shake it off.

Mr. Wasden reiterated the invitation for the class to share their talents and to spread positivity in the student body. In the morning announcements that day, the principal had repeated the rules of the mural, explaining that she didn't want to hear that any one of her students had done anything hateful or crude. There had already been a couple of instances of having to paint over someone's crude depictions. Ireland had no idea how those images had shown up without anyone seeing who'd made them and realized it was impossible to underestimate idiots. Mr. Wasden had been the one to clean up the deviant art. "Be the people I know you are," the principal had said.

People were talking about the mural in her art class, pointing out things they had added to it, when Wasden approached her.

"Any chance you can stay a few minutes after school to talk when you're done putting things away?" he asked.

"Sure." She shrugged. She was already staying. What difference did a few more minutes make? And where did she have to go, anyway?

Throughout the day, Ireland couldn't stop herself from walking past the art room and peeking in to look. She wanted to witness all the ways that the mural was changing. It felt like it was something living. Every time she walked past it, it had taken a new breath. She felt a fulfillment she'd never known before in having been a part of the mural project.

At the end of the school day, she sought out Kal before going to Mr. Wasden's classroom. She wanted to make sure that they were still on for Geppetto's later that night. It was more than just the food for her now. It was him. His music. His voice lulling her into a place of joy and peace. The food was vital too, obviously, but more important was her being with him. That was a hunger that no number of calories could fill. He had asked her to meet him on an official date and had even offered to pick her up, but she had declined, saying she'd meet him there.

Ireland found Kal in the art room, which was a good thing since she was pretty sure she could count on him to help her clean up.

"It's pretty great, isn't it?" she asked. He jumped at her voice as if he'd been caught doing something terrible. She wouldn't have thought too much about that, except for the fact that when he looked at her, he appeared guilty. She narrowed her eyes. "What are you up to?"

He blinked several times before answering. Ireland knew from dealing with people who lied consistently that everybody had a *tell* that they revealed right before the moment they were about to say something untrue. Her dad's tell had been licking his lips. Was Kal's tell rapid blinking?

"What makes you think I'm up to something?" he asked.

"Oh, I don't know. Maybe it's the way you look like somebody about to steal the candy jar the principal keeps in her desk."

"Well, obviously. She *does* keep some pretty good candy in there, so, you know . . ." His gaze finally met hers fully.

"I wouldn't know. I've never been given the opportunity to partake from the illustrious principal candy jar. I've only heard rumors."

Kal leaned on the table of art supplies, which Ireland thought was pretty brave since it had spilled color splotching the butcher paper in more than a few places. "I think she's in the cafeteria right now. We could sneak in and just . . ."

"So you really *were* thinking about pulling a candy jar heist. I'm in. I'll be the lookout."

Kal had visibly relaxed as they talked. Ireland all but melted with gushy happiness at the thought that she could help alleviate some of the stress of whatever it was that bothered him. She loved it when his dimples carved twin canyons in his cheeks. She loved it best when it happened because of something she did or said.

More, there was a very real possibility that she just loved Kal. Where had that thought come from?

Now she was the one blinking rapidly. But instead of her blinking as a tell for some lie she was about to blurt out, Ireland felt certain her blinking stemmed from a truth that had been revealed to her.

Sure, she knew she didn't feel the type of love that required declarations of commitment or anything like that. Her feelings were a step off the path of just liking somebody and onto the path of truly caring for them. Was she staring at him as she battled these thoughts in her head? Yes. Could he feel the heat in her gaze? Her face certainly felt hot to her, but could he see the shift in her? Maybe. But then, Kal was looking at her in the same way that she looked at him. She was sure of it.

His eyes held an intensity that had never been there before as he leaned closer. As if pulled by his gravity, she leaned as well. She tilted her head up. His eyes dropped down to her mouth. Was that her heart beating so fast that it sounded like drumming in her ears? Or was that his? Ireland didn't know. She didn't know anything except that she was about to have her first kiss. Her eyes fluttered closed in anticipation of the moment of contact. But the feel of his lips on hers never came.

She snapped her eyes open and found that Kal no longer leaned toward her. He cleared his throat, a blush darkening his cheeks. "Tonight? Geppetto's? You'll be there?"

Ireland swallowed hard against the lump that had suddenly formed in her throat. She tried to speak, but no sound came out, so she merely nodded.

Kal's smile was softer than it had been earlier. It was filled with . . . what? Love, maybe? Anticipation? Definitely promise. He was promising that they'd continue this little conversation later. Ireland felt a smile crawl across her lips. "Definitely. I wouldn't miss it."

For the first time in days, Kal's hand reached toward her. He held it out, waiting for her to take it. She did, of course.

His fingers tightened over hers as he gave a squeeze. "You are truly something special, Ireland Raine."

"You're something special too." Ireland felt like she could tell Kal anything, like she could trust him. She *did* trust him. She almost opened her mouth to tell him about how she had been living in a bathroom in the woods but promptly closed it again. No. She didn't trust him that much. She barely trusted herself that much. It was a secret bigger than the world, and she wasn't about to tell anyone. She couldn't risk it.

"I'll see you tonight, okay?"

She nodded and Kal released her hand and walked away, but he looked back at her three times. Wasn't that how you knew if a person was really interested in you? If they looked back as they were walking away? Ireland certainly hoped so.

She stood alone in front of the mural for what seemed like forever. Her feet had no desire to leave the place where a promise had been given. Kal Ellis cared about her. Maybe more. Maybe he had taken a step off the path of like and onto the path of love as well. Ireland sucked in a breath of delicious contentment at the thought.

Her life was going so well. For the first time ever, she had control over her situation. Her destiny. She had friends. She had emotional connections.

She glanced at the mural.

She had a purpose.

The students' artwork that was already starting to fill in the lines she'd created felt like a connection to a world she had always felt unplugged from before. Someone had painted the face of a russet-colored dog within the framework of her tree trunk. Not too far from the dog was a guitar. Above that was a Groot. Next to the tree was a flower with rainbow petals. Someone else had painted stars within the ocean wave that Mara had done. Next to that was a skull. There was a cute little bumblebee hiding on the border of the mountain lion's head and a Cthulhu in the tree branches. Ireland spotted five different happy faces.

Mr. Wasden had been right about the idea of this project being unifying. Ireland felt the tendrils of connection flowing from her and the other members of the art club to the student body and back again.

Mr. Wasden. She was supposed to meet him after she cleaned up. She'd almost forgotten. Her feet finally managed to shuffle to action so she could hurry through the task. Mr. Wasden's desk was in the gallery on the other side of the right wall. It was more a long cubby than it was a room. If he was in there, he had probably heard her conversation with Kal, which was so horrifically embarrassing. Ireland would have to be more aware of his possible presence in the future. How awful would it have been if she had been getting her first kiss and he walked in? She grunted out loud at the thought and then snapped her mouth closed since he would have heard her make that noise too. Apparently, she was going to do all the embarrassing things. She finished her work, squared her shoulders, and entered the gallery.

The teacher was sitting at his desk and appeared to be studying some paperwork, which was weird because Mr. Wasden didn't give out a lot of written homework. It was an art class. The assignments were all thumbnail sketches, actual sketches, and full-on paintings with the occasional cardboard or origami project thrown in. Where she would expect to see any other teachers studying paperwork on their desks, she didn't expect to see Mr. Wasden doing it.

Ireland stopped in front of him, but he didn't seem to notice. "Hi, there."

Mr. Wasden jolted, his hands slamming a file folder shut as if a swarm of hornets was trying to escape from the pages inside.

"Sorry to startle you. But you wanted to see me?" She hadn't been nervous when he'd first asked because she assumed it had been about the mural. But at the pity, compassion, and resolve that flashed over his face, it occurred to her that she probably ought to be nervous.

"Have a seat, Ireland." He waved her to the chair in front of his desk. It wasn't the typical chair that sat in front of teachers' desks—hard and uncomfortable and meant to put a kid on the spot. Mr. Wasden's chair was an old armchair. Lots of students kicked off their shoes and snuggled into that chair to do their work.

But Ireland sat and felt anything but comfortable. "What's going on?" No reason to beat around the bush. That had never been her style anyway.

He, apparently, didn't want to beat around the bush either. "So I hear you're unhoused."

Ireland felt the blood in her veins freeze, and her oxygen puffed out of her as if he'd punched her hard in the gut. She wasn't sure she would ever be able to take a breath again.

He knows. How could he know? No one knew. What would happen now? Would he call the police? Was she breaking the law? Would she be suspended from school?

Ireland had once seen a mouse that had its paw caught in a snap trap. The little creature flipped and jerked itself and the trap all over trying to escape, until it finally went perfectly still. Ireland felt like the mouse. She might have been sitting there perfectly still, but her insides were flipping and jerking in panic. She wanted to leap from the chair and flee. But flee where? Nowhere. Nowhere was safe. It took her a moment to stop mentally flailing. Mr. Wasden would not be allowed to see her tells. She schooled her features and flattened her expression into unconcern. She'd had lots of practice to refine this particular look. "I don't know what you're talking about."

Mr. Wasden's fingers flicked the corner of the folder under his hands. Nervous. He was nervous. "Sure you do. I've heard from a reputable source that you don't have adequate living accommodations. So I checked into it. What I found is enlightening."

"Oh yeah? So enlighten me. What did you find?" He couldn't know. No one knew.

"Well, my first discovery was that your dad is currently in jail . . ."

Nothing could have prepared her for that news. She was hot. No. Cold. And sweating. Cold and sweating at the same time. And numb. Tingling too. Was she going to throw up? Yes. No. He must have seen all of her emotions playing out on her face because he said, "You didn't know."

She shook her head. Her stomach lurched, and she worried she really might throw up on Mr. Wasden's desk. The room spun. In jail. How was she still sitting upright? *In jail!* She wasn't surprised. *Yes, I am*, she thought. Her dad was good at cons. He'd never been caught before.

Mr. Wasden's features softened into an even deeper pity as his body sagged and his head tilted to the left. "Sorry. So sorry to be the one to give you that news. Sometimes not knowing is easier. Sometimes it isn't. I don't know which way that goes for you. But I *am* sorry, Ireland."

"It's fine," she said. It wasn't. "Whatever he did to get him locked up, he deserves to be there. If not for whatever they put him in for, then for a million other things. Anyway, about the other thing. I'm not homeless. I have a roof over my head, and I'm perfectly safe. So you don't need to worry."

"Where is this roof over your head located? And you should probably tell me the truth because you have to assume that I already know the truth."

How? How did he know? *Nobody* knew where she was at. The only person who had any indication that anything was amiss in her life was . . . *Janice.* The custodian. Ireland *had* told Janice that she was on her own and needed to borrow cleaning supplies.

"I'm not homeless," she said. "I'm staying in a bathroom at the edge of the woods."

"Oh, okay. Well, in *that* case . . ." Mr. Wasden looked exasperated. "Ireland, that's the very definition of unhoused. I appreciate you telling me the truth, but we can't let things stay this way. Let's fix that situation so you *aren't* unhoused. Let's get you safe."

Hadn't she, just moments before talking to her teacher, felt a delirious sense of freedom and independence? Hadn't she just barely been happy? But now? Now someone knew her secret and had ripped away her independence with that knowledge.

No. She wouldn't let that happen. She straightened up in the armchair, squaring her shoulders and planting her feet directly on the ground. "I'm almost eighteen. So it's not like you can put me in the system. I'm fine. You don't need to worry about me."

Mr. Wasden didn't flinch, but he did give her an exaggerated, pained look. "See, you're kind of right. *And* you're kind of wrong. The thing is that you're still in school. And while you are technically *going* to be an adult, you're not one yet. And I would still have to inform child protective services about your situation and get you taken care of until you graduate."

"Why?"

"Because you're not in a position to support yourself, and it is my legal responsibility to report when students are in an unsafe living situation."

Ireland leaped to her feet. "No! You cannot do that! You can't put me in the system! Who knows what kind of creepy people I'll end up with. And would they even keep me in the same school? I'm doing really well here. Why would you want to take me away from that?"

"Whoa." Mr. Wasden waved his hands for her to sit down again. "Slow down, Ireland. No one's talking about putting you into the system just yet. I actually have a proposition for you. One that I can legally suggest because you are an adult, or will be soon enough that it makes no difference, and one that will allow you to graduate from this school safely without you having to go into the system."

She sat, but her legs felt coiled, ready to spring up and run. "I'm listening."

"There's a family that is financially self-sufficient. By that, I mean they're rich. Sounds crass, but it's true. Without naming you directly because I wanted to protect your privacy, I told them about your situation because they are good people, and I know they can be trusted. The good news is that they have lots of extra room in their house. They've offered for you to live with them. And they already have a girl going to our school, so getting you to and from school is no big deal because you can just drive in with her."

Ireland didn't want to live with one of her classmates like some freakish charity case when she wasn't friends with anyone. How awkward would that be? "And if I decline this offer?"

Mr. Wasden shrugged. He opened the file. Ireland's name was at the top of one of the papers there. "I really don't think you should decline. If I see a student who is neglected or abused, I have to turn that information in to child services, whether you're eighteen or not. It's the law."

"So, if I say no, then you rat me out to CPS, and they what? Come take me away?"

"They could. Or you could choose to accept this other opportunity. If you do, your class schedules will be the same, the people you know will be the same. Your teachers will all be the same. Your life will go pretty much uninterrupted, except you'll be safe and snug inside a home where you will be fed and cared for and protected. The choice is yours."

He waited.

She waited.

It didn't seem like much of a choice. When it became apparent he had no intention of talking anymore, she asked, "Who's the family?"

"The Washington family. They own the bakery chain . . . On the Rise."

"Are you kidding me? Mara Washington's family?" They weren't even in March yet, weeks away from April first, so it couldn't have been an April Fool's joke. If she hadn't liked and respected Mr. Wasden as much as she did, she probably would have thrown his art pencils at him.

His hand was at the back of his neck, as if he were trying to massage away a brand-new tension headache. "What? They're a good family."

"Maybe, but Mara hates me. She and the hag and—I mean, *her friends* look for every opportunity to make my life miserable. I can't live with her."

Mr. Wasden did look concerned then. "What are you talking about? I've seen you and Mara work together side by side for several days. I've never once seen any hint of you two not getting along. Has she ever done anything to you?"

"Well, no, not exactly . . ." The truth was that Mara herself hadn't ever really done anything against Ireland, but her friends had, and she hadn't stopped them, so it was the same thing.

Mr. Wasden leaned back, the sudden relief evident. "Okay, then. Tell me where you're currently holing up. I can have a few of your friends go and help you pack up your belongings to take to the Washington home. Mrs. Parker can drive you."

"I thought you knew where I was staying."

"I know the situation. Not the GPS pin drop."

Her leg bounced like it was having a personal earthquake. She couldn't have stopped it if she'd tried. "I really don't want to stay with them," she said in one last desperate plea for him to see this from her perspective.

"I know." His soft voice calmed her marginally—enough that she could see this from his perspective. He wasn't trying to ruin her life. He had a responsibility, and he actually cared. That was the one thing about Mr. Wasden she was completely sure about. He was a guy who taught school because he cared. "But it's your best option. It's not safe, and not legal, for you to be living in a public bathroom by yourself."

"I don't want to owe anybody anything." Ireland's dad owed everyone. She would not be like him. He was in jail now. She didn't know why that made her feel so ridiculously sad.

"You won't owe the Washingtons anything. They have the means to do this without it putting them out in any way. They've only got Mara and their youngest daughter, Jade, at home now, so there's plenty of room for you and plenty of resources to provide for you. They only require that you stay the course. Keep doing what you're doing. Go to school. Get good grades. Be the person you already are. They're excited to take you in. Once I told Grace about you, she about knocked me over because she wanted to go get you right that minute."

"Who all knows?" she asked.

"I told the principal, and I gave her your name. Other than that, the only people we talked to were the Washingtons."

"How long have you known? You couldn't have arranged all of this and found out about my dad in an afternoon."

"It's been a few days," he confessed.

"Why didn't you say anything to me?"

Mr. Wasden's shoulders twitched. He didn't love what he was about to say, but he said it anyway. "Honestly, we worried if we tipped our hand before we had things arranged, you might disappear on us."

"So, you're saying you thought I was a flight risk?"

He cringed but nodded.

"Huh. Well . . . that's fair, I guess."

"So . . . who do you want to help you get your stuff together?"

No one. She didn't want anyone to help her. She didn't want anyone to know she was living in a bathroom—especially not Mara, who would tell her friends, who would then tell everyone else. The jokes would be nonstop. "Does Mara know where I live?"

"No. Right now, the Washingtons don't even know your name. And I didn't tell them where you were living exactly, only that you were on your own."

Ireland's breathing felt like the oxygen wasn't making it to her lungs. "You won't tell them, will you?"

"Not if you don't want me to."

She leaned forward and rubbed her hand down her face. "There's a Lutheran church on Sixteenth and Bayview. I'll meet you in the parking lot."

"Mrs. Parker can take you to get your things, and I'll meet you at your new house."

He looked at something behind Ireland, and she turned her

head to see what it was. The principal had come in sometime during the conversation.

Right. Flight risk. They weren't going to let her go anywhere on her own until she was settled. She shook her head so slowly that she felt like maybe she wasn't moving at all. Her thoughts felt like they were swimming through mud. How had she let herself get caught like this? How had she become the charity flavor of the month? Wasn't she doing okay on her own? Why was any of this necessary?

"I'm sorry you're taking this so hard, Ireland. I wouldn't strong-arm you into this if I wasn't truly concerned for your safety. It's just until you graduate; then you can make your own choices without my meddling. And though I'm sorry this is stressing you out, I am not sorry to get involved because you matter, Ireland. You're too important to let circumstances cause you harm."

Her head shot up as she met his eye.

She mattered? She was important?

Ireland wasn't sure why his saying those words struck her so forcefully, but it brought the burn and sting of tears behind her eyes. She blinked hard.

She nodded and stood. "I . . . kind of have a date tonight. With Kal at Geppetto's. I can still go out tonight, right?"

"Of course. I'll let the Washingtons know. Their daughter has a social life too, you know. So it's not like you're going to be under house arrest. You might have a curfew, and they'll want to know where you're going and who you're with, but it's normal parent stuff."

Normal parent stuff. He said that like she had any idea what it meant. "Right. Okay. I better go get my stuff."

She started to go with Mrs. Parker but turned back to him. "Mr. Wasden? Can you not tell Kal? I don't want him to know." She didn't wait for Mr. Wasden to agree. She turned and left with the principal. She had packing to do.

CHAPTER TEN

Kal

Kal snapped his fingers as he paced in the school parking lot. Part of him wanted to storm back into Wasden's art room to make sure Ireland was okay. Another part—the rational, sane part—wanted to drive away and wait to see her until it was all over. She'd meet him at Geppetto's. She would tell him what all went down then. Wasden had assured him that he had a living arrangement set up for Ireland and that he would get her moved in after they met together. He assured Kal that Ireland wouldn't spend any more nights alone in the woods.

Gotta trust the guy, Kal thought and finally stopped snapping and pacing and instead got in his car and drove home.

Of course, he still snapped and paced once he got home and made it to his room. His out-of-control emotions were awesome times zero. He needed to have it together so that when he saw Ireland that night, he could be there for her.

His bedroom door opened, and his friend Cooper poked his head in. "Dude, 'sup?"

"Not much." He had to lie because there was no way to

explain to Cooper about Ireland without it being weird. "What about you?"

Cooper sat at the desk. "Yeah. Same. Not much. Just feel like I'm in a Wonkaverse sometimes."

"Am I supposed to . . . ?"

"What?" Cooper pulled a couple of pens from the Darth Vader mug and drummed them on the desk.

"Know what the Wonkaverse is?"

The drumming stopped. "You know. When the whole universe feels like it's all wonky."

Kal laughed. "You just made that up, didn't you?"

"No. Maybe. I'm not sure, actually. I mighta heard it somewhere. But maybe not."

"You're early." Coming home to worry about Ireland suddenly seemed like a good idea. The band members were either on time or a few minutes late. No one was ever early.

Cooper frowned and checked his phone as if he thought Kal was lying about him being early. "Yeah. Needed to get out of my head for a minute."

"You okay?"

The drumming on the desk had started up again. "Yeah. It's just the Wonkaverse."

Kal had his own case of nuclear anxiety and didn't have the ability to deal with Cooper's nerves too, so he moved to the door. "Let's head to the back building. The others should be showing up pretty soon." The back building was a mother-in-law apartment. They'd meant to have Kal's grandpa stay there so he would still have his autonomy, but when they realized how bad off his grandpa was physically, they decided to keep him with them in the main house. Kal's parents had let Kal take over the back building for the band's practice. They'd been using the back half of Asha's garage before. Her parents were glad to have the whole operation relocated so they could use that space to park an Indian Sport Chief motorcycle that Asha's dad had been wanting.

Cooper followed Kal to the back building. Once inside, Kal opened the mini fridge and got himself a bottle of seltzer water. "Want one?" he asked Cooper, who had wandered over to Bailey's drum set and tapped his fingers on the cymbals, making a slushy *tisk* sound with his every tap.

"No. Thanks. Maybe a Coke?"

Kal fished a can of Coke from the fridge and handed it to Cooper, who opened it, took a long swig, and then moved like he was going to set the open can down on the vintage amplifier that Kal had adorned with stickers from his favorite bands. Kal narrowed his eyes at his friend and gave a small shake of his head. Cooper caught the meaning and pulled his hand back, still holding the can.

Sometimes that guy didn't think things through. He knew what the amp meant to Kal. If anyone spilled anything on it, Kal was pretty sure he'd lose it. It had been his grandpa's. Two of the stickers on it were old and weathered. His grandpa had been the one to place them. One for Rush and one for Queen.

Kal's dad had wanted to throw the amp away, but Kal had saved it from the garbage heap.

Cooper finished his drink, his fingers tapping out a rhythm on the can as if he was anxious about something.

Asha came in just as Kal was about to ask Cooper what was up again. Her blue-green hair was in one long braid that hung over her shoulder. It matched the little blue-green heart she'd painted on her cheekbone. Asha pulled her guitar from its case and started lightly tugging the strings, running her fingers up and down the length of them.

"New strings?" Kal asked her.

"Yeah. It was time." She turned on a tuning app on her phone as she adjusted the tuning keys and saddle.

"Hands off the drums, Cooper."

Cooper jumped up at hearing Bailey's voice and splayed his hands out as if to prove they were empty. "I was just sitting there. I wasn't touching them."

"I heard the cymbals as I was walking up." Bailey walked around the wires coiled together on the floor like spilled pasta and shooed Cooper out of her way.

Asha laughed at Cooper getting caught.

Bailey smirked. "Pick up your sticks, and let's play. We don't have a lot of time before we have to get to Geppetto's," she said, settling herself in front of her drums.

She was right. The late afternoon light coming from the back building's windows was now so dim that it cast elongated shadows across the whole space. They plugged in and started rehearsing the songs they'd agreed to play for the night.

Asha adjusted the strap on her shoulder and struck the first few chords, her fingers dancing along the fretboard, producing an upbeat sound to set the tone for the song. Cooper on bass added depth to the melody, and Bailey smiled full on as she powered through the complex rhythm, her sticks a controlled sort of chaos. Kal was pretty sure the only time Bailey smiled with her whole face like that was when she played.

The celebratory song, "Cry Free!," burst with positive energy. Asha had written it, and the song seemed to match her personality. Kal began to sing the lyrics, with Asha joining in after the first stanza. When they got to the chorus, Cooper joined in.

> *Cause we're livin' in the moment, lookin' to a future so*
> *bright,*
> *We're dancin' in the moonlight all through the night.*

Come take my hand. We'll make new memories.
We're gonna shout out to the world, "I am free!"

This particular song had done well for them. The audience loved it. They loved shouting "I am free" along with the band. By the third night they'd played it, they'd gained a modest following of people who came just to hear that song. It was fun and shifted Kal's mood as he locked into the music, lifting the energy of the back building into something light, making him feel as free as the song declared him to be.

It ended with the last beat of Bailey's sticks on her drums, and they all burst out laughing—even Bailey. It didn't matter how many times they played it; that song always set the tone for a good time.

Even Cooper seemed lighter. They played a couple more songs, then gathered their gear and headed to Geppetto's.

Kal's anxiety spiked again. Would Ireland be there already, waiting for him? Wasden had promised to not mention Kal when he handled things with Ireland.

When he walked into the restaurant, his eyes scanned through all the people, but he didn't see her. Ireland wasn't there yet.

"You look like you might be sick, Superman. You okay?" Asha asked.

"Me? Sure. 'Course."

She clapped his back. "You looking for Lois Lane?"

"Lois Lane?"

"Ireland. I see the way you light up when she's around. It's magic, I tell you. I even started writing a song about it. I'll let you see it when it's done."

"She's just a friend."

"Right. And I'm just an average guitarist . . . See what I did there? Because you *know* there is nothing average about me, and there's nothing as average as basic friendship with you and this girl."

Kal grinned at her. "Nothing average at all."

"Who's average?" Cooper had joined them.

Asha made a tsking sound. "Well, Coop, we didn't want to make you feel bad or anything, but yeah, we've been talking about your lack of practice lately . . ."

Cooper's face splotched like a crushed tomato. "You kidding me? Check these calluses and tell me I don't practice."

Kal and Asha both laughed. "Dude, she's messing with you. You know you're a rockstar. Let's go play and show off all your practice."

Asha checked her pink-rhinestone-bedazzled phone. "Yep. We're up."

As the band got into place, Kal swept his gaze over the audience once again to search for any sign of Ireland. Was she not coming? Had she ended up in a home where they didn't let her go out with her friends? What if he'd landed her in a situation that was worse than her living alone in the woods?

That wouldn't make sense. They had a date. Whoever she went to live with would understand that. Right? He really should've talked to Wasden before he'd left school. It would be good to know where Ireland was going and what her life would look like once she got there.

He took a deep breath as Asha led with the first few chords. He forced thoughts of Ireland out of his head for the moment. He had to stay present so he didn't mess things up for the band. They had a good gig with Geppetto's and had even booked a few extra appearances outside of the restaurant. Not that he thought they were going to be the next big-deal band, but what they did was good and fun. And he didn't want to be the reason they broke up. He began to sing, with Asha joining in after a moment.

They were almost through the second set with only two songs left, and Ireland still hadn't shown up. That could only mean she wasn't going to show up at all. Kal just had to face the fact. He hated it, but what could he do? The smell of baking cheeses and meats churned his stomach for the first time ever. He didn't want to be there anymore. He had every intention of leaving as soon as this last set was done.

The next song, "Checkmate," was more of a breakup ballad. Asha had written it when her last boyfriend ended things with her. Even though they were playing mostly love songs in honor of the holiday, this one still felt like a love song. It had a haunting quality to it that most people liked, and Asha and Kal sang it as a duet. He worried his thoughts might spill out into the lyrics as he sang, but he forced himself to focus. Asha's clear voice wove with his. The words tasted like salt and sugar fighting for space on his tongue. Through a lens of relationships, more specifically of his relationship with Ireland, the song's deeper meaning burrowed its way into his soul.

> *Our pieces chase each other on the black-and-white-checked*
> *board*
> *A violent sea between us, our moves tallied, each one scored*
> *The game is silent subterfuge. Am I the queen? Am I the*
> *pawn?*
> *No. Don't tell. I'll know the truth when one of us is gone*
> *Gray shadows mock the two of us, more than hinting at our*
> *fate*
> *How my marble heart will sink at the inevitable checkmate*

Kal didn't love singing about breakups when it felt like he was in the middle of one. Of course, they hadn't really been together, so how could they be breaking up?

You are ridiculous. But he didn't have time to think about it since the band finished "Checkmate" and was shifting gears into the energy needed for their last number.

The rolling force of the song "Cry Free!" swept him up along with it, reaching tsunami heights that felt like it all crashed down when Ireland opened the door and entered the restaurant.

She sat down at the table they'd sat at before. The pizzas were out and waiting for them already, but she didn't reach to take any. Had she already eaten? Was she okay with the new living arrangement? She had to be, right? She had to be happier with the idea of being safe.

Kal tried to check the temperature of her emotional well-being, but she didn't make eye contact with him. Was she mad? Maybe. But if she was mad at him, would she have bothered to show up for their date? He'd almost kissed her earlier, and now he realized that he might have missed the chance forever.

"I am free!" The crowd shouted with the band, making up for the fact that Kal's voice faltered. He steeled himself against the anxiety that swelled in his stomach so he could finish the song. When the last shout of "I am free!" filled the room, the crowd erupted with cheers and applause. Kal rolled his head to stretch out the tension in his neck muscles and tried to smile and wave at the audience. He thanked everyone for coming to hear them play and invited them back for Saturday. He put his guitar in its case, hopped off the stage, and hurried to join Ireland at the table.

"You made it!" He tried to sound cheerful. Could she tell that he was forcing it? He'd never been a very good liar.

"Yeah. I uh . . . I made it." Ireland avoided eye contact as if he were Medusa and she'd turn to stone if their gazes met.

Kal lowered his voice to keep Asha and Bailey, who were just now joining them, from overhearing. "You okay?"

"Yeah. I'm okay. Are you done for the night?"

He bent his head to try to force her to look at him. "Yeah.

We're done. Want to get out of here?" Cooper had bailed as soon as the set was over so he could meet his other friends wherever they were partying for the night.

"And go where?" she asked.

He shrugged, even though she wasn't looking and couldn't see. "Wherever you want."

"I have to be back by eleven."

She spat those words with fiery fury. His blood pressure spiked.

"Me too." It wasn't true exactly. His mom liked him home earlier, but she gave him until midnight when he played with the band.

"We can stay here."

So they stayed. Not because he wanted to. He wanted to be alone with her so they could talk, so she could tell him everything that had happened. No way could he try to coax information out of her with everyone at the table.

Kal could almost hear time ticking down on the vintage Coca-Cola clock on the wall, each tick of the minute hand taking them closer to eleven. Asha and Ireland talked about the mural and their favorite things that other people had added to it. Bailey ate pizza and scrolled through her phone. He just sat there, trying to figure out what to say or do. "I better go," Ireland said, checking the time on her own phone, even though Kal felt certain she'd been sneaking glances at the Coca-Cola clock too.

He stood. "Okay. I'll take you home."

She opened her mouth with a look that made him brace himself to be told by her, yet again, that she didn't need a ride home. But she just said, "Thanks. I appreciate it. See you around, guys." She nodded to Bailey and Asha.

Kal scrambled to gather his gear so that Ireland didn't take off without him. Since she'd done it before, he didn't think he was being paranoid to worry. Once they were outside and loaded into his car, he started it and flicked the seat heaters on since the night was stupid cold and Ireland was already rubbing her hands together to warm them up.

"Where to?" he asked. This was the moment he would find out what happened. He would know where she now lived. She would tell him where she had been living. She would tell him how she got there. She would trust him. She would tell him everything.

Except she didn't. She pulled out her phone and read an address to him.

Kal felt like she'd kicked his kneecaps. Was she really not going to tell him anything? Not that she owed him her story if she didn't want to give it, but over the past couple of weeks he'd told her everything about himself.

Not everything.

He hadn't told her about Brell.

When Kal made the turn Ireland had indicated, his headlights flashed over the familiar neighborhood.

"Here," Ireland said.

He stopped and looked at the mini mansion. "This is Mara's house."

"Yep." She took several deep breaths like she was practicing yoga.

"You're staying at Mara's house?"

"Apparently."

"Are you guys friends?"

"Nope."

"I don't think I . . ."

"My dad's in jail. I needed a place to stay. Mr. Wasden arranged this."

"Oh. That's nice. I mean, not nice about your dad. Nice of Mr. Wasden."

"If you say so."

He wanted to insist that he *did* say so, mostly because her being grouchy toward Mr. Wasden for helping her felt like she was being grouchy at *him*. "It's better than—" He almost said that it was better than living in a bathroom but stopped himself since she didn't know that he knew. "Being alone," he finished.

"Mara's a shrew."

Kal was suddenly positive that Ireland had no intention of telling him about her living in the bathroom in the woods. He was also certain that she would never talk to him again if he revealed that he'd played any part in her relocation to Mara Washington's house, which hardly seemed fair because Mara's stone-and-stucco house was more like a manor. *Anyone* would want to live there. He searched for something to say but couldn't come up with anything. Ireland opened the car door. "I better go in. Thanks, Kal. I'll see you later."

"Want me to walk you to the door?"

"I'm pretty sure I can manage."

That wasn't exactly what he'd asked. He was pretty sure she could manage too. He was asking if she wanted to be with him for that extra moment. He hadn't been prepared for the resounding *no*. "Right." His hands gripped the steering wheel until his muscles cramped in his fingers. He had thought that the evening would be something fun and romantic. Watching it shatter into a classic disaster had not been part of the plan.

She shut the car door.

He waited until she was inside the house before muttering, "Awesome times zero."

CHAPTER ELEVEN
Ireland

Mr. and Mrs. Washington, or Jarrod and Grace, as they insisted Ireland call them, were sitcom-family perfect. The house was almost museum perfect, all cold marble and warm stone and masterwork paintings. But it wasn't so flawless that it didn't look lived in. The house felt very much like a home. Family pictures hung on the walls along with the expensive art. It reminded Ireland of Kal's house and how there had been little bits of handmade kids' art alongside the expensive decor.

So that's what being in a well-off family looked like.

"You're home early." Grace lounged on the couch. She looked a lot like Scarlet Johansson, who played the Black Widow in the Marvel movies. Her honey-colored hair was up in a bun and her silky-smooth feet were propped up on the coffee table. Her toes were painted red and looked like they'd just been treated to a pedicure. She closed the book she'd been reading, a romance, if the pink cover art that looked split in half between modern and historical was any indicator.

Ireland checked her phone. 10:28. She *was* early. She shifted uncomfortably under Grace's gaze. She wasn't quite sure what to say about being early. Was that a bad thing? Didn't adults want children to be early when they came home from something? Maybe they didn't. She jiggled her head and shoulders in what might have been a shrug but probably came off looking like an allergic spasm.

Grace slid her feet off of the coffee table and patted the spot next to her on the couch, waving her other hand to beckon Ireland forward, her several gold bracelets jangling together against her thin wrist. "Why don't you come sit down by me, and we can get to know one another."

Grace's tone went a pitch higher than usual, as if she had just offered cotton candy and a pony ride to a small child—as if she'd offered something fun. The idea of getting to know each other being fun felt like a top-ten lie on Grace's part. At least they wouldn't be going over house rules again. They had done that before Ireland left to go to Geppetto's to meet Kal. Mr. Wasden had been with her during the house rules part and while they took a tour of the house. But now it was just her and Grace and the get-to-know-you game. Since Grace was the new adult authority figure in her life, Ireland sat.

"So how was your date? It was with the Ellis boy, right?"

"Yes. His name is Kal. He plays in a band." Of course, this was all information she had told Grace when she'd first shown up at her house with nothing but her insecurity and a duffel bag. Happily, Mara had been nowhere to be seen when Ireland first arrived to invade her home, and Grace assured Ireland that Mara knew about the move and was completely on board.

Grace's tell was a tilt of her head. Not the curious kind of a tilt, but the kind where she looked off to the side as she tilted her head so she could avoid eye contact. The tilt felt like she was distancing herself from the lie she told.

Clearly, Mara was *not* on board with another teen moving in to her home. Plus, Mara hadn't known it was actually Ireland. She would be less on board when she discovered the truth.

Grace closed the book and set it on the coffee table. "I think we've heard him play before. Is his band the only one at Geppetto's?"

"I think so. I haven't ever seen anyone else."

"Well then, he was very good. So, tell me what sorts of things you like." The whole scenario struck Ireland as weird. Getting to know an adult like this. Being taken into somebody else's home like this. Ireland had once believed that if the devil had offered to trade her soul for a warm bed and a hot meal, she would take the deal with no hesitation. She never imagined that she would find herself wishing she was at her bathroom in the woods. But here she was, wishing she was alone in her bathroom instead of playing the twenty-questions game about her life. Not that she didn't like Grace. Grace was a nice lady. But it was hard not to hold it against her that Mara was her daughter. After all, how nice could Grace really be when she'd raised such an elitist snob?

"I like art."

At this, Grace lit up like a Christmas tree festival with all its lights turning on for the first time of the season. "Me too!" She hopped to her feet. "Let me take you on a tour of my gallery." She laughed as if she had told a joke. And then she explained her joke: "Sometimes I call my house a gallery because I buy so much art. I know you've seen all the rooms, but it was all new at the time, and how much attention could you have paid to the art on the walls? My husband tells me I have to stop buying art because we're running out of wall space, but I just can't make myself do that. So sometimes I rotate pieces, keeping some in storage so I can display others."

There were people starving in the streets of her very own city, and this lady had enough money to rotate through pieces of expensive art? This explained the slippery slope of how Mara became such an elitist snob. Ireland stood up too because Grace was already across the room and turning to explain the picture above the fireplace. The image wasn't very big compared to the rather intimidating solid, dark-wood frame that surrounded it. It was a piece by John Bauer—apparently Scandinavian . . . Swedish. The image was of a ghostly woman with long, white curly hair. A crown of some sort with tall leaf-looking things topped her head. She wore a long white dress that ended at her ankles to reveal her bare feet. She walked between two terrifying-looking trolls, big, gnarly, knobby-looking things. It seemed like she was their prisoner. Yet she glowed—a bright shaft of sunlight compared to the shadows that were the trolls.

Grace explained that this particular piece had been incredibly hard to find. But she'd loved it from the moment she saw it at some art auction. She said it made her feel peaceful.

That was the thing about Grace and her art. Nothing about her explanations was anything to do with the price or the value of the piece but of the way it spoke to her soul or made her feel or made her think. Ireland found herself warming to the tour of the art in the home—each piece spooning a soothing trickle of hot cocoa into her soul.

Grace's art spanned continents. She had some from South America and North America, Africa, Europe, and Asia. There wasn't any from Australia or Antarctica. At least not that Grace specifically mentioned as such. But who knew? Maybe there were pieces from those places as well.

"How did you get all of these?" Ireland asked once they had come full circle and were seated back on the couch.

"Travel is one of my favorite hobbies. I try to buy something every time I go somewhere new. You would not believe the things that you can find in old thrift stores in other countries. It's incredible. Really. I know maybe this looks like I spent a lot on it, but not really. All things considered, this represents a pretty low output of resources for acquiring new art."

"I got my sleeping bag at a thrift store." Ireland offered this as an example of something they had in common.

"Brilliant. I'm a huge fan of thrift store shopping. I think everybody should do it. It's so much better for the environment than buying new things. And people donate some unique and incredible things. I got these pants at our Goodwill here in town." She rubbed her hands over the thighs of her beige, pleated cotton-twill pants. Ireland didn't know a lot about fashion and clothing, but she knew what expensive looked like.

The conversation was not one Ireland had expected to have with a woman who lived in a home that could only be described as palatial, especially when they only had four kids.

Ireland smirked inwardly at that thought. Only four kids? Four kids were a lot by today's standards. Still, the house occupied a huge chunk of land for not very many people.

Regardless of how ostentatious the sprawling household was, Ireland found herself warming up to Grace. She wasn't anything like Mara. Ireland had a hard time imagining people who shopped at thrift stores to be elitist snobs. Ireland was almost certain that Mara didn't wear anything that didn't come from designer boutiques.

Ireland, on the other hand, only had things that came from thrift finds. She was fine with that. That's what she told herself, anyway. Sure, it might be a nice change to have something that was brand new and never worn by anybody else before, but Grace made a great point. Thrifting was doing her part to commit to an eco-friendly lifestyle. Instead of being sad about the whole thing, she could understand herself to be an environmental crusader. *Thanks, Grace*, she thought.

Mara came in and stopped short when she saw Ireland sitting next to her mom on the couch. Her mouth tightened into a slash and her arms crossed over her chest.

"Hey, honey." Grace checked her watch. "Right on time tonight. Good."

The way Grace emphasized "tonight" made it seem like Mara wasn't always home on time.

"Is Daddy already in bed?" Mara asked her mom.

Wow. *Daddy?* As if Mara were a four-year-old. Ireland didn't think she'd ever called her dad "daddy" even when she *was* four. She smirked. She was sure she didn't scoff out loud, but Mara still shot her a sharp look of disapproval.

Maybe she had scoffed out loud.

"Yeah," Grace said. "He's got to be up at three. Which means *you've* got to be up at four, so you should go to bed too."

Mara's lips tightened again.

"Why do you have to be up early?" Ireland asked.

"We own bakeries," Mara said with a tone that implied Ireland was an idiot. Ireland must have looked confused by the answer because Mara added, "Bread doesn't bake itself. Family business. Family responsibility." That last part sounded like a parroted mantra. Ireland wondered if it was on a plaque somewhere in the kitchen.

"I could help," Ireland said.

Mara narrowed her eyes. "Why?"

"To say thanks for giving me a place to stay."

Mara's mouth was obviously in the middle of forming the word "no" when Grace interrupted. "That's a great idea. We actually pay Mara to work, and we'd do the same for you if you want a job."

"I would love a job. I want to pay my own way. Thanks, Grace."

"Great." Grace beamed sunshining happiness at the idea of

the two girls working together for the family bakery. Mara made a grunt of evident disapproval and said, "I gotta get to bed. I guess I'll see *you* in the morning." She cut a glare in Ireland's direction. "Be up on time. I won't wait for you."

Grace's face twisted in discomfort at her daughter's snark. "Mara, that is not how we treat our guests."

Mara's shoulders slumped and her eyes dropped to the ground as she mumbled an apology. She clearly didn't love that she was humbled in front of Ireland. An apology hadn't been necessary since Mara's acid didn't bother Ireland as much as it probably should have. She didn't expect anything different from Mara.

She excused herself to go to bed as well. Once safely behind her closed bedroom door, she allowed herself to shake her head at the insanity of . . . well, *everything*. From the moment Mr. Wasden had accused her of being "unhoused" to this moment as she leaned against her door, there was nothing except insanity. Ireland shook with rage and fury at Janice for ratting her out and getting her into this situation. The old custodian had to have followed her. There was no other explanation. Ireland regretted ever helping to clean the bathroom with the woman. She could hear her dad's voice say, "See? That's what helping people out gets you. A fat lot of nothing. You can only be in it for yourself."

She frowned and swatted out her hand as if she could swipe his memory from her mind. In jail. Idiot. "See, Dad? That's what being a self-centered Smeagol gets you. A fat lot of jail time." She cringed when she realized she'd spoken louder than a whisper. In the house tour they gave her when she'd showed up, Ireland had discovered she was room-adjacent to Mara. Absolutely not convenient. Their rooms were connected by a Jack and Jill bathroom. At least, that was what Grace had called it. That meant Ireland was expected to share a bathroom with Mara Washington.

She straightened at the thought of the bathroom because it

reminded her of something truly magical. She could take a *real* shower with *real* hot water. No more chattering teeth while she rinsed her hair in the glacial water coming out of the sink tap. There would be a towel to dry herself off with. And if her short time in the house told her anything, it told her that the towels would be big, fluffy cotton cuddles.

With a shiver of excitement at the prospect, Ireland opened her door to the bathroom. It was empty and there wasn't any light coming from under the door into Mara's room, which meant she might already be in bed. Ireland considered locking the door on Mara's side to avoid getting an unwanted guest during her shower but couldn't make herself take the steps in the dark over to that side of the bathroom. She certainly didn't want to turn on a light that could be visible from Mara's side of the door.

There had been another bathroom at the end of the hall. Grace had called it the boys' bathroom, but the Washington boys were away at college. It's not like they were going to be using it anytime soon. Ireland backed up and shut the door with a quiet click. Quiet or not, she still cringed at the noise. She waited to hear any sound of irritation coming from Mara's room.

Nothing.

Good.

She opened her duffel bag and pulled out what passed as her toiletry kit. She had several tubes of travel toothpaste she'd stolen from the sample bowl when the school had career day and one of the booths had belonged to a dentist. Her dad had formed a habit several years ago of finding motels where maid carts were sometimes left unattended. He pilfered them for soaps, shampoos, toilet paper, and, every now and again, towels. He'd left a meager supply of those necessities when he'd jumped ship. She still had two soaps, one shampoo, and two toothpastes. She gathered the little bit that was there and peered out into the hallway before deciding the coast was clear. Once inside the bathroom at the end of the hall, Ireland flipped on the light and got down to pampering. Maybe Mara wouldn't consider a steamy, hot shower pampering, but Ireland certainly did.

She stepped into the warm embrace and sighed in relief as the water washed away the homeless girl she'd been. Not that she was a girl who had a home exactly. This place didn't feel like home.

"Unhoused," Mr. Wasden had said. She was now a girl who was "housed."

She stayed under the spray of the shower a long time, letting the buildup of that bathroom in the woods swirl down into the drain.

No. Not just the bathroom.

Ireland rinsed away *everything* from before.

She might not have wanted to live with Mara, but she could appreciate the opportunity to leave her previous life and settle her feet on solid ground.

Ireland didn't end up using the shampoo bottles she'd stolen from the motel. Grace had this bathroom stocked with bottles that looked like they cost more than Ireland's sleeping bag and smelled like citrus and vanilla. She luxuriated in the opulence of the experience, certain she would regret it since four in the morning was only a few hours away.

She stepped out of the shower only after the water had grown tepid, rinsed herself off, and went to bed. She didn't have to imagine wide-open, warm fields as she snuggled into cool, clean bedding. She fell asleep immediately.

When her birdsong alarm went off the next morning, Ireland groaned. No way could it be healthy to be up at such an hour. She got up because Mara would absolutely leave her behind if given the chance. As if to prove Ireland right, Mara was on her way to her car parked on the side of the garage when Ireland caught up with her.

"Oh goody. You're coming after all," Mara muttered, clicking the fob on her key ring to unlock the Fiat.

"I just want to do my part."

"How sweet. Remind me to get you a participation trophy."

"Is there something you want to say to me?" Ireland had no intention of letting Mara pick on her without clapping back.

"I'm just not loving you moving into my house and taking over my life."

"Awesome. I'm not loving it either." Top-five lie. Ireland could not remember ever sleeping so comfortably in her life. Being under that comforter had felt like being swaddled in pillowy angel clouds. And the shower was magical in a way that only glittering pixie dust could compare to. They both got in the car. Mara slammed her door shut. Ireland closed hers normally because the Fiat still had those cute little eyelashes, and Ireland didn't want to make the car sad.

"Then leave." Mara started her car and shoved the stick into drive with more force than was strictly necessary.

"Would if I could. But apparently, it's not legal for me to be living on my own until after I graduate. This wasn't my idea. Mr. Wasden found out I was on my own, and he basically strong-armed me into this arrangement. As soon as we graduate and those caps fly in the air, I promise, I'm gone."

Mara scowled and growled and ran a red light. "Fine. If you're not leaving, then you better just stay out of my way. I have no idea how to explain any of this to my friends."

"By friends, you mean the hag and the harpy?"

"Cut the dramatics. Just because you now have to sleep at my house doesn't mean you can hang out with me at school."

"Right. Of course you'd think I want to be your new bestie.

I forgot you believe the world revolves around you. Don't worry. I'd rather swallow slugs than spend any time with the hag and harpy."

"Don't call them that."

"If the dark soul fits . . ." The argument came to an end. Not because they were done arguing, but because Mara turned on the radio and blasted Taylor Swift at her. And then they'd arrived at the On the Rise, and, apparently, neither one of them wanted to be bickering when they got out of the car since Jarrod was unlocking the door to the restaurant. He grinned widely for them both and said, "There they are! Glad you could join us, Ireland. Grace left me a note saying you'd be here too." He let them in and then locked the door behind them so no one would try coming in while they worked.

Jarrod's white durag covered the tight fade haircut that Ireland remembered seeing in the family pictures as she toured the Washington's house. He wiped his hands on his white apron that already had spots of flour on it before he reached out and shook Ireland's hand. A spot of flour dusted his brown cheek on the left. He looked every bit like a baker. "Sorry I didn't get to meet you properly yesterday. Work was crazy," he said. He'd arrived only an hour before them, but judging by the floured apron and the floured counter in the back kitchen, he had made good use of that hour.

Mara cut several glares in Ireland's direction. Her dad caught one of those glares and whispered something in her ear. "Sorry, Ireland," Mara said in response to what was obviously a scolding by her father. "I'm not trying to be rude. I'm just really tired." She went to work and didn't say another word to her, not while her dad explained the processes of making the breads, not while they worked, and not for the ride back to the house. Mara had apparently decided to ice Ireland out. Ireland couldn't blame her since she'd been chewed out now by both parents and it was all because Ireland was in her life.

Ireland decided it might be best to stay in her room for the rest of the day and not get in anyone's way, but Grace knocked on Ireland's door. "How was it making bread?" she asked when Ireland opened it.

"Good. I had no idea how fun bread could be. It was like a science project that you get to eat afterward."

Grace laughed. "Well, I'm off to our Trinidad location. I already asked Mara, but I was hoping you'd help out in keeping an eye on Jade."

"Sure. Be glad to help." Ireland had no idea what keeping an eye on someone meant but figured it didn't mean she could stay holed up in her room.

She went downstairs to the living room where Jade was watching TV. When Jade saw Ireland, her plump little seven-year-old cheeks rounded out in a wide grin. "Want to play a hidden-objects game with me?"

"Sure." Was Ireland going to say "sure" to every question someone asked her that day when she had no idea what the asker really wanted from her? Probably.

Jade switched to a different app on the TV, and the screen showed an animated scene with a mansion swathed in moonlight. The words *Mansion Mystery* floated onto the screen. The plotline was that the lady of the mansion had disappeared, and her brother was trying to find her. There were puzzles and clues and hidden object boards. Ireland had never heard of such a game before but was having fun playing it with Jade. Until, that is, the room temperature dropped by fifty degrees when Mara entered.

"I'm going to Emily's house. Don't go anywhere, Jade."

"Mom said you were supposed to watch me," Jade said.

"Yeah, well, Ireland seems to be taking over that job. Like

everything else." Mara muttered the last part, narrowed her eyes at Ireland, and was gone.

"I don't really like Emily," Jade confessed with a shake of her head, making her beaded braids click together.

"I don't like her either," Ireland agreed.

"She treats people mean."

"Right?" Even as Ireland agreed with Jade, it occurred to her that she had been guilty of treating people meanly as well. She hadn't exactly been nice to Kal the night before. She had been cold and distant and . . . well, mean.

She sent him a text while Jade solved a puzzle that was completely beyond Ireland's ability to help with. "Sorry about yesterday. It was a pretty confusing day."

Her phone chirped, indicating he'd responded immediately. "Tell me about it."

Wait. Was he saying tell me about it as in "yeah, me too," or as in he wanted her to elaborate? "Too much to put in a text," she wrote.

"I'll be right over."

Ireland blinked at her phone. He'd be right over? As in he was coming to Mara's house to see her?

But then, it wasn't only Mara's house anymore. It was hers too. "Hey, Jade?"

"Mm-hmm?"

"Am I allowed to have friends over while we hang out together?"

"'Course."

"Even if it's a boy?"

Jade giggled. "As long as you're not slobbering all over each other."

Fair enough. Ireland texted back. "Okay. Come over."

CHAPTER TWELVE

Kal

Kal was at Mara's house and ringing the doorbell faster than Superman could change clothes in a phone booth.

Ireland answered and smiled when she saw him. Progress. Last night, he worried she wouldn't talk to him again.

She opened the door wider to let him in. As he passed her, he gave in to the impulse to reach out and pull her into a quick hug. She stiffened as if surprised, and he worried he was blundering his way into the whole thing, but she softened against him and hugged him back.

"So . . . I live at Mara's now," she said against his shoulder.

He pulled away, regretting that he needed to. "So I see."

She took him into the kitchen and cut off a slice of bread from the fresh-baked loaf sitting on the cutting board. She set it on a plate, cut off two more slices, and put those on their own plates.

"I don't know how Mr. Wasden found out my dad wasn't taking care of me," she said. "I have my suspicions of who told, and I'm so mad about it, I can't even think well enough to plot out my revenge."

Kal froze. She *was* mad. He figured as much, but he didn't love to have the information verified. "Who—" His voice cracked. He cleared his throat and tried again. "Who do you think told him?"

Ireland frowned, her lips twisting to the side in a way that made a little crease in her cheek that was super adorable. He looked away to try to shake off the desire to kiss that little crease. The moment when she told him she knew he'd betrayed her secret without talking to her was not the moment he should be thinking about kissing her.

And Kal *had* betrayed her secret. He'd spent all night going over it in his mind, trying to see it the way she would see it. Not that he was sorry she wasn't living on her own because that had been all sorts of not awesome. She hadn't been safe. He'd seen the hungry way Rowan had watched her when she'd left school the other day. The guy had practically salivated on his own shoes. If anyone knew Ireland was on her own in what was basically a rudimentary lean-to, she would be vulnerable to whatever malevolence they could imagine. He'd heard Rowan talk about girls with his friends. And Rowan wasn't the only guy in their school Kal didn't trust. Kal knew there was a lot of malevolence to be had in the world.

But Kal thought maybe he should have talked to Ireland first.

"Janice," Ireland said, tugging Kal back into their conversation—the one where she was revealing who had betrayed her.

Kal tried to process the name—process that it wasn't *his* name and figure out whose name it actually was. "Who?"

"The school janitor. I helped her a few times to do her work, and she figured out I was on my own. I can't believe she'd do this to me. I was fine, and now . . . ugh!" Ireland threw her hands in the air and then settled them on the granite countertop as if needing to hold herself up.

"Maybe she did you a favor though."

"You think living with Mara is a favor?"

Kal looked around at the kitchen he stood in. At the fact that there was a loaf of bread on the counter to slice into, at the fact that there was a stocked fridge and pantry just a few feet away. Did Ireland not see all the ways she was lucky in this? "There are worse places to land," he said, not sure if he was landing himself in an argument with her by pointing it out.

Ireland's shoulders slumped and she turned and leaned against the counter. "I know." She covered her eyes with the palms of her hands. "I know." She put her hands down. "You're right. And her kid sister's pretty cute, so there's that. I've never had a kid sister, so that part might be fun."

And you're safe, he thought. He had done for her what he hadn't been able to for Brell. He'd made her safe. Kal leaned against the counter next to her, close enough that their arms were touching. "So what are your plans for the day?" he asked.

"Oh, you know . . . world domination. One hidden-objects game at a time."

"Huh. Never knew hidden-objects games were so ruthless."

Ireland shrugged, her shoulder sliding against his, her touch sending his pulse racing.

"Need a minion for the hostile takeover?" he asked.

She made a gagging sound and playfully shoved him away. "No. No minions. Sycophants are the worst. But . . ." She eyed him as if sizing him up. "You might make a handy sidekick. What do you say? Wanna be my sidekick?"

"Maybe. What's the dental plan like?" They were facing each other now, close enough for him to see the white nebula pattern in her blue eyes.

She leaned closer to him. "Free popcorn on the weekends. But don't tell anyone else. It's a secret perk for my favorite sidekicks."

He leaned closer as well. "That's not a dental plan, unless you're an evil dentist." How had they moved so close together? His gaze dropped to her mouth.

"I thought all dentists were evil," she whispered.

"Only the ones who wear capes," he whispered back.

"Can I kiss you?" she asked. The question was so soft he almost didn't hear it over the thundering of the blood rushing past his ears.

Instead of responding, he moved his mouth slowly to hers, giving her time to pull away in case she hadn't meant to ask for a kiss, in case he had heard wrong. She didn't pull away.

Instead, her fingers curled into his shirt and pulled him closer to her until their lips touched lightly, like a gentle breeze. Kal wrapped his arms around her and she melted against him. He was kissing Ireland. Tender, a little awkward, but not uncomfortable awkward, not insecure awkward. Just *new* awkward. She smelled like oranges and vanilla and warmth and sunshine. He was kissing Ireland Raine. When they broke away, they both let out a nervous laugh as if they weren't quite sure what to do next. At least *he* wasn't sure.

"What are you guys laughing about?" Mara's kid sister asked, making both Ireland and Kal jump a little farther apart.

"World domination plans," Ireland said with a smirk.

"And top-secret sidekick perks," he added.

"Are we still playing?" Jade asked.

"Sure," Ireland said. "I was just getting us all some bread that I made this morning. Asiago sourdough." Ireland picked up two plates and tossed Kal a sassy wink as she followed Jade out of the kitchen.

"I, for one," Kal whispered to himself, "am legit *not* playing."

He picked up his plate and followed them into the living room, where they spent the next few hours in the game, moving from room to room in the mystery mansion while solving puzzles and finding hidden objects. He didn't play many video games—who had time? Between the band and school, he didn't have a lot of leftover minutes to dedicate to a hobby. But when he did play, it was usually a game with zombies of one kind or another. The hidden object game was a fun kind of different.

Jade went to the kitchen to get herself a drink but said, "No slobbering," before she left.

"What was that about?"

"I think she means no making out while she's gone."

Kal's face flamed hot at Ireland's being so casual in talking about kissing him. He refused to be the one to act awkward about it. If she could be bold, so could he. "Dang. That's too bad."

She laughed, a sound that he was quickly learning to love.

"You don't really hate it here, right?" he asked.

"No. Not hate it. I made bread today. That was so seriously . . . *everything*! Ten degrees of the best awesome. But Mara and the hag and harpy have treated me like I was trash since the first minute I walked into the school."

"Hag and harpy?"

"Mara's friends. I don't know. I was doing fine on my own before. I don't need this in my life. It causes me so much anxiety."

"You seem calm right now." He wanted to make her living situation seem okay since it was his fault she was in it.

"It's easy to be calm right now. She's not home."

Just by her bringing it up, he felt the tension rise in Ireland. Time to shuffle the playlist. "So what are your plans after graduation?"

But if he'd thought that conversational direction would improve things, he was wrong.

"Moving, for starters." She became more agitated and got up from the couch to wander the room. "I know most people have big plans after graduation. Mara's going to Europe." Ireland twisted her face and rolled her eyes to tell him what she thought of that. "Isn't that just so one percent of her. Argh!" She threw her arms over her head as if protecting it from falling rocks. "If only Janice would have just minded her own business."

Kal hated that she blamed Janice. The custodian was innocent. She hadn't betrayed Ireland. He had. "What about college? You could go to college after you graduate. It's what all the cool kids are doing." He flashed her a grin but then wanted to kick himself. Could he be any more glib when she was having a crisis?

"Oh yeah. I should do that. 'Cause college is super affordable."

"I could help you apply for scholarships."

She was already shaking her head. "My grades have never been good. We moved around too much."

By the time Jade came back into the room, Ireland had gone from happy to contemplative.

Mrs. Washington came home not too long after. She greeted them all, but before Kal had time to worry about whether it was okay that he'd come over, Mrs. Washington was asking where Mara was.

"She went to Emily's." Jade provided the needed information.

Mrs. Washington didn't seem to love that answer but didn't say anything more.

"I better get going," Kal said finally. "We play Geppetto's tonight."

"Oh. Okay." He and Ireland both stood. She walked with him to the door. Once they got there, he put his hand on the handle and twisted it open. "You can come with me if you want. I promise to get you home before eleven."

Ireland looked back in the direction of the living room where they'd left Jade. "I should probably stay. We've almost got this game solved. I wouldn't want her to think she wasn't important enough to stick around for."

He felt all the meanings in that statement. She'd been living on her own for who knew how long. "Are you going to be okay? I didn't mean to make you feel sad."

She nodded. "You didn't. I'm fine. Or I will be. Just a lot going on. Sometimes I'm just so angry. I want to hit something but don't know where to throw the punch."

"You could go ahead and hit me."

Ireland let out a small laugh. "You didn't do anything to deserve it. But thanks for the offer. Thanks for everything." She leaned over and hugged him. Then she kissed him, a light quick sweep of her lips on his before she pulled away, touched her fingers to her lips, and smiled. "Thanks for letting me do that. It's way better than punching you."

He smiled. "But the offer of you punching me is still on the table."

"Can't do it when you don't deserve it." She grinned and closed the door.

Except that everything she'd said proved that if she knew it was him who got her into her situation with Mara's family, she would absolutely think he deserved it.

CHAPTER THIRTEEN
Ireland

Mara had come home from Emily's to meet a very unhappy Grace. Grace didn't yell at Mara in front of Ireland but instead took her to the back office, where she and Jarrod did work from home for the bakery cafés. Even still, the argument got loud enough for Ireland to hear from the living room. Ireland heard her name a few times and Jade's name a few times. It was evident that mother and daughter were fighting because Grace was mad that Mara left when she was supposed to be watching Jade. And Mara was mad that Grace took in a stray—she was referring to Ireland—without consulting how Mara felt about the whole thing.

"Don't let it bug you," Jade said. "They do that a lot."

Maybe they had fought before, but Ireland would bet every dollar she would ever earn in her life on the fact that they hadn't ever fought over *her* before the last few days. She was a new element to whatever struggles they had between them.

If Mara had seemed frosty before, the fight with her mom had turned her into something glacial.

The following Monday, when Mara drove them to school,

Ireland tried to start a conversation. It wasn't like they could maintain total silence when they were living in the same house. But Mara just rolled her eyes and said, "Oh no you do not. Boundaries."

"What's that supposed to mean?"

"It means I have set a boundary. I don't want to be friends. You live in my house, eat my food, play games with my sister, get loved on by my parents—whatever. But the boundary is that we don't need to be friends."

"Fair enough." Ireland could sort of see Mara's point of view. Ireland really had taken over Mara's world. Her little sister, Jade, loved Ireland. Her mom loved that Ireland helped around the house so much, and her dad was thrilled to have another set of willing and happy-to-be-there hands in the bakeries. Ireland, in just three days, had found her groove in the Washington household. Mara had a great family. Ireland could see why Mara might not want to share.

Even though it was obvious Mara didn't want to talk, Ireland asked, "Can I ask you if you like Kal Ellis?" She had to know because if Mara did like him, Ireland would have to back away from that relationship. She did not need the drama that would come from her liking the same guy Mara liked.

Mara laughed. "Superman? You mean like am I into him? That's a big no."

Ireland breathed out her relief. "Is there anyone you're interested in?"

"Boundaries."

"Right."

The rest of the ride was in silence.

At the school, Mara locked up the car, flipped back her box braids, and stomped off without so much as a backward glance.

Ireland shrugged and sighed. She couldn't let it get to her. It's not like she chose to live with the Washingtons. As much as she loved the comfort and the full stomach and the hot showers, she didn't love Mara hating on her.

Mara hadn't told her friends about Ireland, which was fine. It's not like it mattered to Ireland that Tinsley and Emily didn't know. If Mara didn't want them to know, Ireland would respect it. In fact, it was probably better that the hag and harpy weren't in on the information. If they had been sort of petty before, they would become outright savage if they thought Ireland was intruding in their queen bee's life.

She shrugged it off. She had her own work to do at school that had nothing to do with Mara Washington, Mara's boundaries, or the hag and the harpy. Ireland pulled out the paints and brushes from Mr. Wasden's art room and set them up on the worktable by the mural, then went to get the water so people could clean their brushes off.

Once everything was set up, she inspected the mural to see what new things had been added. Over the course of the weekend, she had made her peace with Janice. Janice was a responsible adult. It was her job to do her part to keep the students safe. If only Ireland's parents had felt that same sort of obligation, how different would her life be? Ireland walked the length of the wall, not wanting to miss anything new. She smiled at the picture of the velociraptor sticking his head up out of the tree branches. He wore reading glasses and looked mildly annoyed. He had a clawed finger in front of his lips with the word "Shh!" next to him in pine bristles.

Ireland's gaze went from the tree branches down to the ground where a flower had been added. She stopped short when she saw some terrifyingly familiar words. They were written in hot pink paint instead of lipstick and made up the bud of a flower next to the tree. The flower was the size of Ireland's palm and the paintbrush used to write had to have been thin to be able to fit so much in the compact space. There was a small flourish at the flower's base that wasn't paint, but the lipstick she'd seen in the bathroom. Ireland was sure of it.

My every heartbeat is now a wracking sob, wrapped in a cloak of betrayal. I'm a hideous beast now—scarred, repulsive, and howling at the uncaring moon.

Ireland stared at the words. She knew those words. Knew that handwriting in lipstick. Spending the night scrubbing them off her bathroom wall had seared them into her brain. Her personal vandal went to her school.

"What's wrong?"

She jumped, startled by Kal coming up behind her. "Nothing. Why?"

He pointed at her face. "You're scowling at the mural as if it personally offended you."

Direct hit. How was she so transparent? She tried to laugh off whatever remnants of scowl might have existed on her face. "No. It's just this here." She pointed at the prose. "Any idea who wrote it?" *So I can sock them in the shoulder for vandalizing my home.* She hoped she didn't say that part out loud. Sometimes it was hard to tell what she thought in her head and what she let escape her lips.

She must not have said it out loud because Kal leaned to read over her shoulder. Her eyes fluttered closed at having him so close. He couldn't see her eyes, right? He couldn't know that she was drinking in the scent and nearness of him, could he? She snapped her eyes open again, just in case.

"That's not paint, is it?" he asked, pointing at the bottom of the flower.

"Nope. Lipstick."

"Huh."

"Is that against the rules?"

He snorted. "I didn't think I'd have to make a rule about that, but I dunno. It looks like it belongs there. I say we leave it." He read the last of the words out loud. "'Howling at the uncaring moon.' I like that. Don't know who wrote it or why they chose a lipstick and paint duo, but it's high-key awesome."

Ireland turned her gaze back to the flower, shimmering with the glitter that had been in the lipstick. A bright flower with a dark message. "How does it make you feel?" she asked. It made her feel scared. But she wasn't sure if that was because she'd come in and found what she'd initially thought was blood on her bathroom wall, where someone had trespassed into her life.

Kal shrugged, still standing close enough that his shoulder brushed hers as he did. "Sad. Whoever wrote this sounds like they're hurting from something."

Ireland looked back to the mural, tilting her head as she focused on the words from a different perspective. Sad, not scary. Hurt, not haunting. Except why couldn't they be all of it? Sad *and* scary? Hurt *and* haunting? For the first time, she felt pity for her vandal. They were going through something hard, and she'd let a little thing like lipstick smears get in the way of compassion.

"You're scowling again," Kal said.

She glanced at him to find he was staring at her, his gaze heavy, as if he were puzzling her out. She could almost feel him moving her pieces around to try to lock them together to see the whole picture.

"Is it against the rules of the mural if I respond to this?" she asked.

He considered the question, then shrugged again, his shoulder brushing against hers once more in a rustle of cloth that made her involuntarily shiver. "I think a conversation on the wall could be interesting—even artistic—especially if you flow the words down the flower stem so it's a clear response, and as long as it doesn't violate any of the other rules."

She nodded, then went to the table of art supplies to find a small, thin paintbrush. She wanted this person to know that they weren't alone in whatever they were going through. They had come into her home and cried to her on her wall. And now, here they were again. "I'm listening," she said out loud.

"What?" Kal asked.

She startled, realizing she'd spoken out loud. "Nothing. Just talking to myself. Again."

He grinned. "It's cute that you do that."

"You don't think it's crazy?"

Kal shook his head. "Nah. Sometimes saying the stuff in our heads out loud helps keep us from spinning the words over and over and over until we're dizzy and sick. It lets the stuff get out, you know? Escape. I think it can be healthy. I do it all the time."

She nodded, grateful he wasn't judging her. Kal Ellis had said she was cute—innocuous enough. But did he mean like puppy-dog-tripping-on-ears cute? Or endearingly charming, and I-want-to-kiss-you-again cute? She really liked him. Her heart had taken another step on that path to love. He was gentle and observant and smart and interesting. He was everything a person should be if a person could at all help it. He made *her* want to be a better person when she was with him. And if he liked her even half as much in return . . . well, *that* would really be something. Jade had asked her if she had a crush on Kal after he'd left on Saturday. The word "crush" felt so juvenile. Ireland was practically a grown-up now. She'd even lived on her own. She was not a child who gave way to juvenile thinking. And she'd had crushes in the past, on boys who were interesting to her in some way or another, boys she'd liked from afar and made up stories about in her head. Ireland wondered if she was the only person who did such a thing or if there were others like her having whole relationships from first glance to breakup in their heads.

Or maybe there wasn't anybody else doing that sort of thing, and she was just a little different in yet one other way from everybody else.

Either way, what she felt for Kal was so much more than a crush. And yet, at the same time, it felt exactly how a crush should feel. Because she would be well and truly crushed if he ever went away.

Ireland twirled her paintbrush in the green paint and considered how she might respond to her vandal. She finally turned to answer the message on the wall.

"Most people only see the outside. Live your life like they can see the inside. Remember the moon has cycles. Soon it'll turn its full light to your beauty." She paused, having run out of space on the stem, wondering if she should end it there. But she decided to go into the grass because she had more to say. "Keep howling until your voice can find a different melody."

CHAPTER FOURTEEN

Kal

Kal watched in fascination as Ireland wrote her message on the student mural. She painted the letters with deft precision, as if she were creating a brand-new typeface, which she totally was. From a design standpoint, the font was full-on fire. How she'd managed such a thing with a paintbrush and paint was nothing short of miraculous. In spite of his art skills, Kal had rather crappy penmanship. It was one of those things that he always meant to work on and never did. Wasden had given an art assignment at the beginning of the year that involved creating pictures out of words they wrote. He'd done a guitar out of words that were lyrics to a song he'd written. He was still proud of how that project had gone down—even if his penmanship sucked.

Kal realized he was hovering over Ireland when she hesitated for a long moment. He went back to the art table to make sure the tubes of acrylic had their lids put back on. No reason to let the paint dry up.

He saw that someone had drawn a bird flipping the bird. They had to think they were being pretty clever with that, but it made him mad since this person could ruin the mural for everyone.

He'd promised Wasden that he'd help monitor the wall to make sure nothing inappropriate went up. He and the other members of the art club had sworn to do their parts to keep the project positive, which meant if something ugly went up, they had to take it down. Kal swirled a brush in the red that had been squeezed out onto a paper plate and then left to dry because someone squeezed out too much.

This was the second time something needed to be painted over, and if he hadn't been paying close attention, he might have missed it, since it was pretty subtle. Wasden had found the other one. It had been subtle too.

Kal had complained about it to Cooper and Asha when they were practicing in the back building one day. Asha had been peeved that someone would screw up the mural while Cooper had stayed quiet about it. Cooper usually had an opinion on everything, which meant it was probably someone he knew who'd done it. Probably one of his drinking buddies. Any one of the trust-fund frat boys Cooper hung out with could have been the guilty party.

Kal couldn't prove it was one of those guys though.

"Hey," he said to Ireland. "I'll see you in class, okay?" He wanted to talk to Cooper.

She didn't look up as she worked on her message, which she was now painting in the grass. "Sure." Ireland was a woman of few words. Where he could take ten seconds to say something, she could take two words and get the same point across. Sometimes it made him feel a little insecure that he talked so much. But she didn't seem to mind, and he didn't mind that she talked so little. It made them good friends. Easy friends. He liked it. And her kissing him made them . . . well, he wasn't sure what it made them, but he liked the kissing part of her too.

Kal turned to go outside, where Cooper would be warming up for track like he did every day.

But from the hallway as he approached the doors leading outside, Kal overheard Cooper's voice coming from a classroom. It was low enough that he couldn't discern what was being said, but he knew Cooper's tones. The conversation sounded serious. It was early—too early for Cooper to be showing up to meet with a teacher unless he was flunking out of a class, which Cooper's dad would never let him do. Kal didn't want to interrupt something serious and had decided to go back to the mural and walk to his first class with Ireland when he heard something that made him stop.

"I'm not sure what I saw, but it looked like he was forcing himself on you."

Who was Cooper talking to? What in the actual . . .

It was a girl's voice that responded, one that sounded familiar to Kal, but she spoke quieter than Cooper, so Kal couldn't quite place it.

"I wasn't going to say anything," Cooper said. "Every time I've seen you since then you've acted like you were fine, but then when he was talking to the guys last night, I just thought maybe what I'd seen was right."

"You need to mind your business." This time the girl spoke loud enough to understand what she was saying.

"But I don't think I'm wrong about what I saw. You need to tell someone. If you don't, I'm going to."

"You seriously just need to leave me alone." Footsteps were coming to the classroom door. Whoever the girl was, she'd had enough of dealing with Cooper. Kal quickly ducked into the boys' bathroom so he wouldn't get caught eavesdropping.

He stayed there until the first bell rang because he wasn't

really sure what he'd overheard, and he felt oddly unsettled about it. Whatever it was hadn't been good.

He made his way to class and slid into the seat next to Ireland. She crossed her eyes and stuck her tongue out at him. She was definitely goofy, but goofy had never looked more amazing than it did on her. "Hey," he whispered.

"Hey." She grinned at him. She seemed happier than before.

The moment with Ireland made Kal forget whatever had been going on with Cooper. "We should go on a real date sometime, one where you aren't stuck listening to me play."

"I like hearing you play."

Mr. Nichols had stood and was moving to the front of the class.

"You *might* like hearing me play, but I want you to be my girlfriend, not my groupie."

Her smile vanished and her eyes dropped to her hands on her desk. He realized what he'd said. He'd used the "girlfriend" word. Ridiculous.

But did she think he was ridiculous?

Maybe not.

He kept staring at her even after Mr. Nichols brushed back his comb-over and began the class. After a moment, Ireland pulled out some paper and a pencil. She scribbled something on it and then slid it over so Kal could see.

"I'm in. When and where is this date? Please say we're finally going to pull off the great candy-jar heist."

He laughed out loud.

All eyes in the classroom turned to him.

"Did you have something you wanted to add to the discussion, Mr. Ellis?" Mr. Nichols asked. What discussion had Mr. Nichols been talking about? It was history class, so chances were good Mr. Nichols hadn't said anything worth laughing at, which meant Kal had no reason to laugh. School never covered the funny parts of history. Surely there had to be some funny parts, didn't there?

Kal cleared his throat and said, "Umm. No, sir?"

"Is that a question? Do you not know if you have something to add?" Wow. Mr. Nichols must have been shorted some sugar packets in his coffee that morning.

"I don't have anything to add, sir. Except that your choice of tie is fire today." Kal pointed to Mr. Nichol's tie, which was emblazoned with Thor's hammer. "You can never go wrong with Thor, can you? I mean, historically speaking."

"Thor is not a historical figure, Mr. Ellis."

"Oh yeah. I know, but certain people in history believed he was a real figure."

Now several people were laughing. Mr. Nichols sent Kal a withering stare but ultimately must have decided it wasn't worth the effort because he went back to his lecture.

Ireland pulled back the paper, scrawled something new, and then moved it so he could see what she'd written. "Nice save."

His eyes caught what she'd written before. "I'm in." Did that mean she was in on the candy-jar heist or that she was in with the plan of her being his girlfriend? He really hoped it was the girlfriend option because *that* would be more fire than a Thor tie.

He wrote on his own paper and turned it so she could see. "Is tonight too soon?"

The smile that curved her lips was his answer.

"Pick u up at 6?"

She nodded.

It was a date. Kal had a date with the most enigmatic, incredible person he'd ever met.

CHAPTER FIFTEEN
Ireland

A date with Kal. Ireland had a date with Kal Ellis. One where he would pick her up and take her somewhere and probably let her kiss him again before it was all through, which sent an involuntary shiver up her spine and back down again.

She needed to hurry to meet Mara at the car. Part of her worried that Mara would leave her, except Grace had been adamant that Mara's new chore was driving Ireland to and from school—no exceptions.

But she'd had to stay at her last class to get clarification on an assignment, and she still had to clean up the paints at the mural.

As she entered the art room, something bright and new caught her eye. Another pink paint-and-lipstick flower.

Ireland frowned. She needed to hurry because Mara could leave, but . . . the mystery lipstick writer had struck again. She needed to know what the new message said. She moved closer to read.

"The moon will turn away in shame because I look like this . . ."

The words were bigger than before, so they took up the entire flower. Hanging off one of the petals was a distorted creature. The creature was a beast as hideous as the first flower had claimed it to be. The creator had used paints for the monster, which looked like it could have been a woman but bald, with gouges scarring the head, face, and limbs as it hung from one arm and looked out as if staring straight back at anyone who might be staring at it.

It could have been a thing from nightmares, looking human enough but also "off" enough to be twisting to the eye. But as Ireland gazed on it, she saw what Kal had seen in the words. She saw the sad.

The eyes looked like they were on the verge of tears.

The little creature had obviously been done quickly, the brushstrokes having an unfinished quality to them, but it was still striking. Ireland glanced at the door. She needed to leave, or she'd *get* left. But the idea of rushing off to placate Mara felt like abandoning her mystery lipstick artist. She hurried to dip the small brush into the green paint so she could respond.

As Ireland pulled the brush from the paint, she realized what she could say. She took out her phone to look up a few images so that her own picture would look proportionately right. Then she began carefully tracing the words into the stem. She cleaned her brush and squeezed out a few colors of acrylics onto the edge of one of the used plates that had been left.

She got to work on the message.

When she was done, she felt satisfied by the end product. She'd never created any kind of art that made her as happy as this did. She took a picture of it, making sure both of the flower messages were in the frame because all of it together was what made it powerful.

In the stem, the message read, "You must be using a twisted mirror that distorts images. I got you a new one to see yourself clearly." Hanging from one of the leaves, she drew an intricate silver mirror with the words, "You are beautiful," in the reflection.

She took a deep breath, satisfied, and then hurried to clean up the art supplies, getting all the tubes capped and the brushes properly cleaned. She put the bin of supplies under the table.

Mr. Wasden poked his head out of his gallery. "Hey. I thought I heard someone out here. You ready for me to lock up?"

"Yeah. All ready. See you tomorrow."

At the car, Mara was waiting. She turned her full glare on Ireland. "Where have you been?"

Ireland would have laughed because Mara sounded like a stern mom at that moment. And Ireland would know what that sounded like since Mara and Grace had gotten into an argument the night before, and Grace had started the argument with those exact words. But Ireland didn't think Mara would take being laughed at very kindly.

"I have to put the paint stuff away. You know that."

"If it's going to take that much time every day, you'll need to find somebody else to do it."

They both got into the car, with Mara shutting her door harder than necessary. Again. Maybe she wasn't slamming the door. Maybe the driver's side didn't close tightly unless it got slammed. Because it seemed that was all Mara ever did when she was closing the door around Ireland.

Mara started the car and huffed when she saw the clock on the dash display. "Seriously. You're going to need to find somebody else. I cannot wait for you every single day. This is ridiculous."

"You could make it go faster by helping me out," Ireland suggested. "After all, you're in the art club too. This should be your responsibility as well."

Mara cut a glance at Ireland before she pulled the car out onto the road. "Are you kidding me right now? You're trying to delegate to me? Seriously?"

"Just saying. If you're in a hurry . . ."

"I'm not the one who volunteered."

True enough. Mara hadn't volunteered. The task was Ireland's responsibility. The extreme amount of time it had taken that day hadn't exactly been fair to Mara either. Ireland had been doing much more than simply putting away the supplies; she'd taken the time to craft her own piece of art. Mara wasn't wrong to be irritated.

The conversation Ireland was having with the lipstick writer on the wall had shifted a few things in her. Maybe she didn't dislike Mara as much as she thought. Maybe, like the lipstick writer was both scary and sad, Mara could be both monstrous and misunderstood.

Since Mara had initiated conversation, Ireland assumed it was okay for her to keep it going. "So, I have a date tonight. With Kal again. Not sure what I should wear. Do you have any advice?"

Ireland assumed that if she brought up the topic of fashion, Mara would be more inclined to keep the conversation going since she seemed all but obsessed with her clothes.

Ireland was wrong.

"Boundaries," she said. If anything, Mara looked more annoyed with Ireland than she ever had before.

"What boundaries? It's not like I asked anything about you."

"You're talking to me. And I already told you we weren't friends."

Ireland rolled her eyes hard enough to make her wonder how she didn't give herself a concussion.

"I wasn't talking to you, princess. I was talking to myself because the conversation is better. So, as I was saying before we were so rudely interrupted, I'm not really sure what to wear. I mean, we look great in the plain white shirt with the black jacket. It's both dressy and casual at the same time. And it makes us look like we have a figure, which is always nice."

"You do know you can keep the tea to yourself, right?" But Mara no longer glared at Ireland. Instead, her eyebrows were furrowed in a confused knot above her nose.

Confusion, Ireland's father had taught her, always worked to off-balance people who thought they were in control. It allowed you to pull the control back to yourself.

Ireland gave her head a small, firm shake. She would not be taking lessons from her father. The guy had landed himself in jail, so what good could any advice from him be? And Mara was right. Ireland could keep the tea to herself. She pressed her lips together and stayed silent for the rest of the car ride.

At the house, Grace was home and helping Jade with homework already. "You guys are home late."

Mara pointed at Ireland. "It's her fault. She had to stay after."

Just in case Grace thought that Ireland had to stay after to do detention or some other activity caused by or leading to delinquency, Ireland hurried to explain herself. She talked about the mural and how the principal's agreement to allow the mural to happen was partly dependent upon her willingness to clean up.

"Well, that's nice. I hope you helped, Mara. Since you're in the art club."

Ireland wondered if Mara would lie and say that of course she was involved. But Mara ignored her mom's question and started up the stairs.

"Yeah," Ireland interjected. "Mara helped. Also, Mara painted the ocean waves. You should go see it sometime. It looks great. She's really talented."

Ireland's view of where Mara stood on the stairs was limited, cut off so she could only see Mara's legs and feet. But those legs halted on the stairs. For a moment, Ireland worried Mara would stomp back down and yell "Boundaries!" at her.

But that hesitation on the stairs was over, and Mara continued up until her feet disappeared altogether.

Ireland took the moment while Mara was gone to ask Grace if it was okay if she went out with Kal that night.

Grace gave her permission as long as Ireland promised to get her homework done first, which Ireland had already intended to do.

When she entered her room, she noticed that there was something on her bed that hadn't been there when she left. Clothes. It was a whole outfit. The gray sweater with silver threads woven into it had a whimsical asymmetrical hem and paired perfectly with the midi skirt and the low-heeled boots.

Ireland recognized the outfit because she had seen Mara wearing it on several different occasions.

Mara had loaned her clothing? Ireland stood perfectly still for a moment, waiting to see if any other apocalyptic event might happen. She listened hard for any siren announcing an alien invasion and peered out the window to see if a meteor was hurtling toward the ground. But all was quiet. She glanced at Mara's door. It was quiet there too. Ireland contemplated knocking on Mara's door to say thank you but couldn't figure out how to do that without being awkward and weird and maybe making the entire thing blow up in her face. She decided the best option would be to quietly accept the gift that had been quietly given and be grateful for what it represented.

For all Mara had insisted that they weren't friends, this loaning of clothing seemed very much like friendship to Ireland. Wasn't that what girls did for each other when they were friends? Loan clothing for dates?

Ireland grinned because, for the first time ever, she was going to go out wearing something that hadn't been salvaged from a thrift store. Although maybe that wasn't true. Grace had already declared she thrifted every once in a while. For all Ireland knew, this outfit came from the local Goodwill.

But even if that were the case, Grace's budget for that type of shopping and Ireland's budget for that type of shopping weren't anywhere in the same neighborhood. They weren't even on the same planet. Ireland was pretty sure they weren't even in the same solar system. Even at the thrift store, Ireland looked for the clearance stuff.

She hurried with her homework, getting it done quickly so that she could get dressed.

When she'd buttoned the last button, she brushed her hair off to the side and did a single braid that would lay over her left shoulder. Only then did she allow herself to look in the mirror. Her breath caught at her reflection. "I look like. . ." She frowned as she tried to put into words what it was she saw. "Like I belong."

She wanted to knock on Mara's door to thank her now more than ever. The fairy-godmother-gift Mara had given was a night of normalcy.

As her eyes felt glued to her reflection in the mirror, she thought of the mural and what she'd written to the mystery lipstick artist. She hoped when that person stared in the mirror, she could feel like this—like she belonged.

When Ireland went downstairs to wait for Kal to show up, Mara was in the living room wearing yoga pants and a bulky sweatshirt. Her hair was up in a sloppy ponytail and she'd washed off all of her makeup, so her face was clean and fresh. It was like Mara and Ireland had swapped places with each other in some *Freaky Friday* kind of moment. They inspected each other for a long moment, with Mara finally giving a nod of approval and

Ireland saying a soft "Thank you" before the doorbell chimed and Ireland broke eye contact so she could answer it.

Kal let out a small puff of air as if looking at her knocked the wind out of him. "You look amazing."

"Thanks. You do too." He wore a black, long-sleeved shirt with a black jacket and jeans. The whole look came together like he was about to be in an ad for guy's cologne. Grace met them there at the door to greet Kal and to verify that he would get Ireland home early since it was a school night. When Grace asked where they were going, Kal answered, "Humboldt Observatory. It's clear out, and it's 'observe the moon' night. There's an activity there that's open to the public."

"How sweet is that?" Grace asked "Well, you two have fun. Have her home early."

Kal agreed again that he would and led Ireland to the car.

"How did you even hear about something like this?" she asked once they were driving up Fickle Hill Road.

"My grandparents were both members of the Humboldt Astronomy Society. Whenever we visited my grandparents before moving here, they would take us to the observatory. One time, we even managed to see the northern lights."

"That's cool. I didn't know you could see those in California." The forest swooshed past Ireland's window.

"It's rare, and it doesn't look like you would think. At least it didn't when I saw it. It was a bright red, like the sky was on fire."

"Okay, that sounds terrifying, actually."

Kal laughed. "Not at all. Just cool. Ten times awesome."

When they arrived and were out of the car, Kal held out his hand to Ireland. She would never get tired of holding his hand. Never in her whole life.

"It looks abandoned," Ireland said softly. She couldn't help it. She tucked herself into Kal just enough to feel the warmth of his energy next to her. Most parking lots had lights to help people be safe while getting to and from their cars, but this parking lot was entirely dark.

Kal explained that the lack of lights on the outside of the building had everything to do with the light pollution interfering with proper observation of the heavenly skies.

"So why the observatory?" Ireland asked.

"I wanted to give you the stars tonight," Kal answered.

That statement qualified as next-level, heart-stutteringly adorable. Kal had been right about the facility being open to the public. There were several other people there using the equipment. Kal and Ireland waited their turn to view through the telescope. As they did, she overheard a couple of people using the term *earthshine.*

"What's earthshine?" Ireland whispered to Kal.

"See the crescent moon there?" He pointed up through the opening without looking into the telescope. "It's the sunlight reflected by the earth that lights up the dark part of the moon. See how you can kinda see the image of the full moon along with the crescent moon? That's earthshine. It only happens a few times a year, which is why the society gathered tonight."

Ireland gazed into the nighttime sky that was visible through the telescope and hugged her arms to her. The observatory was cold thanks to the crisp, clear night, which meant that even the sweater and the jacket she wore weren't enough to keep her warm. It might not have been a great idea to wear a skirt.. But she wouldn't have missed the earthshine for anything. Cold legs were a small price to pay.

"I like that word. Earthshine."

"Yeah. My grandparents did too. I think I remember my grandpa telling me that Leonardo da Vinci came up with the idea of earthshine."

Ireland nudged Kal with her shoulder. "Wow. Impressive that Leonardo da Vinci created the idea of the earth, the moon, and the sun. I kinda thought they were here before he was."

He nudged her back. "You know what I mean." She could hear the grin in his voice.

He put his eye to the telescope, and Ireland watched him watch the universe. The jacket he wore accentuated his broad shoulders. She'd never considered herself the kind of girl who noticed things like shoulders, but she'd discovered that once she'd started cataloging Kal's features and found so much to approve of, she could consider looking at him a worthwhile hobby. Her own time at the telescope wasn't nearly as satisfying as looking at him.

After they were back out in the parking lot and heading to the car, Ireland looked at the sky. Even without the telescope, the earthshine on the moon was easy to see. Kal's hand enveloped her own in warm safety. "I've looked at the sky millions of times, but I don't think I've ever seen it before tonight. Thank you."

Kal stopped and tugged at her hand so that the distance between them moved from several inches to nonexistent. "I have a confession to make," he said, his breath warm on her lips in the cold night air. He maintained eye contact. His thumb traced the curve of her cheekbone.

"Yeah?" Could she breathe? No. Ireland was drowning in him. In his warmth. In his gift of the stars.

"I was really mad at you for ignoring me all those months you sat by me."

Ireland winced. "Sorry. I wasn't sure if I was—"

"Sticking around. I know. I'm glad you decided to stick around because I really, really like you."

"I really, really like you too," she said, her lips brushing lightly against his as she made her own confession. He then pressed his lips to hers, his kiss tender, careful, as if she were some fragile bit of crystal that could shatter at the slightest touch.

The thing was . . . she didn't feel fragile. She felt strong and capable. She wrapped her arms around him, her fingers in his dark wavy hair, and kissed him with greater insistence.

In this place where the stars tracked the time, Ireland lost time completely. Had they been there a whole minute? A half hour? A day? It felt like eternity in an eyeblink.

When they broke apart, his forehead leaned on hers as he gave a low laugh. "Wow," he breathed. "Just wow."

She could not agree more.

He drove her back home, and it wasn't until he was pulling up in front that Ireland realized she actually considered it her home. They walked to the door hand in hand and he kissed her all over again, and the universe felt good and right and perfect.

Ireland entered the house and was slammed with a charge of tense energy from the people inside, shattering her euphoria. Mara was fighting with her parents. Again.

Maybe the universe wasn't good or right or perfect after all.

CHAPTER SIXTEEN

Kal

Kal drove home with a grin perma-plastered to his stupid face. That girl though . . . she completely owned him.

The next day at school and several days after, he spent every moment he could with Ireland: in between classes, during lunch, and for a brief moment before and after school. Ireland couldn't do anything with him after school because she'd decided to take on a waitressing job at the Washington family's most local café in addition to the time she spent on Saturday mornings helping to make the bread.

She said she wanted spending money and a savings account, which he could understand, but it seemed like an emotional nail puncturing a tire on the way out of town for a road trip to have her get a job just as they were getting to know each other— getting to *like* each other.

Ireland had promised she would meet him at Geppetto's on Friday and that she could go out with him Saturday night, but by Wednesday, he wasn't sure he could wait that long to spend actual time with her. The few minutes here and there weren't enough.

"Still keeping up with your pen pal, I see," he said Wednesday afternoon. Ireland was supposed to be cleaning up for the day, but she was instead creating another piece of the wildflower field under the tree. Kal had started doing the cleanup so she could work. He had to admit, from an artistic point of view, the work that the lipstick writer and Ireland created together was interesting.

The carefully written pink-lipstick message that Ireland now contemplated was tucked into the petals of a flower that had been made to look like reflective shattered glass shards. "Someone broke my mirror," the message read.

Kal toted the art supplies to the back room. He was starting to worry about the conversation between Ireland and the mystery writer. This cry for help made it seem like the person needed an intervention, more than what Ireland could do with a paintbrush. He wondered why the principal wasn't doing anything about it. But maybe the principal wasn't paying close enough attention to the mural to know that one of her students was literally screaming on the wall. There was also the fact that there wasn't much the principal or any other adult could do. The artwork was anonymous, and even though the art club kept a close eye on the mural to make sure no one did anything that broke the rules, the mystery artist remained in total stealth mode. Kal worried about what it would do to Ireland if the person on the other end of these messages ended up hurt in a real way and Ireland found out about it. Would she blame herself like he blamed himself for Brell, even though there was logically nothing more she could do than what she was doing?

He worried that Ireland would spiral like he had. He wanted better for her than the guilt he carried for himself.

When Kal came out of the back supply room, Ireland was still working. He watched her painstakingly paint the words that made up another flower stem and leaves. He waited until she was

done before he peeked at the finished product. "Not broken ir-
reparably. Your mirror is like a pond. A pebble might ripple the
surface, but no one can truly shatter a pond."

"You have the heart of a poet," he said softly.

"I wish there was more I could do." Ireland stared at her response to the shattered mirror-flower message.

"You're doing as much as you can. Especially since you don't
know who it is," Kal said.

Ireland made a noncommittal noise low in her throat as she
scrambled to her feet. "I know. I better go. Mara doesn't like to be
kept waiting."

"I'll walk you out." He'd parked not too far from Mara's car.

Mara wasn't alone at her car. She had her friends with her.
Kal held Ireland's hand in his and felt her grip tighten around
his fingers as they approached. When Tinsley started talking, he
understood why Ireland had tensed.

"So what's the latest with the hobo in your house?" Tinsley
asked Mara. She said it in a whisper, as if she hadn't wanted to be
overheard, but she had to know they were close enough to hear,
right? Tinsley turned, made eye contact with Ireland, and smiled
with a dismissive curve of her lips as she turned her attention to
Kal.

"I heard you play last week, Kal. You were lit." Tinsley's eyes
slid briefly to where Kal's hand connected with Ireland's, and then
she let out a light laugh as her brow furrowed in evident disbelief.
"I'll be there this weekend too."

Kal hadn't ever liked Tinsley. The girl was an oil spill in the
ocean. He always left every interaction with her feeling saturated
in her toxic waste. But that was probably because Tinsley had a
thing for him, and her obvious attempts to get him to pay attention to her irritated him.

Why did she think he'd be okay with her hating on the girl he was obviously with? His mom always told him that ugly behavior got ugly results. Tinsley had a collection of ugly results coming if she kept it up.

Kal decided to ignore her. "Hey, Mara," he said, turning his attention to her instead.

Mara nodded at him. She looked tired, as if even *she* felt exhausted by her friends.

"Do you have to work at the café tonight too?" he asked.

"No." Tinsley interrupted. "Our girl's coming with us. Party at Cooper's."

"I told you guys," Mara said. "I can't tonight."

"You have to come. Rowan's gonna be there!" Tinsley insisted.

"Yeah," Emily agreed. "You don't want him to get tired of waiting for you and find someone else. Besides, this party is going to be brill."

Mara popped a hip and gave Emily a flat stare. "How brill do you think a Wednesday night party is really going to be? Cooper's parents might not be home tonight, but everyone has school tomorrow. It's going to be basic."

"But Rowan's gonna be there!" Tinsley insisted.

"Tinsley, stop," Mara said.

Tinsley closed her mouth, as if Mara had clamped it shut by force with that one word. Wild that Mara could hold so much power.

Kal walked Ireland to the passenger side of the car and opened the door. "You okay?" he whispered low enough that Tinsley couldn't hear him.

She slid onto the seat. "Fine."

Maybe she hadn't overheard Tinsley talk smack about her.

"I'll see you later then."

She nodded and shut the door.

Mara, who had also got in, turned the car on. The stereo blasted

Taylor Swift's music as they drove away. Ireland had told him she was starting to worry she might go deaf with the music that loud.

"So, you coming tonight?" Tinsley asked Kal as he watched the car leave. He had to step back since she'd entered his personal bubble.

"Can't see why I would." He turned to his own car.

"I'll be there!" she called after him.

Exactly why he wouldn't be. But he didn't say that out loud. He did not want to get pulled into her drama. And there was no reason to hurt her feelings, Though he wasn't sure she had any.

Except as he was driving home, Cooper called him. He hit the hands-free button. "'Sup Coop?" he said.

"Party at my house tonight."

"Yeah. I heard."

"Oh good. So you're coming."

"I didn't say that."

"C'mon. You have to. Alison's coming. And you know I'd die for this girl to like me."

"That involves me how?"

"She likes our band. I figured we could play a few songs and woo her with the music."

Kal laughed. "Dude. You know I'm not taking you seriously now. Did you just say 'woo'?"

"Woo is a word." Cooper's tone sounded belligerent, which made Kal laugh.

"A hundred years ago maybe."

"Whatever. Will you come?"

"Fine, but I'm not staying long."

"You are the GOAT. Thanks, Superman."

"Uh-huh."

He stopped home to let his parents know that he was going to Cooper's and to grab his guitar, but when he walked in the door, his mom called from the kitchen, "Oh good. You're home. Any chance you'd be willing to help your grandpa with an early dinner?"

"Why'd you bring him into this?" His grandpa's voice came from the kitchen before Kal could respond.

"I need his help," his mom answered.

"I can make my own dinner."

"Donuts don't count."

Kal laughed. He'd actually had that same argument with his mom just that morning. He joined them in the kitchen.

His mom was looking in the fridge. "We don't have any donuts anyway because *someone* ate them all." She glanced back in Kal's direction.

"I was in a hurry this morning. I needed something that would be quick."

"Should've blamed the dog," his grandpa muttered.

His mom, who had never had an issue with hearing, said, "We don't have a dog."

Kal's grandpa slumped down in the chair he was sitting on at the table. "Well, this is just embarrassing. I wonder whose dog I've been walking every morning."

He tossed Kal a wink.

"Hey, Grandpop. How you doin'?" Kal pulled out some eggs. If he was cooking, they were having cheesy scrambled eggs.

His grandpa noted the eggs and gave him a thumbs-up. Kal enjoyed having his grandpa around. They had a lot in common. "Is it okay if I go to Cooper's?" he asked his mom as he cracked an egg into the pan.

"As long as you're home at a decent hour. School tomorrow," his mom said.

"I will."

Something crashed to the floor, and Kal jumped as he was

splattered with liquid. His grandfather had dropped his glass on the floor.

His mom rushed to clean up the spill, but Kal beat her to it. "I've got it, Mom."

His grandpa apologized over and over again. "I'm so embarrassed. I hate that my grippers just don't grip as much anymore." He flexed his fingers and frowned. They all knew why his hands weren't working like they used to. He'd lost muscle mass due to forgetting to eat, or not eating the right kinds of food. He'd just stopped taking care of himself. It was why they'd moved to Arcata. They'd bought a bigger home to accommodate all of them living together comfortably under one roof.

"It's just bodies doing what they do," his mom said. "Nothing embarrassing about it."

But his grandfather kept apologizing anyway. Kal agreed with his mom. Bodies were weird. No use making it weirder by getting awkward.

"Sorry, boy," his grandpa said as Kal mopped up the liquid.

Kal had to shuffle the conversation playlist, or his grandfather would be apologizing to him all night. So he told him all about taking Ireland to the observatory. It was enough of a change in topic that his grandpa seemed to forget what had been causing him distress.

"You like her?" his grandpa said when his mom left the kitchen to run errands.

"Yep."

His grandpa nodded. "You kiss her yet?"

When Kal's face heated, his grandpa grinned knowingly and pointed a bony arthritic finger in his direction. "Never take a girl's kiss for granted. They're special from the first to the last."

Kal knew his grandpa was thinking about his grandma. They'd been a good couple, the kind of couple-goal people should

aspire to if they wanted to succeed in relationships. Kal was glad
his mom had stopped him to help so he could have the chance to
hang out with his grandpa. He and his grandpa ate their cheesy
eggs and talked about dating.

When they were done with dinner, Kal hated leaving for
Cooper's house. It wasn't that he didn't like being with Cooper;
Cooper's friends were just not his scene.

Most of the people in their area would be considered middle-
income kind of people. Kal was. Cooper was. But Cooper hung
out with the few who towered over middle-class standards by a
stratosphere. Some of them were okay enough, like Mara, but
more often than not, Kal would rather eat a scabby Band-Aid
than hang out with any of them. Usually, he didn't have to because he wasn't in their sphere or whatever, but sometimes, like
today, Cooper called in a favor.

Kal wasn't late or anything, but Cooper still acted relieved to
see him—as if Kal had ever bailed on him before. "Why you so
tense?" Kal asked.

"She's here." Cooper pointed to a pretty, dark-haired girl who
was talking with the basketball team's hero, Nathaniel Fredericks.
"Her name's Alison. Alison Lopez. And she's . . . dude. She's all
the things."

"Well, I'm here for you, man. Literally. I'm here. So let's get
started."

The good news was that Asha and Bailey were there too,
though Bailey voiced displeasure at the number of jocks, cheer-
leaders, and trust-fund kids. Asha, in typical Asha fashion, didn't
seem to mind who anyone was. She was just glad to be there.

They played two songs. The standard "Cry Free!" and "Sink
or Swim," which was a cute little song about love and getting the
girl. Cooper had handpicked the music selection with the very
obvious intent to woo Cooper's girl. Just thinking the word *woo*

made Kal laugh. When they finished, the small crowd cheered and clapped, and Alison had eyes for only Cooper.

Achievement unlocked.

Kal meandered to the snack table to see what looked interesting.

"You must get a lot of love with an act like that."

Kal looked up to see Rowan standing there. He made some noise that was neither agreement nor disagreement. Speaking to Rowan wasn't exactly something he'd been dying to do all night. Luckily, or unluckily, Rowan didn't really need Kal to say anything. It was like the guy couldn't get enough of hearing himself talking.

"You know that girl Cooper's talking to? Yeah, she hit on me earlier, but I know my boy Coop likes her, so I told her no way."

Lie, Kal thought. Asha had already told Kal that Alison was dying to talk to Cooper as much as he wanted to talk to her. She would *not* have been hitting on Rowan. Kal looked around for a way out of the conversation. He didn't want to start anything at Cooper's party, especially when Rowan was the school's golden boy, but it seemed Rowan was determined to talk only to Kal, because as Kal walked away, Rowan followed.

Rowan pointed at one girl with straight red hair and said, "Sadie's a total swipe left. Just not very good, you know?"

"Dude. Seriously?" Kal said, shaking his head. "Not cool."

"What? I let her down easy. She can't help that she's not my type," Rowan said and then pointed to a blond. "Not like Meg. She wanted to be serious, though, so I had to cut her off, if you know what I mean."

The word *lie* was on repeat in Kal's head. Because there was no way Rowan's brags could be true. Kal doubted Rowan had ever gone out with most of the girls he was pointing to. The guy vibed skeeze.

"So you dating that Raine chick?"

Kal tensed. "Yep."

"Well, that's too bad." He smacked his lips. "Too, too bad." He grinned at Kal as if they were sharing an inside joke. Kal didn't get the joke. Didn't want to get the joke. And he did not want king skeeze thinking about Ireland.

Rowan went back to talking about the girls at the party. But he'd gone from insisting they all wanted him to disparaging their looks and getting crude about it.

Kal thought about his grandpa and the way he respected women and realized that listening to Rowan was not respecting anyone. "Look, Rowan. Let me just stop you right there. I think maybe you believe that this is guy-bonding talk or whatever, but really, it's not."

Rowan barked a laugh. "Lighten up. I'm just having some fun."

"It's not fun for me to know your social disease status, okay?"

Rowan's features darkened. He shoved Kal's shoulder. "You kidding me right now?"

Kal backed up in case Rowan threw a real punch. "Not kidding. Trash-talking women is not very cool of you, bro. You need to stop. Now."

Rowan probably would have hit Kal, except Mara's friend Emily showed up at that exact moment and asked Rowan about something. The distraction was enough for Kal to slip away.

He turned back when he was at the door. Rowan was sitting on the couch with Tinsley and Emily. It was like a gathering for a vapid competition. Kal shook his head. Why or how those girls could want to be with this guy baffled him. Regardless, Kal was determined to make sure Rowan stayed away from Ireland.

CHAPTER SEVENTEEN
Ireland

Ireland stayed late at the café. Mara had driven her there, but she was going home with Jarrod. And though he'd intended to leave early, something had happened to one of the ovens, and he wanted to fix it before the morning baking needed to be done. It was okay. She had her homework with her and her sketch pad. But she didn't sketch. Once she was done studying, she got up and began looking around at what needed doing. She wiped down baseboards, organized the walk-in fridge, and deep cleaned the bathroom.

"Mara could sure take a lesson from you," Jarrod said.

He meant it to be a compliment, but hearing herself compared to Mara and having Mara come out on the short end made Ireland feel uncomfortable. Like her skin was too tight.

She didn't know how to respond, so she stayed silent.

Jarrod obviously wanted a back-and-forth conversation, so he tried again. "You have good natural skills with people too. I'm glad you've come to work with us."

With us. Not for us. The way he worded it shouldn't have

made a difference, but it did. It made her feel like they were on the same team, working toward the same cause.

"I'm glad too. I honestly didn't know I liked people until recently."

He laughed as if she had made a joke, which was probably better if he thought of it that way. She'd been dead serious.

He was behind the oven, removing a gas filter or something. She'd heard what he said he was doing but hadn't actually understood it. The oven door was open and his muffled voice behind it made it seem like the oven was talking to her. "Tell me about school. How are things going there?

She told him about her classes and gave him a report on where she was at gradewise, figuring that was what he really wanted to know since he'd taken her in and likely felt a responsibility there. There were no lectures or even hints of disappointment when she reported several Cs.

"You thinking about college?" Jarrod asked with a grunt as he shifted position behind the oven.

She wasn't about to mention that she couldn't afford it. She already owed this man and his family enough. She didn't want him thinking she was asking for more. "I don't really have the grades for it."

"Have you applied anywhere?" he asked.

"No."

"You should apply. Your grades aren't so bad you won't get into a state university. College is a good choice while you figure out what you really want to do with your life. It'll give you a path you might not have considered before."

"Sure. I'll think about it." There was nothing to think about. Ireland couldn't afford it, even if she was accepted somewhere. And she wouldn't take a handout for something as expensive as school. She was not her father.

"What are some things you like about school?"

Wow. The poor guy had to be desperate for conversation if he was going to keep circling the same topic like a buzzard checking out roadkill. "I like my art class."

"Oh yeah?" He strained, obviously trying to reach something in an awkward, unreachable place. "Mara likes her art classes too. Mr. Wasden has created something that looks like magic there. Mara got an art scholarship to Humboldt. It's not full ride or anything, but it kicks in a couple of thousand dollars every year, and I'm not mad at that."

"That's cool." Mara hadn't mentioned getting a scholarship, though she wouldn't have. How many times had she insisted they weren't friends? Why would she tell Ireland anything about her life? "What about you?" Ireland said. "Did you go to college?"

"Yep. Believe it or not, I majored in finance." Jarrod scooted out from behind the oven with some small object in his hands. "Had an accounting job at a major firm, a company car, a pension, and a whole lotta misery."

"You hated it?"

"Oh yeah. So one day, after Grace and I had a weekend break when I spent the whole time baking because it relaxed me and I seemed happy for the first time in two years, she asked me why I wasn't looking for other options. The restaurant that used to be right here in this very location was available for purchase, so we cashed in my retirement, handed in my two weeks' notice, changed the name and the menu, and changed our lives. It's been a good choice. And now, with four restaurants, that accounting degree has really come in handy. My books are cleaner than anyone's." He blew into the object he held, polished it on a rag a little more, and then went back behind the oven. "So what kind of art do you like?"

Buzzard-circling-roadkill conversation. Ireland smiled at her inside joke and shook her head, but then she told Jarrod about the mural and how it all worked and how connected she felt to people at school because of it and how there was this mystery writer she wished she knew how to help. She told him everything about it, including all the ways she worried.

"Sounds like trauma," Jarrod said, scooting back out from behind the oven. "Let's try this." He turned on the oven and peered through the open door, putting his hand in to feel the air. "We've got heat!" he declared. "Tomorrow's loaves are back on the menu!"

"What do I do to help this person?" Ireland asked.

Jarrod swiped a hand over the sweat that had beaded up on his forehead below the brim of his durag. "Sounds like you're doing all the right things already. Trauma is complicated. We don't know the nature of the trauma. Could be physical. Could be sexual. Could be mental or emotional. Could be anything. The biggest thing that somebody who has experienced trauma needs is to know that they're not alone. The fact that you responded and continue to respond helps them to know that they're not in it by themselves. That's huge. Shows you've got a lot of heart. I'm proud of you."

Ireland squirmed under the compliment. A father, even if it wasn't her father exactly, had said he was proud of her. She felt warm and weird and happy and embarrassed all at the same time. "I just don't know what advice to give," she said, trying not to give off any vibe of embarrassment.

"I doubt the person on the other end of that mural is looking for advice. They're looking for acknowledgment. They want to be heard, to know that their voice matters. You're already doing everything you need to do. Just listen to them."

"It's good advice."

"It's all I've got, from one good listener to another. Let's get home before Grace does something dramatic, like order takeout because she doesn't like cooking." He scrambled to his feet and she followed him.

When they got back to the house, Mara was sitting on the couch and flipping through channels on the TV. She wore sweats again. Not the cute activewear kind that showed off a nice figure, which she totally had, so she totally could do. But the frumpy, shapeless, baggy kind that almost hid the human inside them.

"How's my smart girl?" Jarrod planted a kiss on the top of Mara's head.

"Hi, Daddy. I'm good." She didn't look away from the TV.

"I thought that Cooper kid had some sort of shindig going on at his house tonight." He put a hand on Mara's forehead. "You not feeling good, baby?"

Mara finally looked up at him. "I'm fine. Just not feeling like hanging out with friends is all."

"Hm. What's this world coming to? You not wanting to hang out with friends is like Santa Claus going on a cookie-free diet. It's like me hoping the Lakers will lose. It's like . . ." He lowered his voice to a whisper. "It's like your mom deciding she wanted to make dinner tonight." He started laughing.

She joined in. "And you know that's not happening."

He held out his fist. "True that."

She bumped her knuckles to his. "I'm just tired."

"Too tired to help with dinner?"

She flipped off the TV. "Never too tired to cook with you."

Ireland almost offered to help as well but then thought maybe Mara needed this time alone with her dad. She'd already accused Ireland of moving in on her territory with her family. Giving her some time to just be herself with her family was probably a good idea.

Later that night, after dinner, and after everybody had gone to bed, Ireland couldn't sleep. She kept thinking about the mystery lipstick writer. Of course, Jarrod was right. There really wasn't anything more she could do than what she was already doing. But it didn't stop her from worrying about it. And it didn't stop her from worrying about her own problems.

Jarrod had talked about college. He wasn't the first person to bring up college to her. He probably wouldn't be the last either. But it was the first time she'd considered the idea as an option. She could probably get a student loan. She could also work. Lots of people did that, the student-loan and work option.

Jarrod had made an excellent point. She needed to do something until she figured out what it was that she *actually* wanted to do. School was a good way to discover whatever it was that she wanted to spend the rest of her life working on. And even though school hadn't worked out for him exactly the way Jarrod had expected it to, he still felt like he benefited from it. On the way home from the restaurant, he talked about how grateful he was for the opportunity he had to go to school and figure himself out.

Ireland was absolutely certain she needed to figure herself out.

After staring at the ceiling above her bed for what felt like eternity, she realized she needed to go to the bathroom. Like desperately. There was no time for her to make it to the bathroom at the end of the hall. She got up and decided to brave Mara's bathroom. She crept into the dark space, shoved a towel against the door to block the light, and then flipped the light on.

She cringed when she flushed, not realizing how loud that sound could be when everything else was quiet. As she washed her hands, she spied a piece of paper sticking out of the top drawer with writing on it, writing that was familiar, and words that were even more familiar because they were her own. She turned off the water and quickly dried her hands so she could pull out the paper to inspect it closer. "Keep howling until your voice can find a different melody."

Sucker punch.

Ireland considered all the options. Mara worked on the mural too. Maybe she saw that written there and liked it so copied it. Except the handwriting was done with the same flourishes as those in lipstick. Ireland glanced at the door to Mara's bedroom. Then she carefully opened the drawers in the bathroom and rifled through them, searching for further evidence. Nothing in the drawers.

She opened the cupboard under the sink and saw a small, black, rectangular-shaped case. In gold metal on the outside were the words Kate Spade. Ireland unzipped it and found what she was looking for. A tube of lipstick. The tube was quite beautiful, covered with swirled colors. It was as if some artists had done an impressionist painting and shrunk it to fit on the tube. Ireland pulled off the cap. Bright pink.

In shock, Ireland dropped the lipstick tube as if it had bitten her and then made shushing sounds at the tube clattering on the floor as if she could somehow call back the noise.

Mara. Mara was the mystery lipstick writer.

"Did not see that coming," Ireland muttered before wincing because Mara's room was right next door. She really had to stop talking to herself.

She stared at Mara's door. Mara? How could it be Mara who was broken? Mara who was howling at the uncaring moon? How could it be when Mara was also a shrew? The leader of the hag and harpy?

And what could Ireland do about the information she now had? She put the lipstick back in the case and tucked it back under the sink. She flipped off the light, hung the towel back on the rod, and eased the door on her side closed again.

Then Ireland paced. And paced. And paced.

Mara. The mystery writer was Mara. What could be so out

of place in Mara's perfect life that she could call herself broken? Mara was the girl everyone wanted to be. Even *Ireland* wanted to be Mara—a little bit, anyway. "This is ten degrees of the worst ever thing to happen." She allowed the muttering since there were now two doors and a bathroom between her and Mara. She needed to mutter. Needed to process out loud. Honestly, the household was lucky she hadn't resorted to shouting yet. "What to do? What to do? What to do?" She couldn't help Mara with anything. Mara wouldn't even want her help if she knew it was Ireland on the other end of these messages. *What to do?*

"Get a snack. Yeah. Get a snack." Ireland always thought better when she had a full stomach. And maybe she'd watch something on the Washington family's many streaming services so she could calm the erratic beating of her heart. Then she would be calm and know what to do.

The house was quiet as Ireland crept to the kitchen, her feet making soft taps against the stone-tiled floor.

Grace and Jarrod had insisted that the kitchen was open to her anytime she needed it, as long as she cleaned up after herself and didn't take something that somebody else had made for a specific purpose. Even so, guilt gnawed at Ireland's insides. When she turned the corner to pass through the living room and into the kitchen, she was surprised to find the light from the gas fireplace on and a shadowed silhouette sitting on the couch. Probably Grace, reading again. Ireland would have turned around to go back, but there was no way to hide the fact that she had been there. She hadn't been *that* quiet.

Rather than look as guilty as she felt, Ireland decided to face the situation directly, so she rounded the couch to greet Grace and maybe chat for a few moments before getting her snack. Granted, there would be no watching TV, but the snack was still a good idea. Ireland stopped short when she found Mara sitting there instead.

"Hey," Ireland said since she didn't know what else she could say.

Howling at the uncaring moon.

"Hey." Mara stared into the flickering flames. Her tone flat. Her body curled into itself as she hugged her knees to her chest.

Ireland considered leaving her alone so that she could do whatever it was she was doing.

Someone broke my mirror.

Ireland stopped midway into turning and swiveled back. "You okay?"

"Sure. Okay like Santa Clause on a cookie-free diet or my mom cooking dinner."

"So not okay?"

Mara's dark eyes were suddenly glassy. Holy brick to the head. Was Mara going to cry?

"What's going on?" Ireland sat on the recliner next to the couch. She waited for Mara to say "Boundaries" in her snotty elitist voice while also declaring them not friends. But Mara didn't say boundaries. She didn't declare them not friends.

"Am I okay?" Mara repeated. "I'm perfect. Everyone says so. There goes Mara Washington. Isn't she perfect? Perfect clothes. Perfect hair. Perfect car. Perfect grades. Perfect family. Just perfect."

Ireland wanted to snort in derision while declaring, "I get the point." Except Mara was the mystery lipstick writer. Except tears were now slipping down Mara's face.

She sniffed. "Please ignore the perfect monster boyfriend, everyone."

Wait. What? Ireland straightened. "Wait. Rowan?"

Mara laughed, though the sound was more alarming than

humorous. She finally tilted her head to look at Ireland. "Even *you* don't believe it, and I'm pretty sure you're the only girl in the school who doesn't wish I would walk into traffic so they could have a shot at him. I mean, you might want me to walk into traffic, but not because of him."

"I legitimately don't want a shot at him. The guy is hair-in-the-drain gross—no offense, and yes, I say that fully knowing that I was being offensive. And I don't want you to walk into traffic either."

"Rowan attacked me." Mara whispered it as if trying the words out loud for the first time and frowned at the unexpected nature of the way it sounded.

Ireland's extremities went cold with this revelation. "He ra—"

"No!" Mara hurried to interrupt. "Not that. Not for lack of trying though. I fought him off. I don't know how it happened. We were just kissing, and then . . . it was something else. When I shoved him away and got out of the car, he shouted some really terrible things at me. He left me. In the woods. Alone. What kind of slithering snake does that?"

Ireland had gone from *what to do* to *what to say*. Her head spun with the nightmare Mara had lived through. If she hadn't fought him off . . . Trauma. Jarrod had called the messages from the lipstick writer trauma. He hadn't known he was talking about his own daughter. He hadn't known how right he was. "Where were you?"

"Redwood Park. I left a perfectly good clambake for that."

"Did you tell anyone?"

Mara's typical look of shrewery briefly returned to her face as she rolled her head and eyed Ireland like she was stupid. "Who would believe me? You know who his family is."

Ireland did know. Rowan's dad had made a lot of money in the stock market. He'd bought some land and built a house of obscene proportions and then thrown his money around every-where so people remembered how important he was. Ireland's dad had complained that the guy owned practically everything. He'd complained that Rowan's dad was as obscene as the house he'd built.

"I think people would believe you. *I* believe you."

"Maybe they would, but they wouldn't want to. Rowan is the school's ticket to the track team's fame. He's faster than anyone else." It was weird to hear Mara compliment Rowan after what she'd just revealed to Ireland. "If I told, even if anyone believed me, it would be a fight. I don't need that kind of attention. My family doesn't need that kind of attention. My dad's business doesn't need that kind of attention. So it's not gonna happen."

"You could tell your mom and dad. They would believe you."

Mara sniffed and nodded. "They would. They really would. But I shouldn't have even been there. I shouldn't have let it go so far. It's partly my fau—"

"Oh no you don't. You do not get to victim shame yourself." Ireland thought about kissing Kal and considered how she knew he never would take anything further than she wanted. Poor Mara. What she had to be going through all on her own.

"So why tell me?" Ireland asked softly.

Mara's gaze turned back to the fire. "I don't know."

Ireland thought about the messages on the wall. Mara didn't know that Ireland was already her friend, and yet she still trusted her on this side of the paint with her secret.

Ireland stood up and sat on the couch next to Mara. "Is it okay if I give you a hug?" Ireland held out her arms. She didn't have a lot of experience giving hugs, but she figured if any-one ever needed one, Mara did. Mara hesitated a moment be-fore she reached out and let Ireland embrace her. And then she cried in earnest. Ireland thought about what Mara's dad had said regarding how she should handle the situation with the mystery lipstick writer. He had told her to listen. To make sure they knew they were not alone.

She could do that.

She could do that for Mara.

They didn't stay like that for very long because Mara pulled away while mopping at her eyes with her sweatshirt sleeve. "Thanks, Ireland. Sorry to dump all of this on you, but it's been tough to keep to myself. You won't tell anyone, will you?"

Ireland hesitated. She wanted to tell. She wanted to go pound on Jarrod and Grace's bedroom door and tell everything. They would know how to help their daughter.

"Promise me, Ireland."

Ireland nodded. "I promise."

Mara and Ireland both went to bed after that, but Ireland didn't really sleep, maybe a few mangled minutes at a time here and there. Mara apparently hadn't slept either. Not that Ireland asked her. She could tell from the bloodshot eyes. Mara was quiet, but not the quiet that came from boycotting conversation with Ireland. It was the quiet of someone who was sifting through the thoughts in her head. Like Mara's dad sifted the flour to make it lighter and easier to mix with the other ingredients, Mara was sifting thoughts to make herself lighter so she could make something out of the ingredients of her life.

Ireland didn't interrupt the sifting process. Her job in this was to listen, not to talk. She didn't know what else to do. The thing was that Mara had stopped talking. There was no new message on the mural, and throughout the whole day, Mara never said anything of any significance. But by the next morning, after enduring another drive to school with nothing but the music from the Eras Tour between them, Ireland had an idea.

CHAPTER EIGHTEEN

Kal

Kal met Ireland at Mr. Wasden's classroom to do mural duty. This was the last day of the mural being open to the student body. After that, the art club would fill in the gaps and make it cohesive. Then the principal would decide if it stayed as a permanent part of the school wall or if it would only be up for the promised month and then painted over.

Ireland greeted him with an anxious hello and a quick peck on the lips before she started gathering everything from the back supply room. "Are we in a hurry for some reason?" Kal asked.

"Yes," she said without elaborating. She put the tote of acrylics and pitcher of clean water in his hands.

"Why?" he asked.

She hefted the other tote with the cans, brushes, smocks, and plates, and then she rushed back out to the mural. "Because I finally know what to say!" she called back.

He couldn't keep up with her without spilling the water pitcher, but he went as fast as he could and felt pretty good about the fact that he'd only splashed a small puddle at the very end by the table. He tried to point out his heroic efforts to Ireland, but she was already pulling the acrylic tubes from his tub and squirting dabs of color onto a paper plate. She yanked a few brushes from her tub and said, "Would you be willing to set this all up while I get started?"

"Sure," he said. He would have asked her more, but she was kneeling by the flowers she and the mystery painter had been creating and had already gone to work. She looked at an image she'd pulled up from her phone that she was using as inspiration. He peeked over her shoulder to see a picture someone had taken of a gray wolf in the wild. With each brushstroke, a similar image appeared next to the wildflowers under the tree but with a few notable differences. The wolf was small but stood tall and proud, its ears pointed up and its muzzle raised skyward in a howl. As the image took shape, Kal could almost hear the howl echoing through the woods and into the sky. The words she painted inside the wolf's body were "Howl Out Loud!"

Ireland stood and viewed her handiwork. She sucked in air as if she'd been in gym class, not sitting in the art room. She glanced around at the classroom, which was starting to fill with people, either coming to start class or to check out the mural. She was clearly worried she would be caught painting on the wall, which was weird since they were supposed to be doing that.

"It's coming along really well, don't you think?" Kal asked as they went to their first hour.

"What is?"

"The mural. Hey, Ireland, what's going on?"

"Nothing," she said.

"You hesitated." He tugged her hand lightly so they could slow down before entering the classroom, where Mr. Nichols would shut them up.

"Did not."

"Yes way."

She scowled at him. "I didn't say 'no way' either."

Kal kissed the little wrinkle above her eyebrow that made up the scowl.

"I can't tell you about it." Her eyes dropped from his.

He fully stopped then, not caring that the kid behind them said, "Dude. Watch it."

"You can tell me anything, Ireland."

"Not anything. Some things I can't." She shook her head, her long, single dark braid swishing like a cat's tail.

"Like what things?"

She laughed and shot him a look of incredulity. "If I told you what, then I would be telling you the thing I can't tell you. C'mon." She pulled at his hand to try to get him to move forward again. "We gotta go to class."

"Okay. But I don't want you to shut me out. I don't know what I would do if anything happened to you. You can trust me."

"I do trust you. You are my person—the one person I can count on. But I'm fine. I'll let you know if that status changes at all, okay?"

He wanted to argue more, but she was right that they needed to get to class. Mr. Nichols wasn't exactly forgiving of tardiness. And Kal's dad had been zero times awesome about grades lately. He'd allowed the art and the band because he'd worried about Kal's mental health after everything with Brell. But the more time that came between that event and the present day, the less Kal's dad felt like indulging those hobbies and the more he stressed good grades—even though Kal had already been accepted to Berkeley. It wasn't like his grades were slipping.

Kal understood why his dad worried. His grandpa had spent his life as an artist, which meant there had never been enough money during his dad's childhood and that Kal's grandma had to work extra hard to help keep the family supported. Kal's dad didn't want that to be his son's future.

Not that Kal had huge aspirations about being a rock star. And he knew his artistic skills were good, but not as marketable as Mara's, so he didn't mind his dad insisting he go to a good school and get a good education. He would have done it whether his dad wanted it or not. He just wished his dad didn't get so intense about it.

Ireland's leg bounced in an erratic pattern as she sat through class. Kal could tell she wasn't paying attention. She spent half the class looking out the window. The other half she spent staring at her hands on her desk as her fingers tap-tapped a rhythm that sounded like the chorus to Taylor Swift's "Shake It Off."

If only Kal could be graded on studying the subject that was Ireland Raine. He would be sure to get an A+.

When he got to Wasden's class, the teacher asked Kal about how Ireland was doing. He did it quietly so that no one who had already come in could hear the question. Kal dropped his voice so no one would hear the answer either. "She's good. I mean, she used to say that Mara's a shrew, so she wasn't thrilled with where she'd landed. But she hasn't said it in a while." He glanced around to make sure Mara wasn't anywhere around because he didn't want her to overhear and get her feelings hurt—especially since he liked Mara well enough. "I think they're working it out."

"That's good. The Washingtons were the best choice in her situation. They're good people. Anyway, just checking."

"'S all good, man."

Kal breathed a sigh of relief that their conversation had come to an end because Mara did walk in then. A frown creased her forehead, and she took her seat without looking at anyone. Weird.

Her leg bounced up and down like Ireland's. She was

tap-tapping a rhythm too, only this one sounded like Taylor Swift's "Look What You Made Me Do."

Apparently, it was a Taylor Swift kind of day. Not that he knew for certain what the two girls had been tapping, but he was pretty good with rhythms and patterns. Whatever was going on seemed like it was between the two of them. He briefly considered asking Mara about it, but if Ireland had shut him down, Mara wasn't likely to spill.

After school, Ireland wasn't at the mural like he'd expected. He walked around to try to find her and discovered her talking to the custodian. He panicked because he remembered that Ireland blamed the older woman for telling on her regarding the homelessness situation. Kal hurried over to interject and save the poor woman from underserved wrath.

When he got there, Ireland wasn't berating the woman. Instead, they seemed to be having a fairly laid-back conversation. "Everything good here?" he asked warily.

Janice tucked back a silver strand of hair that had pulled loose from her bun and said, "Everything good." She gave no further information.

"I better get going. I'm glad your son's doing better." Ireland waved at the custodian. "See you, Janice."

"See you."

"Want to hear something weird?" Ireland said once they were back in the art room at the mural.

"Absolutely."

"Janice wasn't the one who told Mr. Wasden about me not having a place to live. She said she didn't know."

Kal's blood slowed to sludge in his veins. "Huh. Weird."

"How would Mr. Wasden have found out?"

"It's a good thing he did though, right? You're happy where you're at. You said you liked working at the bakery, right?"

Ireland shrugged. "Well, yes, but . . ." she kept looking down to where she and the mystery lipstick writer had been communicating. She went silent as she inspected the wall. "I am so stupid," she blurted.

"You are *not* stupid."

"I am though. I totally overstepped," Ireland said in a rush of panic-laced words. "Jarrod told me to just listen. But no. I just had to give advice because I felt like I knew what was right, but I don't think she was ready for advice. She's not ready. She just needed someone to listen. Like he said. Why couldn't I do that? Why couldn't I just listen?"

"Ireland. Pause. Time out. I don't know what you're talking about."

She licked her lips and glanced nervously around before she lowered her voice. "Look." Ireland pointed to the mural.

Kal looked at the wolf Ireland had painted earlier that day and saw that the howling wolf was now muzzled. Tears were streaming out of its eyes. When he looked back up at Ireland, tears were in her eyes too.

"I just don't know how to help her. What could I possibly say to Mara that she would listen to?"

"Wait, what?" Kal was sure he'd heard wrong. "Mara?"

Ireland's eyes went from sad to straight-up, high-key panicked. "Mara . . . nothing about Mara. Sorry. I was just talking out loud. Never mind."

"Ireland. Is Mara the mystery artist?"

"Kal . . ."

She was totally about to lie to protect that secret, but Ireland didn't need to respond. The answer was written all over her face. He looked back at the mural, seeing it through the lens of its creator. Of course it was Mara. There was a level of skill in the art that no other student in the school owned except her. How had he not seen it before?

"How did you find out?" he asked.

Ireland opened her mouth, probably to lie to him, but he shot her a look, and she finally said, "I found her lipstick in her bathroom the other night."

"Oh. Oh boy." Kal didn't know why it bothered him so badly that this person in such desperate need was Mara. Perfect Mara. Her life was the one in this school that seemed to have nothing lurking in its shadows. If perfect Mara could feel like a shattered mirror, what hope was there for any of the rest of them?

What could he do? What *should* he do? It was like finding out about Ireland living in a bathroom all over again. He wanted to help, but like Ireland had said, he didn't want to overstep.

The nervous energy coming from both girls all made sense now. They must have had a talk about it, and now neither one knew how to act. At least that was what he assumed. "So you told her you knew?"

"No!" Ireland insisted. "How could I? But I talked to her last night, and she told me things, more than she's said on the wall here. Oh, Kal. I should have just listened. Why did I try to solve her problems with my unsolicited advice? Even my dad used to tell me that no one appreciates unsolicited advice, and here I am handing it out like people are trick-or-treating and I'm the only house with candy."

Kal put his hands on Ireland's shoulders and gently massaged them. "Hey. Hey, Ireland. Breathe, okay? What happened?"

"Kal, someone hurt her. He hurt her, and now she's just . . . gah! Why are guys such trolls?" She leaned into him, resting her head on his shoulder.

He slid his arms from her shoulders until he had them

wrapped around her. It was cute that she insulted people using fairytales. Shrew, hag, harpy, and now troll. "Not all guys, right?"

"No not all guys. But Rowan is the biggest—"

"Rowan?" Kal pulled away to look at Ireland directly. "Rowan?" Why did everything come back to that guy? "Rowan hurt Mara?"

Ireland's eyes widened. "I need to stop talking. I can't think. And I'm saying everything I shouldn't. This isn't my stuff to be sharing. And it's what you think but not as bad as you think. At least that's what she told me. Look, Kal. You can't tell anyone. I shouldn't have told you. I hate that I can't tell the difference between talking out loud and talking in my own head sometimes. I promised her. I didn't mean to break that promise. I'm just so freaked out because I thought about it all after she told me, and I really thought I was helping her by giving her advice by using our connection here on the mural. I thought telling her to howl out loud would give her what she needed to tell someone, but Kal, she muzzled the wolf. She didn't need advice. She just needed me to listen."

"Does she not know you're the one responding here?"

Ireland shook her head. "I didn't tell her."

"Rowan is such a piece of—"

"Sh! Someone's going to hear you!" Ireland said as she scanned around them to see who might have overheard. There were people in the hall outside the classroom, but none close by, and their tones had been hushed up until Kal had decided to verbally abuse Rowan.

Thankfully, Mara always waited for Ireland in the car.

Ireland held Kal tightly again. "I have to go. Will you finish up for me? I don't want to keep Mara waiting. And seriously—no one can know you know. Okay?"

Kal didn't respond, but it didn't matter because Ireland had already gone to meet Mara.

Kal slowly packed up the acrylic tubes and cleaned the brushes. He threw away the used plates and used some paper towels to wipe up where some paint had accidentally spilled onto the tile. The more he worked, the angrier he became. He read over the messages between Ireland and Mara. Mara was clearly in real pain—all because some guy was a "troll," as Ireland had said.

A guy like the ones who had been with Brell that night.

Mr. Wasden entered his classroom and saw Kal standing there, nearly dizzy with fury, like he might throw up and pass out all at the same time.

"Whoa," Wasden said. "You do *not* want the cleanup that comes from crashing with that." He pointed to the pitcher of old paint water that Kal held at an awkward angle.

"Right. You're right." Kal returned to the worktable and dumped the supplies there rather than taking them all the way back to the supply room.

"Something buggin' you, Kal?" Wasden asked.

"No. I'm right as rain."

"So something's bothering Miss Raine then?"

Kal didn't mean to. He really didn't. But everything tumbled out of him, from Mara being the one writing the cryptic messages to Rowan being the . . . Kal ran out of expletives when describing Rowan. Ireland had called him a troll. And while Kal found it adorable that she insulted people based on fairy-tale monsters, he didn't think her verbal slam of Rowan was nearly dark enough.

Kal felt defeated after ranting to Mr. Wasden, like a balloon that had been expressed of all of its air and now had no purpose. "What can I do?" he asked his teacher.

"You can't do anything. This is an assault charge, and it's something I have to take seriously. But it's also hearsay. You heard it from someone who heard it from someone else. I can't do anything about it at the moment. I'll set up an appointment with the school counselor for Mara. For right now, keep your word to Ireland. Don't go telling people. Don't make trouble for Mara. Let this be her story where she controls her own narrative. It's not your story, okay, Superman? I get that you're into saving people, but this time, she needs to be the one to tell her story, not have someone tell it for her. I'll get her into the counselor. That's all you need to know."

Kal nodded that he understood. He didn't. Not really. But he'd respect it.

CHAPTER NINETEEN
Ireland

Going home with Mara had been something that terrified Ireland all day, but once she was in the car, it was Mara and her and singing along to Taylor Swift. The drive home had been no drama considering everything Ireland knew about Mara.

They didn't talk about it. Ireland waited for some hint of their previous discussion, but there was nothing. Mara seemed bizarrely normal. Even after Ireland had painted a wolf howling. Even after Mara had muzzled the wolf.

They got home and went to their separate rooms like no big deal. The music came on within moments.

Mara loved Taylor Swift. The singer was always blaring from her car radio, her phone while she was in the shower, and the family digital assistance in every room when her parents weren't home. Seriously. Taylor Swift in every room. In every space. All the time.

At first, Ireland's instinct was to be critical. The whole T-Swift thing felt trendy and clichéd. But once Ireland listened to the lyrics of the songs over and over, she found herself pulled into a world she'd never imagined wanting to belong to. Taylor Swift's music spoke to her soul. Deep. Visceral. Like somebody finally understood her. And it was strange how much she liked the song "Mine." It was the phrase "a careless man's careful daughter" that got her. It felt like somebody had seen her for the first time.

Ireland had a guy in her life who said things like, "We won't be like our parents." Not that it would be bad to be like Kal's parents, because his parents were truly "ten out of ten—totally recommend," as Mara would say. But *her* parents? Those people hadn't stuck around to see her grow up. Ireland didn't want to be anything like them. Kal knew it, which was why he'd told her she didn't have to be anything like them. Her father was a careless man, and Ireland was his careful daughter. And Kal belonged to her.

Ireland's phone rang. An unknown number. Frowning, Ireland answered. "Hello?"

The muffled, computerized voice crackled with static at the other end of the line as it said, "Hello. You have received a collect call from—" The robotic voice broke off, and she heard a recording of her Dad's voice say, "Derek Raine." Her blood froze in her veins as the computer voice continued. "This call is from Humboldt County Correctional Facility and is subject to monitoring and recording. Do you accept the charges?"

Ireland could barely breathe. She tried to say something—to answer the recorded voice. Would she accept the charges? No. Yes?

Her finger pressed the end-call button on her phone. She dropped to her knees on the ground. Her stomach roiled, but she didn't throw up, which she was thankful for, since she didn't know how to explain getting sick all over the carpet to Grace and Jarrod. So her dad was in jail. She knew that. Why did she feel so taken by surprise? Why feel frightened?

With a deep breath, she forced herself back to her feet. He

didn't get to dictate to her whether or not she stood her ground on her own two feet. She would not crumple like debris in the street because of him. When she'd finally leveled her emotions to merely turbulent instead of crashing and burning and felt more furious than anything, it occurred to her why she felt afraid. A glance around the room that she was able to call her own was enough to help her understand herself.

The stocked fridge and pantry, the support from adults that made her feel valued, the legitimate job that she enjoyed, and the money she had started to build up in a savings account at an actual bank instead of a jar in a field all whispered to her that her fear was justified.

Ireland finally had something to lose.

The very idea that her dad was trying to get in touch with her made her new life feel like it was teetering on the edge of a deep chasm. One slightly gusty breeze could send it crashing.

"Girl, you do not look well." Mara stood with her hand on her cocked hip in the open doorway of Ireland's bedroom.

"Don't you knock?"

Mara showing up made Ireland feel dizzy enough to send her back to her knees again, but she sat heavily on the bed instead. She hoped she didn't look like she was collapsing but merely flouncing down like Mara seemed to do whenever she sat.

Mara gave a flat stare before twisting her mouth to the side in a smirk and rapping her knuckles on Ireland's doorframe. Then she walked in as if the mock-knock counted as an invitation.

"Thank you for helping me to understand why girls complain about their sisters," Ireland said.

"Whatever. So, my friends and I are going to the beach for a bonfire tonight."

"Okay."

"Do you want to come?" Mara's habit of touching things

when she was in Ireland's room would have been annoying if Ireland wasn't too busy being surprised at the invitation.

"You're inviting me?" She felt instantly pathetic for voicing her surprise. If Mara was going out with her friends, there wasn't a reason for her to take Ireland. Her friends hated Ireland, and the feeling was so mutual.

"Mom says I have to," Mara said, with the smirk set more deeply on her face. She didn't mean it. Not really. The conversation from the other night was enough that they had found legitimate friendship, even if Mara didn't want to make it into some big thing.

"Right. Again, thank you for helping me understand why girls complain about their sisters."

"Do you want to come or not?"

Honestly, Ireland didn't want to. Spending any time with the hag and the harpy and the idiot boys they hung out with made Ireland's hackles rise, but she didn't want to be left alone with her thoughts and her phone. What if he tried to call again?

"Sure," she said. "Let me get my jacket."

Mara said, "Okay. I'll be in the car."

Ireland grabbed her sweatshirt, jacket, and fingerless gloves before snagging her drawstring backpack with her wallet. Hanging out with the rich kids meant she would likely need money for something.

She joined Mara in the Fiat and buckled her seatbelt. There was no reason to try to engage in conversation since Mara had Taylor Swift on loud and hadn't wanted conversation since the other night.

Ireland would have complained about the music being so loud again except now that she was a superfan, the louder it was, the better. Not that she would ever admit that to Mara. No reason to give Mara anything more to gloat about. If she'd discovered she'd converted Ireland to her music, she would count the personal victory as if it were of Olympic proportions.

The sun was sinking toward the horizon when they pulled off the road.

Once they were parked at the beach and treading over the sand to where silhouettes stood or sat against the firelight's glow, Mara's mood shifted. She began talking as if needing a distraction.

"You ever been to a clambake before?"

"Nope."

"Oh. Well. It's fun. The clams aren't exactly ten out of ten. More a two or even a one. But the fire is kinda perfect, especially since it's still so cold out, and Cooper usually brings a guitar, which is cool because we do sing-alongs, and—"

"Sing-alongs?" Ireland wanted to say so much more about how corny that sounded, but Mara suddenly seemed so completely different, and not in a good way. She appeared nervous for some reason.

"Yeah. He usually plays songs we all know, and we sing, and it's fun."

"Okay." Ireland was not convinced of the "fun" review, but she kept her opinions to herself. Besides, they were in Mara's world, and Mara had the car keys. Ireland did not want to get left stranded at the beach with the rich delinquent crowd.

Get stranded . . . It finally occurred to Ireland why Mara's nerves were off the charts. She dropped her voice and whispered, "Is he here?"

Mara's eyes widened into two sad, terrified twin moons. "Don't say anything. Remember, you promised."

"Why are we here if he is here?"

"I'm howling out loud, okay?"

"What?"

"Never mind. You wouldn't get it." But Ireland did get it. It was her fault they were there. Mara was proving something to herself. Ireland just didn't know what. This was not what she'd meant when she'd said to howl out loud. What she'd meant was for Mara to talk to the police. File a report. Send Rowan to juvenile detention. She did not mean to go eat scorched clams at a bonfire with her attacker.

"These are my friends," Mara said. "I'm not giving them up just because he thinks he has first dibs on this space. Emily and Tinsley are here."

"Ugh! We're here because of them? Why do you even hang out with them?" Ireland asked Mara. "Those two are like accidentally touching old chewing gum stuck to the bottom of the table. They're just gross."

Mara's eyes turned pleading. "They're my friends, Ireland. C'mon. Please."

"They hate me."

"You're not here for them. You're here for me. And I don't hate you. You're the best friend I have right now, and I need you to not leave my side tonight. Please?"

Ireland finally nodded her assent that it was fine. But in that moment, she knew she had finally told the number-one biggest lie. It was not fine. None of it was fine. She did *not* like being here with these people. Not one bit.

They approached the group. There were two large, open fire pits, both constructed out of weathered concrete. One of the concrete pits contained actual flames. The other was filled with hot, crackling coals. Someone had placed a large barbecue grate across the concrete sides surrounding the coals and then spread a thick layer of seaweed over the top of the grate. Steam rose from the whole setup, and the fragrant smokiness filled the general area in a way that was surprisingly pleasant, especially considering Ireland's unsettled mood. "I'm here for Mara," she told herself.

The thrum of Cooper's guitar carried over the waves lapping at the shore. There was no wind, and the waves were pretty mild. By the time she and Mara were close enough that Ireland could make out individual faces, she immediately picked out Rowan from the crowd. Ireland wanted to go punch him in the face, but she stayed close to Mara's side, like she'd promised. In spite of being in front of a small bonfire, it was a cold evening. The mismatched blankets over people's shoulders somehow matched the mismatched chairs in a way that felt trendy and stylish—like only rich kids could manage.

People said hi to Mara and to Ireland, too, which was surprising, given how she hadn't thought most of them knew who she was. Tinsley and Emily finally pulled out of whatever self-absorbed conversation they were in long enough to jump up and rush to Mara so they could hug her.

"How did you get here?" Tinsley asked Ireland.

Mara interjected before Ireland could. "I brought her with me."

"Aww. Nice. Hobo's got herself a chauffeur." Tinsley smirked, her freckles twisting with the facial expression.

"Well, I'm sure you would have offered me a ride, Tinsley," Ireland said. "But, you know, there's just not enough room on your broom, so I would have had to pass. Thanks anyway."

Mara sighed, and Ireland mentally berated herself. She was here for Mara, not to entertain herself by outwitting the hag and the harpy.

Emily gave Ireland a look more scorching than the coals steaming the clams. She clearly didn't like that Ireland had insulted her friend. She then linked her arm with Mara's and guided her to the fire where she and Tinsley had been sitting. There was only one open chair next to the two they had vacated.

Unless Mara was going to invite her to sit on her lap, Ireland guessed she'd be stuck sitting on the sand—which would have been okay, except the sand felt even colder than the frigid air.

She had actually started to sit in the sand when Mara stopped her and tapped the empty chair next to her. Tinsley had gone over to sit by a little group that had surrounded Rowan.

Mara must have seen Ireland's fury over Tinsley's apparent betrayal. "Don't worry about it," Mara said.

"Worry about what?" Emily asked, thinking Mara had to be talking to her. Because why would Mara be talking to Ireland?

"We shouldn't have to worry about anything, right?" Mara said.

Cooper started up a new song, d4vd's "Don't Forget About Me," and everyone joined in—even Ireland, because she was there for Mara and Mara wanted to sing.

Though she found she was actually enjoying singing along with everyone in the fire's glow while clams popped and sizzled next to them, Ireland kept glancing in Rowan's direction. Did a troll like Rowan join the sing-along like he was a normal person? It turned out that he didn't join in, not exactly. His mock-sing grated on Ireland's nerves as he made his voice louder and more obnoxious than everyone else's.

Ireland thought that maybe she was imagining things, but it seemed like Rowan was keeping an eye on her the same way she was keeping an eye on him. No. Not the same way. His eye was trailing over her in a way that made Ireland's skin crawl like biting into tinfoil-covered spiders. She was about to ask Mara if the point had been made well enough that they could leave, but her phone rang. Panicked, she looked down at the number calling, afraid it was her dad again. When she saw Kal's name and number, she leaped to her feet to move away from the crowd so she didn't disrupt anyone while she took his call.

"Kal, hi!" she said, plugging her other ear so she could hear him better.

"Hey. I was wondering if I could come by tonight. Wait. Where are you?" he asked, obviously hearing the background noise.

"Mara invited me to a clambake with her and her friends."

"Sounds like Cooper singing."

"Yeah. Yeah, it is."

"So it's *all* of Mara's friends."

"A lot of them. Yeah."

He went silent for the space of three breaths. "He's there, isn't he?"

It was Ireland's turn to go silent for the space of three breaths. "Yes."

"You need to get out of there. Seriously. You guys aren't safe there. He is not safe to be around. You are not safe being around him. The creepy innuendos he makes about you . . . Leave. Ireland, leave. Please. If Mara won't go, then ask Cooper. He'll drive you home."

"I'm not leaving Mara. Kal, how can you even ask me to do that?"

"No. You're right. Of course not. You can't leave her. I'm sorry. I'm just really freaked out for you. I'm getting my keys right now. I'll be right there."

"We're in a crowd. We'll be fine." She realized at that moment that she'd wandered away from the group's fire enough that she was in shadow—definitely not in a crowd. "Kal, I . . . don't come. I'm fine."

"It's not a problem for me. It won't take me long."

"You showing up would just be more drama at this point. We aren't alone here, so we're fine. I gotta go though. I'll see you tomorrow at Geppetto's okay?"

"Okay." He didn't sound happy, but he didn't argue about the fact that she needed to hang up, which she needed to do sooner than later. She'd caught his paranoia, and it was seriously dark and anyone could drag her off and no one at the fires would notice.

"Before you go, if you could, please just text me to let me know you got home safely."

She agreed that she would and then hung up.

When she turned to head back to the fires, she had to pass Rowan and Tinsley. The stress she felt made Ireland fumble and drop her phone right in front of Rowan. She hurriedly bent down to pick it up so she get back to Mara. Rowan made a low whistle. "I am loving that view," he said. Ireland realized her V-neck shirt had hung down low enough to be revealing.

Her cheeks flamed hot with humiliation, fear, and anger. She wrapped her sweater tightly over her front. "Do not ever talk to me or about me again, you sick troll," she said, her voice shaking.

"Oh please," Tinsley, who had obviously been drinking, said. "You can't think he's serious. Not about you. You'd give him fleas." She laughed, nearly falling off her chair.

Mara was on her feet and moving toward Ireland at the same time Ireland was trying to move away from Tinsley's laugh and Rowan's leer.

"What's going on?" Mara asked, her expression wild with worry.

"He just . . . He said . . ." Ireland didn't know why, but tears formed in her eyes. She could not cry. Not here. Not in front of these elitist brats who didn't care about anyone else. Why was she crying? Why could she not keep it together for a little longer?

Maybe it was everything Mara had been going through, and she was projecting herself into Mara's situation.

Maybe it had been her dad's attempted phone call.

Maybe it had been how completely victimized she'd felt by Rowan in that moment because she knew who he really was.

Maybe she had just had enough of everything, and it was all just too, too much.

When Mara saw the tears, she whirled on Rowan. "What did you do to her?"

Rowan stood, as if not liking that she was taller than him while he was sitting. "I didn't do anything."

Mara tucked Ireland behind her in an apparent attempt to keep her out of his reach. "That's a lie. You never do anything you'd admit to, but you definitely do things."

"What are you doing?" Ireland whispered in a fierce attempt to get Mara to just turn around and leave with her. All they had to do was leave, and this would all be over, and they could go back to her house where it was safe.

"Howling out loud," Mara said, not whispering.

Rowan lifted his hands in a placating gesture and moved to sit down again when Tinsley jumped to her drunken feet. She wobbled a little but managed to stay upright. "I am sssooo sick of you," she slurred at Mara.

Everyone else moved to their feet too, and not because they were starting an impromptu dance party. Like Mara had put herself in front of Ireland, Tinsley had placed herself in front of Rowan. "I am sssooo sick of you!" Tinsley was slur-shouting now.

"I can't believe you." Tinsley continued, waving her arms. "I *cannot* believe you right now. I can't even—ugh! Rowan, you want *her* after all that she's been saying about you? Do you know what she's been telling people?"

"What do I care what people say or don't say? I've got nothing to hide." Rowan shrugged like he was entirely unconcerned by the spectacle before him. His act would have been believable if weren't for the little guilty tells. His eyes were tight, and he covered them as if saying he was exhausted by all the drama, but to Ireland, it seemed more like he was hiding his eyes from the truth. When he lowered his hand, his fists clenched and unclenched.

Mara noted that everyone was standing and staring. She did not want an audience like this. She didn't want her howl to be quite this loud. And the fact remained that Mara cared about her friends. She didn't want Tinsley involved. "Maybe we should get you home, huh?" Mara tried to approach Tinsley, but it was like Tinsley had snapped. No one could touch her or go near her without her flying into a rage again.

"I'm done! I tell you I am so sick of it. I'm done. Finished. Kaput. Over it. No more. Calling it quits on our friendship. Do you hear me?"

All Ireland got from the rant was that Tinsley must have owned a thesaurus at some point.

"I know what you're saying about Rowan. I heard *her* boyfriend talking to Mr. Wasden." Tinsley pointed at Ireland and all eyes followed until everyone was looking at her. But Ireland didn't look at anyone except Mara, whose face scrunched in confusion.

Ireland's body felt numb. Her thoughts turned to static. Kal had gone to Mr. Wasden? Impossible. Tinsley hadn't said anything to prove that she actually knew what had happened with Mara. Kal would never betray her confidence like that.

As if hearing Ireland's thoughts, Tinsley continued. "Don't act dumb. Kal told Mr. Wasden that Mara was running around telling people that Rowan attacked her. As if he'd need to when everyone knows how thirsty she is for his attention."

"I didn't attack anyone!" Rowan insisted when it became clear people were looking at him through a different lens. He tried to appear calm, but the wild in his eyes matched the higher pitch in his voice.

"She says you did. But you still want her!" Tinsley said. "She does all that and you still tell me I'll never be good enough because I'm not at her 'level.'" She made air quotes and then said, "You mean I'll never *stoop* to her level."

"She's been drinking," someone in the crowd said.

"Everybody just calm down," Kiya from Ireland's English class said.

Emily tried to reach out to Tinsley, but Tinsley yanked her hand away. "No! Listen to me! It's true! Mara's been throwing herself at Rowan since freshman year. He finally gives in, and she does this? Right before the big track meet? It's like she's trying to get him suspended for no reason at all." She'd said all this while addressing the group, but then she whirled on Mara. "You have everything. Isn't it enough? Do you need his dignity too? Do you have to ruin it so that the rest of us don't have a chance?"

"Hey, maybe we just take this all down a notch, huh?" Kiya tried again to deescalate the situation, but no one paid any attention to her; all eyes were glued on the drama unfolding on the sand.

Tinsley swiped her hair out of her face. "You take in the little hobo and become her bestie, as if that makes you a saint or something. And then you blow the rest of us off like we're nothing. I'll tell you what: *Ireland* is nothing. Yeah, I said it." She whirled to face Ireland. "You were living in an outhouse in the woods before you moved in with Mara. I heard Kal and Mr. Wasden talking about it today in the art room. I was in his gallery to talk about my grades and heard the whole thing."

There were murmurs about Ireland's living arrangement, but Tinsley's shrill declarations drowned out what they might have been saying. "If Kal hadn't told Mr. Wasden about you, you'd still be there drinking toilet water and having bugs burrow under your hair, and you just—"

Nathan from the basketball team picked Tinsley up and carried her away from the fire. She kicked and swore at him while Cooper held up his hands. "Nothing to see here, folks. Tinsley's meltdown doesn't concern you. As you were."

Rowan's eyes fixed on Mara, and he took two steps toward her. She scrambled back to get away, but Emily stepped between them. "Until we sort this out, why don't we all go back to our corners. Don't talk to my girl unless she initiates contact with you." Emily shooed him away.

"Seriously. Tinsley's trippin'. I never—" Rowan started but Cooper cut him off.

"I saw you, man. There at Redwood Park."

Rowan floundered a moment, his nostrils flaring. "I don't have to take this from people like you." He stomped off, kicking up sand.

Ireland couldn't mask her surprise. Both at Emily, of all people, keeping a cool, practical head and at the relief that Mara had a witness. Ireland hurried to Mara's side, but she backed up from Ireland in the same way she did when Rowan had tried to talk to her. "You said you wouldn't tell," she whispered.

"I didn't! I mean . . . I didn't mean to." How could Ireland explain? How could she apologize? "It was an accident."

"You made things worse, Ireland. I thought you were my friend."

"I am. I am y—" but Mara and Emily were already moving away from Ireland and back up toward the parking lot.

Was Mara going to leave Ireland alone at the beach?

Mara pulled out her phone to call Kal to get her so she wasn't stranded there, but then she remembered that Kal had been the one to go to Mr. Wasden, not just about Mara but about *her*, too. He had been the one to tell about her living in a bathroom. He was the reason she'd had to go live with Mara. He was the reason

Mara now hated her. Ireland dropped the hand that was holding her phone to her side. She couldn't call him. Never again. Kal had proven himself to be a false friend. A con man just like her father.

Her fingers began kneading at the space just under her collarbone. She couldn't breathe. Her chest felt so tight, she was sure she was suffocating.

Fight or flight? She wanted to run. Run far. To never return to school. To never return to Mara's house. Would Mara even let her walk through the door if she went back?

Fight or flight? She wanted to scream. To punch someone. To howl out loud.

But Mara had been right. The moon didn't care. What good would howling do? Ireland stood there alone in the sand. Unable to flee. Unable to fight. Unable to breathe.

Kal's betrayal cut a chasm deep into her soul. She was falling into that chasm. She might never stop falling.

Ireland jumped when she heard a voice next to her. "I can take you home." Cooper was at her side. He had a girl with him, someone Ireland didn't recognize. She looked like she wanted to ask questions about everything, but once she saw Ireland's face, she changed her mind about saying anything.

Ireland nodded numbly and followed them up the trail to their car.

She didn't know how it had all happened, but like she'd left words in the flowers of the mural, she felt like she was leaving a trail of words in her every footstep in the sand. *Step.* Sad. *Step.* Empty. *Step.* Wrecked, *Step.* Shattered. *Step.* Betrayed. *Step.* Confused, *Step.* Alone. Again.

Alone.

All because of Kal.

CHAPTER TWENTY

Kal

Kal's phone rang, and he nearly dropped it in his rush to pick it up. "Hey, Ireland. You home okay?"

"Sorry, man. It's not Ireland," Cooper said. "I just dropped her off."

"Oh. Okay. Well good, I guess. What about Mara though? I don't want to get into the details, but it's not a good idea for her to be on her own right now."

"A little late to be worrying too much about the details, my dude, because pretty much everyone knows 'em now."

"What are you talking about?"

"Tinsley was apparently in Wasden's gallery when you decided to chat him up. She heard everything."

"Everything?"

"If you're asking if we all know Ireland lived in an outhouse, or if we all know that Rowan assaulted Mara, then yes. Everything. And when Rowan brushed her off tonight, Tinsley went off the rails and spilled everything she knew. It was so much drama."

"Oh no."

"Yep. That's why I'm calling you. Your girl is not impressed. She asked me to call because she said she gave her word that she would let you know she got home safely, and that, unlike some people she knows—she meant you when she said that, by the way—"

"Yeah. Got that."

"Anyway. She said that unlike some people she knows, her word matters. So I'm giving you the message. The other part of the message is that she doesn't want to talk to you, so don't call her."

Kal's heart plummeted into his stomach and then tanked into the floor from there. "What have I done?" he said.

He hadn't exactly been asking for an answer but Cooper gave one anyway. "The words she used were 'betrayal of trust.'"

"Very helpful."

Cooper made a clicking noise with his tongue. "I got you, man. Dude, I'm starving." Cooper morphed from one conversation to another like he hadn't just punched a hole in Kal's emotional life raft. "All that drama meant no clams. I went hungry and expecting to eat. Stupid Rowan messed up my dinner."

Kal couldn't focus on Cooper's hunger pains. He was trying to see around the blind panic in his own head. Ireland knew that he'd told not just one secret but *all* her secrets. What must she think of him?

"Did she mean like she didn't want me to call tonight, or she didn't want me to call ever?"

"It sounded kinda like ever. Can I be real for a minute though?"

"I don't know. Can you? Talking about being hungry doesn't feel very real."

"Tell that to my stomach. Anyway, she might be mad right now—and the night was pretty ugly—but someone needed to tell the truth about that guy. I begged Mara to let me tell what

I knew, but she was worried about dragging her family through something, so I backed off. This is her deal, right? It's not my place to get into it without an invite, or at least, that's what I thought. But whatever happens now, the truth is out. Truth isn't a bad thing."

"I hope you're right, 'cause it's looking pretty bad at the moment."

"I feel that. Don't call her tonight. But definitely call her tomorrow."

They hung up, and Kal agonized over the different ways he could apologize so Ireland knew he meant it. "I never should've told Wasden." It didn't matter how many times he said it out loud; he *had* told. The truth was out.

Somewhere in the middle of the night, he decided that though he couldn't call her, he could write to her. He spent the rest of the night crafting an email. He told her everything—from the first time he saw her taking the pizza, to following her into the woods and seeing where she was living, to watching her sketch and admiring her kindness for other people. He told about the skeezy things Rowan had said about her and other girls and how he worried that she was going alone to the woods, where no one was waiting up for her to know if she made it home safely or not, and that was why he had told about that.

His telling about Mara was more complicated. But Kal tried to explain. He apologized over and over, hoping that one of those apologies stuck. After that there was nothing to do but hit send, turn out the light, and go to sleep.

He didn't sleep.

He thought about all the ways he could've explained better or where he explained too much. He finally got up and went downstairs to forage for food. His grandpa was there. "Good morning," his grandpa said.

"Is it?"

"Come walk with me, and I'll show you."

Kal went walking with his grandfather. The frigid air made his nose run, but it cleared his head.

His grandpa talked about his grandma and asked about how things were going with Ireland. Kal figured he had nothing to lose by talking now, so he told everything. His grandpa was a good listener.

When Kal was done talking, his grandpa said, "You should have asked her what she wanted to do."

"I know that now."

"Give her time."

That phrase made it sound like maybe, in time, she'd forgive him and everything would all be okay, but Kal wasn't so sure. He waited all day but heard nothing back from her. Every time he considered writing or calling her, he put his phone down and walked away. He had to respect her choices. That was what his grandfather told him. What Cooper told him. What his mom told him. Kal was pretty sure if he explained the situation to the guy at the checkout counter in the grocery store, the advice would be the same.

That night, she wasn't at Geppetto's. On Sunday, she was still radio silent. On Monday morning, he waited for Mara's car in the student parking lot, but the little Fiat with the eyelashes on the headlights never made an appearance.

Rowan wasn't in school either. But the rumors about what had happened between him and Mara were on every whisper in the whole school.

"Police showed up and now he's in juvie."

"He's transferred schools."

"No. Mara's transferred schools."

"Mara's being sued for libel . . . or maybe it's slander?"

"Ireland lived in a bathroom."

"Not just any bathroom. It was an outhouse."

"So weird."

With every whisper, Kal's heart sank lower. What had he done?

Mr. Wasden didn't have any more information than anyone else, but he'd declared that even if he did, he couldn't tell him.

And despite all the rumors in school, Kal figured no one there knew anything more than he did. Probably less.

"Proud of yourself?" Emily stood blocking his way to his physics class.

"Not in the least." If his honest response surprised her, she didn't show it.

"You really screwed up Mara's life, Kal."

"So I figured. I'm really sorry."

"She had to make a statement to the police, you know. Her parents are going crazy with the whole situation, and she's stuck living with a girl that you planted in her house like some spy."

"Ireland is not a spy. Mr. Wasden and Mara's parents arranged that. Not me." Kal considered going around Emily but stopped. "Is she okay?"

"No. I just told you. She had to talk to the police. There's this whole thing."

"Talking to the police is not a bad thing. He hurt her. There should be consequences. And anyway, I mean Ireland. Is she okay?"

Emily put a hand on the hip of her canary-yellow miniskirt. "You did not just ask me to verify the well-being of the spy."

"She's not a spy, Emily."

"Whatever."

She finally moved out of his way so he could get into his seat on time, even if she didn't give him any of the information he wanted.

Kal's physics teacher seemed to not care Kal didn't feel like talking because she kept calling on him. "Describe heliocentrism."

Kal looked out at the people. Emily was in the class and giving him a flat stare. Several other people looked curious. He already had a type of infamy for being in a band, and now he was connected to the situation between Rowan, Mara, and Ireland. He cleared his throat and gave a response so he could sit down and mope in peace. "Heliocentrism means the sun is at the center of our solar system, not the Earth. Planets go around the sun. It replaced the idea that Earth was the center, helping us understand our place in space."

Kal moved back to his seat and heard a few muttered comments about Rowan or Mara from people who seemed to think the world revolved around one or the other depending on whose side the person was on. How Mara was being called out confused him. And Rowan running around a track hardly made him worth being the center of anyone's universe.

Since Ireland and Mara were both absent from school, only four members of the art club were left to try to wrap things up with the mural. The detail work required to blend everything while still letting each piece of work stand on its own took way longer than Kal had imagined. If Ireland had been there, they would be swapping puns about chickens or elephants or whatever came to mind or they would be playing would-you-rather games.

Kal missed her.

He was agony walking.

He hated knowing Ireland was out there in the world and hurting and that it had been him who caused the pain.

Would Mara's parents kick Ireland out of the house because of all that had happened? Would she end up homeless again? Not like it was Ireland's fault that Rowan hurt Mara, but Ireland was part of all the rumors taking place.

And Mara. How was Mara in all of this? Kal's eyes kept going back to the flower garden she and Ireland had created on the wall. Ireland had wanted to help Mara. And Kal had screwed it all up.

His phone buzzed with a message from Ireland. His hands shook while he swept his finger over the screen. "Kal, I appreciate you telling me the truth. But I don't think I can trust you. You promised you wouldn't tell. But you broke your word. I know this is my fault too, but maybe that's the problem. Maybe us both being at fault means we're a toxic match."

That was the whole message.

A toxic match.

Kal scrubbed his hand over his head as his brain put those words on repeat.

He had screwed everything up for everyone. He saw the custodian pushing a garbage can on wheels down the hall. He'd even screwed things up for her by letting Ireland be mad at her. But that was one thing he could apologize in person for. He hurried to catch up to her. "Hey, um, Janice."

She stopped and leaned on the can while she waited for him to speak.

"Sorry to bug you." He stopped. She didn't know Ireland had ever been mad at her. Was he making things worse by bringing it up? "Just wanted to say you do a great job. Thanks."

Janice pursed her lips in confusion before she said, "You're welcome." She patted him on the shoulder and started walking with the rolling can again.

Kal breathed a deep, cleansing breath and went back to work on the mural. *The issue doesn't revolve around me,* he thought. *It revolves around Mara and Ireland.* He would work to fix things a little at a time.

It wouldn't change what happened, but maybe it would change how everyone felt about it. Maybe it would change how Mara and Ireland felt about it.

Maybe it would change how Ireland felt about *him*.

CHAPTER TWENTY-ONE
Ireland

Five days later, Mara still wasn't talking to Ireland. Ireland didn't blame her. She'd made a promise and broken that promise. Her total hypocrisy was not lost on her. She wanted Kal punished for doing the same thing she had done. She hoped for forgiveness in the same way he hoped.

She was denied in the same way he was denied.

But her situation was different. She had told accidentally. He had gone out and told on purpose. Premeditated betrayal.

Everything had come to a crashing crescendo the night of the clambake. Ireland and Mara arrived home at the same time that night. Or close enough. Grace asked why they'd driven separately, and then Mara dumped the whole tale about the assault and the clambake.

Mara told them everything because, as she said when she was talking to them, they were going to hear about it one way or the other, and she owed it to them to have the information come from her and be completely true instead of rumor.

Mara left out one thing: she didn't tell her parents that Ireland had betrayed her trust. Grace and Jarrod couldn't figure out what exactly had happened between the girls, and Mara never volunteered the details. Ireland wasn't sure if it was because Mara had reached deep inside herself and found some compassion and didn't want Ireland kicked out of the house, or if she was so done with Ireland that she thought Ireland wasn't even worth the mention.

Ireland hovered in the background as the conversation happened because she didn't want to be alone in her bedroom with only her thoughts to keep her company.

After Grace heard what had happened to Mara, she insisted that they report the incident "for the safety of other girls." Mara protested. She didn't want the drama. She didn't want her family to have to deal with the drama. Her life wasn't anybody else's business. She hated Rowan and didn't want to ever have to deal with him again. She hated herself and what people would think of her. She'd gone to Redwood Park with him. She'd known he had a reputation as a player. She'd made the mistake.

Grace was exactly what her name described her to be. She held her daughter in her arms and stroked Mara's hair while whispering words of encouragement, comfort, love. She gave Mara a safe space to say whatever it was she wanted to say. No judgment. No derision. Except when Mara tried to blame herself—then Grace defended her daughter with a ferocity that made Ireland envious.

What would it be like to have a mom hold her like Grace held Mara? To protect her the way Grace protected Mara?

Jarrod was on the other side of his daughter. He held her hand and told her she would be okay. He told her that whatever happened, she had them.

What would it be like to have a dad who said, "Whatever happens, you have me?"

Ireland had gone to bed that night feeling like someone had

hollowed out her insides and placed them up on a high shelf where she couldn't reach, leaving her empty and numb.

She crept to Mara's door in the bathroom and knocked. "Mara? Mara, I'm sorry. It was an accident. It slipped out by accident. Mara? Please talk to me."

"Boundaries! We are not friends, Ireland."

Ireland hated that days later they still weren't friends. The police had come by and taken a statement. Rowan's parents had also come by. That had been weird. Ireland expected them to defend their son and to insist Mara take it all back. But they did the exact opposite. They apologized for him, said they were putting him into counseling, and asked what they could do to help Mara.

It was classy of them to take responsibility for what they could. Not everybody did that.

It had been on the third day after the clambake blowup that Ireland was cleaning in the kitchen. She'd hoped that she could Cinderella her way into not being kicked out of the house. They hadn't been back to school. Thank the stars because Ireland could not take the back-and-forth drive with Mara's frosty silence, only broken by the word "Boundaries!" thrown in intermittently.

Grace and Jarrod were letting Ireland do at-home study because Mara told them that Rowan had said some demeaning things to her as well. On top of that, they knew Tinsley had announced Ireland's homelessness to everyone, and they also didn't want Ireland to have to deal with all the drama of trying to answer questions about Mara. Ireland didn't have a driver's license, either. Because of all this, they figured both girls needed a break from in-real-life school. So they were keeping up on schoolwork from home, instead.

Ireland's phone rang. She looked at it, expecting Kal's name and number on the display screen. It was Humboldt Correctional

Facility. It buzzed once more while she stared at it. A third time. Her finger swiped up and she answered.

"This call is from Humboldt County Correctional Facility and is subject to monitoring and recording. Do you accept the charges?"

Would she accept the charges? No. Yes?

She had money in the bank. Not a lot, but enough.

"Yes," she said, surprised that her voice box worked.

"Hello? Hello?" Her dad's voice sounded far away. But hadn't he always been far away?

"Hi, Dad."

"Ireland. How are you? How's . . . school?"

Had he ever in her life asked her about school? She glanced at the clock on the oven. If he'd been paying attention, he would have realized that she still should have been in class. That thought made her mad. "What do you want, Dad?"

He stammered. She could picture him raking his fingers through his hair—dark brown like hers. She could see him licking his lips. That was his tell when he was formulating a lie.

"I wanted to hear your voice."

"I don't have money to give you." He needed that information right up front. It would keep him from making promises he wouldn't keep if he knew she had nothing worth him bargaining over.

"I'm not asking for money."

"So what do you want?"

"There's no agenda. I just wanted to hear your voice and to say . . . to say I'm sorry. For leaving like I did. That was not my best moment."

Ireland blew out a breath and tossed the rag she'd been holding into the sink. "Definitely not your best. But hey, in the grand scheme of things, it *is* your typical moment."

"I deserve that."

"Not even close to what you deserve, Dad."

"Are you safe?"

The question made her breath hitch. It was the concerned kind of question a parent should ask a child. "I am *now*."

She heard his breath catch too. Her comment had hit its mark. She wanted him to know that she hadn't been safe.

"I'm staying with a girl from school and her family," she added. Not because he deserved to know, but because she couldn't stop herself.

"Good. Good. I'm probably going to be here for a while. The lawyer did a good job though. He pled me down to a year."

"What did you do?"

"Online romance con."

"You have got to be kidding me." Ireland slumped against the kitchen counter in disbelief.

"What? I'm still attractive enough to make that viable."

"I'm not questioning your looks, Dad. Your moral compass is seriously broken."

"Yeah. I know. But hey . . . I only have another minute. Would you be willing to come see me sometime?"

Ireland pressed her palm against her eye to relieve the pressure building there. "I don't know. Maybe. I'm not promising anything."

"'Course not. Understood. Just think about it."

"Sure. I'll think about it. I gotta go." She hung up. Only then did she allow herself to sink to the floor and hold her head in her hands. "I am the worst," she said to the kitchen. How did he do that? How did he make her feel guilty for not agreeing to visit immediately? "I am the absolute worst."

"Absolute worst what?" Jade asked as she came into the kitchen.

Mara was with her and raised her eyebrows as she said, "Gettin' no arguments from me on that."

"Mara . . ." Jade admonished her sister before turning back to Ireland. "Why are you on the floor? Are you okay? Are you sick?"

"Who's sick?" This question came from Grace, who had only been a few steps behind her daughters.

"Ireland is," Jade said at the same time that Ireland said, "No one."

She scrambled to her feet to prove that she was fine.

"What happened?" Grace put her hand on Ireland's arm.

The gentle touch shouldn't have been a big deal. It certainly shouldn't have shattered her emotionally, but Ireland burst into tears she couldn't control. She instantly felt like an idiot since Mara was there observing the whole thing.

Grace pulled her into a hug like she had done with Mara just a few days before. She made soft shushing sounds, and when Ireland calmed enough, she asked, "What's going on?"

"It's nothing. It's stupid. My dad called."

"From jail? Or is he out?"

Ireland shook her head. "He's still there. For the next year, I guess."

"What did he say to upset you?" Grace looked thunderous, as if whatever Ireland told her was bad enough that she'd go to the jail personally to make him pay.

It shouldn't have, but that made Ireland start crying all over again. "He didn't say anything," she said. "Not really. He asked me to go visit him."

Grace stayed silent for a long moment. Jade had crept forward and tucked her hand inside Ireland's. Mara watched her family comforting Ireland from the other side of the island.

Ireland wished she could turn off the waterworks. How stupid to cry over a guy who was a thief and a liar.

"Do you want to go see him?" Grace asked when it seemed Ireland had control over herself again.

"I don't know. Is it wrong that I do? Even after everything? I mean the guy left me on my own with no way to take care of myself. Am I completely cracked in the head to want to see him?"

"No, baby. It's not wrong. He's your father. If you want to see him, Jarrod and I can take you. If you decide at any point you've changed your mind, we can turn around and come home, okay?"

Ireland nodded, her body shuddering with the after-effects of crying. By the time dinner came around that night, it was decided that they would go the next day to visit Ireland's dad. It's not like she'd be missing school since they had already planned to stay home. The teachers had all been generous with emailing the homework so Mara and Ireland didn't get behind.

As plates were passed around the table, there was an open discussion about going to visit Ireland's dad. The adults didn't shy away from hard topics in an effort to hide anything from Jade. They might have softened the delivery, but Jarrod often said that open and honest communication was key to raising healthy, responsible, capable children. Dinner with the Washington family was like looking in on a living Norman Rockwell painting sometimes. They were the blueprint of what family should be.

It was decided that Jarrod would drive Ireland to the correctional facility so Grace could handle the scheduled interviews for a new employee at the café. Mara stayed quiet for most of the conversation until she finally said, "I don't know why you're going. It's a toxic relationship. You should cut him out of your life."

"I mean . . . I don't disagree," Ireland said, feeling like she might choke on the almond-crusted salmon Jarrod had made. Mara, talking to her without any prodding from her parents? Miraculous. "And I've been thinking that same thing, especially since he called."

"But you going is a brave thing," Grace interjected. "It's okay to cut the toxic people out of our lives. But not if we're going to do it in anger or bitterness. Because that means we didn't really cut them out. They're still in our lives, manifesting themselves in our anger and bitterness. You are making a healthy choice, if it's something you think you're ready for."

"Yeah," Ireland said, feeling herself shrink under the unexpected praise. "I don't want to be angry all the time. But I think I should cut him out in a way that wishes him well in his life and that allows me to move forward with mine. You know? Then I can say I've done what I needed to do. No guilt. At least, that's how I think it should go. I'm not a therapist or anything, so really, what do I know?" Ireland took a deep breath and met Mara's gaze.

Mara stared at her as if Ireland had grown an entire solar system out of her nose. "Some people don't deserve our forgiveness," she said.

"That's true." Ireland felt the *sad* wash over her again and again.

"It is true," Jarrod agreed. "Some people don't. But if Ireland is up for it, she deserves the peace that comes from moving forward."

Mara could have been talking about not forgiving Rowan. Or she could have been talking about not forgiving Ireland.

Ireland knew she didn't deserve unearned absolution from Mara. But she truly believed Mara deserved to feel peace.

I do too. Don't I? Ireland felt like she *did* deserve the peace that came from her letting go of what her parents had done to her. She wanted to move on and couldn't do that if she was feeling trapped in the emotional chaos that those people had inflicted on her. She wasn't going to live like that anymore. Her life was hers, not theirs, and she was not about to give them another second of it unwillingly. How she lived would be her choice from now on.

The thought of Kal shoved itself to the front of her thoughts. Shouldn't she work on forgiving him? Especially since she was guilty of betraying trust as much as he was? But for whatever reason, his betrayal felt worse. His betrayal reminded her of her dad's. Kal's manipulation of her life cut too deep. She wasn't ready to forgive him just yet.

Mara looked perplexed, even hostile. She stabbed her salmon with her fork and continued to eat in silence.

Later that night, Ireland struggled to sleep. A tap came from the bathroom door. "Come in." Ireland sat up.

Mara's black hair was tied back in a ponytail. Her face was freshly washed. She hadn't worn makeup of any kind for days, but Ireland was still getting used to her being natural. Mara's beautiful features looked better without all the products. She wore black dance pants and an oversized orange hoodie with their school mascot on it. She sat on the chair at the desk near Ireland's bed and pulled up her legs, tucking her feet underneath her. "I'm sorry about your dad. Your mom too, I guess."

"It's okay. It's not your fault."

"I was talking to my mom a little bit ago, and she was filling in some of the information about your dad and your mom and your life before you moved in. Sorry I didn't know any of that before."

"It's not like knowing changes anything."

"Maybe. But I wasn't nice to you. My friends weren't nice to you. We should have been."

Ireland smoothed her hands over the white sheets, feeling the soft fibers of the high thread count under her fingertips. "Whether you know somebody's backstory or not, shouldn't you always be nice to them?"

Mara laughed. "Touché. You're right. You're right. I really let myself get caught up in the social scene. It sliced away pieces of me every time I turned around. Tinsley. Rowan. Half the student body. I had people with me almost all the time. But I felt so alone. And then there was you—actually alone. My mom and I were talking about it, and she let me know I could have been more sensitive to that. She's not wrong. I'm sorry."

"It's okay, Mara. It's not like I put out a get-to-know-me vibe. When you've moved around as much as I have from one con to the next, getting to know people just seems like a lot of work with not a lot of payout. That attitude feels like my dad talking. Everything for him was about the payout."

"You still going to go see him tomorrow?"

"Yeah. I think I need to."

They both went silent after that. After a moment, Mara spun in the chair, dropping her head back and closing her eyes as it went around. She stopped the spin and stood. "Okay then. I'll go with you. I'll see you in the morning." She stood and strode to the door.

"Mara . . . why are you talking to me?"

She stretched her arms up over her head and laced her hands behind her neck. "Because you're right. Not forgiving you doesn't hurt you. Well, it might. I don't know. But I do know for sure that it hurts me. I could use a little peace right now. Besides, I actually forgave you a couple of days ago. I just wanted to punish you a little bit more, I think, because . . . well, I don't know why. What happened to me wasn't your fault. And I know you didn't mean to share it with the whole school. Tinsley did that. I'm working on the idea of forgiving her, but that one might take a little longer."

"I really didn't mean to tell anyone. I am sorry, Mara."

She dropped her hands to the side and picked at the hem of her sweatshirt. "I know. I have a tendency to not say what's bothering me. But I got some good advice the other day, and I think I need to start paying attention to it."

"What advice?"

"A friend told me to howl out loud." Mara left, closing the door behind her.

Ireland was now sitting up straight in bed. Did Mara know that Ireland wrote that message to her? Was this her way of saying, "Hey, I know that was you?"

Or was it just that the message mattered, and Mara had taken it to heart enough to pass it on?

Either way, Ireland felt like everything was going to be okay. Whatever happened with her dad, the next day was going to be fine because she had a friend she could depend on.

CHAPTER TWENTY-TWO
Kal

Kal had hoped Ireland would change her mind and contact him.

She didn't.

It had been nearly a week. The gossip had pretty much died down, though he guaranteed it would pick back up if any of the involved parties returned to school. Asha, Bailey, and Cooper had rallied around him—not that he was surprised. They were his friends. Okay, he was a little surprised about Bailey. And when he wrote a new song for Ireland and asked to practice it with them, no one turned him into the latest joke. They practiced the song with him, and on their last run-through, when it sounded near-perfect, Asha gave him a sad look that did not vibe at all with her normally sunny disposition. "That was really beautiful, Superman."

"It's a hit for sure," Cooper agreed. "It hits all the right feels."

"We should definitely play it tomorrow night," Bailey said.

Kal scoffed at that. "Too bad she'll never hear it, huh?"

"Don't say that, Superman," Asha said. "You never know."

He did know. Ireland had made it clear.

"Let's go again," Bailey said, not one to wait around for sentimentality.

They ran through it several more times.

"Definitely a hit, man," Cooper said when they'd finished and were packing it up for the night.

"As opposed to a hitman." Bailey socked Cooper's shoulder on her way past him and laughed when he scowled at her.

"Thanks, Coop."

"I know it doesn't feel right at the moment. But not telling would have felt worse. Believe me."

Kal understood what Cooper meant. Cooper had known about Mara and Rowan and hadn't told. He said he regretted it. Kal probably would have regretted not telling too.

He maintained that he would right his wrongs as much as possible. He had apologized to Ireland, but he hadn't apologized to Mara. Since Mara and Ireland still weren't coming to school, he decided he needed to go to them. Well, not to Ireland because she didn't want to see him. But he would go to Mara. He would explain himself. He would apologize, and then she could forgive him. Or not. Whichever it was, he would have at least done as much as he could, right?

He hated how much he hoped he would see Ireland while at the Washington's house. Maybe if she saw him face-to-face, she would want to talk to him. Not that *that* was why he was going to Mara's house, but it would be a nice perk of going.

Kal checked his phone. It was still early enough to go see Mara. It wasn't even four in the afternoon yet. He put on a nicer shirt and smoothed down his hair. He told himself he wasn't doing it to impress Ireland, but because dressing nice to apologize was just polite.

When Kal arrived at Mara's house, he worried he might throw up. "You're not here to talk to Ireland. Stop being ridiculous." The

self-talk didn't motivate him as much he would have wanted. He
approached the door and sucked in a deep breath of courage before pressing the doorbell.

Jade, Mara's little sister, answered "Hi, Kal. Ireland isn't
here."

He could have kicked himself for feeling such intense disappointment. He stomped down the feeling. "No problem. I'm
actually here to see Mara."

"Okay. But you have to stay here while I check with her if it's
okay." She shut the door on him before he could agree to her stip-
ulation. He waited on the front step until the door swung open
again. This time, Mara stood in front of him, not Jade.

She didn't smile or say anything. She didn't invite him inside.
She leaned against the doorframe and raised her eyebrows in a
look that clearly said, "Get on with it."

"Hey, Mara. I bet you're wondering why I'm here."

"I am curious adjacent."

"Right. Well . . . I wanted to say I'm sorry. I never should
have gone to Mr. Wasden for help without talking to you about
it first. I don't have an excuse, aside from the fact that I think
Rowan is a skeeze, and I worried what he might do next."

"You're right. You should have talked to me."

"I know. I just . . ." He sat down on the step. "It's been a
long year." He told Mara about Brell and everything that had
happened leading up to her funeral and his emotional breakdown
after the funeral. It was all information he was finally ready to
share. He wished he could tell Ireland, but she wasn't talking to
him. And he needed to explain it to Mara so she'd understand
why he'd barged into her business the way he had. As he talked,
Mara sat next to him on the step.

By the time Kal was wrapping up all the events, Mara didn't
look mad anymore. "Asha told me it wasn't my job to save

people," he finished. "But after losing Brell, it's hard for me to see it any other way. I'm just sorry to involve you in my issues. I'm sorry it caused you trouble."

"That was a good apology, Kal. I accept. You're forgiven. The truth is that I wasn't handling the situation very well on my own. I should've told someone right at the beginning. But how do you bring up such a thing, right? I mean, I guess you know because you did bring it up, but for whatever reason, I couldn't. I don't think I would have. And that wasn't good for anyone. You telling was actually the right thing to do even if it made me mad."

"What's going to happen to Rowan?" Kal asked. "If you don't mind me asking. And you don't have to answer. It's fine if you don't."

"Well, what happened to me could have been worse, right? I wasn't sure pressing charges was the right thing to do. But I decided to go ahead and do it. I have evidence and a witness, and it's better to have stuff documented to help keep it from happening to anyone else. He's being charged with misdemeanor sexual battery. Tinsley's peeved. She says I did it all to spite her. As if. Like I'd get myself attacked just to spite someone. Right."

"Sorry."

"I know. You said."

"When Ireland told me you were the lipstick writer, she was freaking out because she worried she'd said the wrong thing when she responded. She hadn't meant to say it was Rowan who hurt you. She'd spoken in generalities. She just slipped up and said Rowan was a troll. I put it together after that. She didn't mean to tell me. So even if you decide to keep being mad at me, don't be mad at her. Please."

"Hold it. Ireland knows about my writing on the mural? She knows about the lipstick?"

"Yeah, but you know that, right? You have to know that the

mural conversation was between you and her, right? I mean, she didn't know it was you at first. She just figured it out." With his every word, Kal realized he'd been wrong. Mara hadn't known. Kal wanted to bang his head against the ground. He had done it again? "You didn't know," he said flatly. "Awesome times zero."

Mara stayed quiet. She wrapped her arms around her legs to ward off the cold.

"Don't hate her. Don't hate me. I mean, it's okay to hate me, but don't hate her. Ireland legit cares about you."

"Huh. And you legit care about her, right?"

Kal's head bobbed in agreement. "I do."

"Sorry she's not here."

"Where is she?"

"Visiting her dad in jail."

Out of all the things Kal thought Mara might say, that was not anywhere on the list.

"I wanted to go with her, but someone needed to stay home with Jade, and Ireland said she wanted to do it on her own. I didn't think she should go. It's not like she owes that guy anything. But she feels like she needs to, so . . . anyway . . . sorry she's not here."

"It's okay. I came to talk to you. She doesn't want to talk to me."

Mara made a sad, sympathetic *tsk*. "Maybe you could write her a letter or something."

"Already did." He picked up a loose pebble from off the porch and flicked it so that it skittered down the stairs. "She told me not to write back. So I wrote her a song, but she'll never hear it. But I guess it's fine because the band likes it, so we'll at least get some play out of it."

"That's perfect!" Mara jumped to her feet.

"Perfect would be her hearing it, not a crowd at Geppetto's."

"I can get her to Geppetto's." Mara was practically doing jumping jacks in her excitement.

"How?"

Mara smirked. "She wants me to forgive her as much as you want her to forgive you. I'll tell her I really feel like pizza."

"Lots of kids from school will be there. There always are."

She tilted her head to the side. "What do I care? I can't stay home forever. Better to get the public viewing done at Geppetto's instead of at school Monday."

Kal stood and blew on his hands to try to warm them up. "I appreciate the gesture. Really. But, Mara, I don't want her to be where she doesn't want to be. We're good, okay?"

She nodded and hugged her arms to herself.

"Go inside before we both freeze to death." He shooed her toward the door and made his way to his car, grateful he had seat heaters. The visit with Mara had been a success. He had been able to apologize, and she had forgiven him. He couldn't ask for more than that. He wanted to. Of course he wanted to.

But he couldn't.

He wouldn't.

CHAPTER TWENTY-THREE
Ireland

Ireland rested her head against the car's seat and closed her eyes as they pulled away from the correctional facility. She hadn't known what to expect, but the nondescript, boxy building had been a little underwhelming.

And overwhelming.

All at the same time.

"You okay?" Jarrod asked.

She didn't open her eyes. "Sure. Ten degrees of fabulous."

What had she expected? Did she expect that her dad would tell her how sorry he was for everything and that he had plans to make a real go of being a family as soon as he got out? He *had* said sorry. But she didn't think he was sorry as much as he was bored. Yanking on her heartstrings was a convenient way to find entertainment. Beyond wanting to have someone to keep him busy for a short while, he actually did want to borrow money.

She'd informed him that she would not be coming back to visit once she realized that he was conning her. The decision, once made, was easy to stick to, no matter how many different ways he tried to manipulate her into changing her mind. She wished him well. Told him she wanted nothing for him but peace, light, and love—a phrase she'd heard when the gym teacher had them do yoga at the beginning of class for a few weeks.

Ireland told her dad not to call because she didn't have the money to pay. She said he could email and she might write back, but that was all he could expect. She didn't give him a mailing address because she didn't want him knowing where she was living.

Now that she was back in the car heading home, she felt exhausted.

"We should get you signed up for driving lessons," Jarrod said. He liked to chitchat while he did things like driving.

"That's expensive," Ireland said, still not opening her eyes.

"Not expensive at all. Not compared to not having a license. You'll need to drive. It's an important skill."

Ireland found it difficult to not compare the man next to her driving the car to the man she'd just left at the correctional facility. The man at the facility wanted to take from her. The man next to her wanted to give. It made her sad that Jarrod had been a better father to her in the short period of time that she had lived in his house than her real father had been to her in eighteen years' worth of life.

She was sad but also grateful. Because she *did* have Jarrod and Grace and Jade and Mara. Maybe they weren't her forever family to keep, but they were letting her borrow them for a while. Family on loan was better than no family at all.

"Okay. I agree with you about needing to know how to drive. But I'll pay for the lessons. I'll work them off with more hours at the restaurant or chores around the house."

Jarrod didn't argue. But that didn't mean he wouldn't argue later on. He liked to do things for people.

At the house, Mara was waiting for Ireland. She greeted her with a hug. Jade squeezed into the embrace too. Jarrod smiled approvingly at his daughters and then went to start making dinner. "So? How did it go?" Mara asked.

"About like one would expect from a guy in jail for grifting some lady in a love con."

"So what that means is you had to send him a wire transfer for your entire life savings? But it's okay because you really love him."

Ireland laughed. Just when she wasn't sure laughing was something she could ever do again.

"So I need you to hear me out," Mara said.

"That doesn't sound ominous at all."

Jade nodded her head like Ireland should tread carefully. "Every time she says that to me, I end up having to do her dishes."

"This isn't anything like that. In fact, it's better than that because there are no dishes involved for anybody, including me. Tomorrow is your birthday, right?"

"Right." Funny that Ireland could forget something like that. Tomorrow she would be a legal adult.

Her dad hadn't even mentioned it. Granted, she had forgotten as well, so how could she expect him to remember?

"I say we celebrate in style. We'll go to dinner and have some entertainment and party like rock stars. I'm buying."

A birthday party. Ireland had never had a birthday party before. Her dad would sometimes buy her a donut to celebrate, and once he'd even put a candle in it, but there hadn't been any matches, so she'd had to pretend to blow the candle out.

"I love birthdays!" Jade said. "Am I invited to the party?"

"Absolutely. But there are a few stipulations attached to your birthday party, Ireland."

Well, that wasn't suspicious at all. "Like what?"

"Like we have to go where I want to go."

"Suspicious," Jade said.

"That's what I was thinking." Ireland agreed. "Where do you want to go?"

Mara fidgeted with her necklace. "Geppetto's."

"Right. And Geppetto's is the celebrating in style that you were talking about?" Ireland walked away so she could put her bag in her room. She knew a setup when she smelled one. Conversation over.

"I'm buying, so we should totally go where I want to go."

"Because we shouldn't let the birthday girl decide where she wants to go for dinner." Ireland had made it to the stairs and took them two at a time to get to her room.

"Kal came by while you were gone. He's really sorry, Ireland."

Ireland turned slowly on the stairs. "I just walked away from one man I can't trust. I didn't do it so I could run to the arms of another one." She continued up the stairs until she reached the top and then headed to her bedroom. But Mara stayed right on her heels. Jade did too.

"You told me you were going there today to forgive your dad."

"And I do forgive him. That doesn't mean I'm going to go hang out with him anymore. That was just today. You're the one who said it was okay to cut toxic people out of your life." She went into her room and tried to shut the door, but Mara put her foot in before Ireland could get it closed.

Mara bumped the door open the rest of the way with her hip. "It *is* okay to cut toxic people out of your life. But come on. You know that Kal doesn't qualify as toxic. He's just a nice guy with a little bit of a Superman complex. But can you blame him? His name is literally Kal-El. He probably uses kryptonite for deodorant."

"Superman can't use kryptonite because it weakens him." Ireland considered leaving the room, but she knew that Mara would just follow her. So she pulled off her socks and fell onto the bed. Jade sat next to her.

"That doesn't make any sense. Why does he use it if it weakens him?"

"I know what movies I'm going to make you watch."

"Whatever. The point is that Kal is a good person. And if you can forgive your dad for abandoning you, but not Kal for breaking a promise, then I'm a little repulsed by you."

"That's a little strong, don't you think?"

"Not strong enough. Just let me take you out for your birthday. Let me celebrate you. Kal will be onstage for the majority of the time, anyway, so it's not like you're going to have to really talk to him very much if you don't want to. In fact, you won't have to talk to him at all if you don't want to. I'll respect that. But if you at least let yourself see him, then maybe you can move into that forgiveness part that you said was so good for you and me."

"I already told him that I forgave him."

"You obviously didn't mean it, or you wouldn't be so freaky about me taking you to get food on your birthday."

Ireland huffed. Then she puffed out her cheeks and huffed some more. She was starting to feel like the big bad wolf.

"I like pizza." Jade's quiet, innocent voice was the linchpin in Mara's argument.

"Fine. You win. But if I decide that I'm not happy in that situation and I want to leave, you have to respect me, and we get to leave as soon as I say."

Mara jumped up and down clapping her hands. "I love it when I win. It's my favorite."

Jade gave Ireland a flat look. "You might think she's joking. But Mara loves to win more than anybody. It's why she always gets her way."

"Trust me. I didn't think she was joking."

After Mara and Jade vacated her room and left her alone, Ireland wanted to call them back. Loneliness wriggled uncomfortably inside her belly.

"Why am I so unwilling to forgive him?" she asked herself.

A knock came from the bathroom door. "Stop talking to yourself and go to sleep!"

Great. Mara heard her talking to herself. Could Mara always hear her when she was speaking to herself?

"I'm going to have to wire my jaw shut." She said that out loud too, but she muttered low enough that she was sure Mara couldn't hear. She frowned. At least, she hoped Mara couldn't hear.

Mara was right though. She needed to get some sleep. She rolled over and forced her eyes closed.

The next morning, everything in the house was eerily quiet for a Saturday. Usually, Taylor Swift crooned from the bathroom or Mara's bedroom. And sounds of activity from either Jarrod or Grace interacting with Jade would float up from downstairs.

But nothing.

Maybe it was early?

Ireland checked her phone, but instead of waking up early, she had slept in. It was 9:10.

She got out of bed and put her ear to the Jack and Jill bathroom. No noise at all. Maybe everybody was gone. Ireland gathered the clothing she planned to wear for the day but then rethought her choices. If she was going to see Kal, she wanted to look her very best.

She stared into her closet for longer than she wanted to admit to anyone. "I really need to hit a thrift store with Grace so she can help me find the good stuff."

She pulled out a top that looked flattering on her even if it was worn out. Then she got a sweater that matched it close enough. She grabbed the pair of jeans that was in the best shape and called it good.

Now armed with her clothing for the day, Ireland opened her bedroom door to go to the bathroom at the end of the hall. And ran right into paper.

The brown paper spanned the entire opening of her doorway. She stepped back. In bright colorful letters was painted Happy Birthday! Ireland recognized the handwriting to be Mara's. There were balloons and candles and party hats all painted carefully around the words.

Ireland felt a burn at the back of her throat and behind her eyes. She blinked away the tears that were going to fall no matter how much blinking she did. Mara had given her a birthday present.

She didn't ever want to take it down, but there was the other problem that she needed to go to the bathroom and had to get through that door somehow. Ireland carefully pried away the tape on one end and slid through the opening she created.

When she opened the door to the bathroom, it was full of actual balloons. The bathroom wasn't very big, so it wouldn't have been hard to fill it, but there had to have been at least thirty helium balloons floating at the ceiling with their strings hanging down for Ireland to walk through.

On the mirror was written the words You Can Vote! with pictures of ballots and an American flag surrounding the words.

Ireland dropped her clothes to the floor, hurried to take care of her reason for being there, and left the bathroom to go find Mara.

Downstairs, the dining room table was set with colorful party plates and streamers. There was a chafing dish in the middle of the table to keep whatever was inside warm.

A cake sat next to the chafing dish. A real birthday cake. It was tall and round and frosted with aqua blue and white stripes circling its base while pink frosting drizzled down the sides. It was topped with white roses and aqua blue macarons and eighteen candles. Ireland didn't have to count them all to know that they were there.

The entire Washington family jumped out from behind the decorator wall and yelled, "Surprise!"

Ireland ugly sobbed. Snot bubbles probably hung out of her nose. She didn't care, which was a good thing because she couldn't have stopped crying if she'd wanted to.

"You said she was going to love this." Jade gave Mara a scandalized glance.

"Those are happy tears, baby girl," Jarrod said.

Grace wrapped Ireland up in a hug. "Happy birthday, sweetheart. When Mara said you guys were going out for dinner, we figured we could do a birthday breakfast instead."

"This is amazing. I *do* love it." She looked at Jade to make sure Jade heard that part. "Thank you."

Jarrod looked pleased. "Mara did most of it. But I made the cake."

"And I made the pancakes!" Jade said.

Grace shrugged. "I set the table. Figured there was no reason to be poisoning you on your birthday with my cooking."

Everyone sat down and ate pancakes together. Then they lit the candles and sang and waited for Ireland to blow the candles out so that they could cheer. Celebrating Ireland. Celebrating family. Celebrating together.

While they were eating the lemon raspberry confection perfection that was Ireland's birthday cake, Mara left the table and brought in a box with a big bow on it.

"But you've already done so much." Ireland would not let herself start ugly sobbing again. She'd just stopped, for crying out loud!

"Open it!" Jade insisted.

Ireland pulled off the bow and took off the lid so she could peer inside the box. Clothing. Brand-new with tags clothing. The only new item of clothing Ireland had ever owned was a free T-shirt a bank was giving away at the grocery store to try to get people to open accounts.

In the box, there were a new pair of jeans, a tee printed with a giraffe that was wearing sunglasses, a patchwork sweater in shades of blue and green, and two pairs of shoes—one flat and casual and the other heels. "This is so much. I don't know what to say! Thank you."

"That's not all!" Jade said.

Jarrod brought out one more box from under the table. "This is a special one," he said.

It was overwhelming to have received so much all at once, but Ireland eagerly opened the new box and gasped.

She reached out a hand to touch the delicate, sky-blue, lacy fabric before pulling the dress from the box. Ireland stood and held it up to her. The midi-length dress had a swing skirt that made Ireland want to rock back and forth just to see it swish. "It's beautiful! Thank you!"

"We wanted to stick to shades of blue to match your incredible eyes," Grace said with a smile, clearly pleased with her choices and with Ireland's reactions to the presents.

From there, the day was filled with a casual hanging-out vibe. Jarrod had to run into one of the bakeries because someone was sick, but other than that, it was chill.

Ireland's insides, on the other hand, felt anything but chill.

When it came time to get ready to go to Geppetto's, Mara insisted Ireland wear the blue dress, even though it was far too bougie for a pizza place.

Mara did Ireland's hair, but Ireland put her foot down when it came to the makeup. She wasn't really a makeup kind of person. Then they were off.

"And you promise I can leave anytime I want to?" Ireland asked.

"Of course. You're not a prisoner. This is going to be fun. It's pizza. And music. And looking at a seriously beautiful boy singing from a stage. What can be bad about that?"

"Only that I'm in a fight with that same beautiful boy."

Mara pulled into the parking lot. "What does that even mean? In a fight? It's not like the two of you are actively boxing. Why don't they ever call it 'in a silence'?"

"You are so weird." Ireland took a deep breath, smoothed her hands over the uneven hem of the dress, and said, "Let's get this over with."

Mara laughed. "Should I have my feelings hurt that you sound so fatalistic right now?"

They went into Geppetto's. Kal's band was already in the middle of a song. It was one of the ones that Asha had written—fun and punchy. The crowd was loving it.

As soon as Ireland entered, Kal's eyes were on her. He skipped a few words in the song, then picked things up again.

Kal never looked away from her, maintaining eye contact the entire time. When the song was over, Kal gripped the microphone and said into it, "Thank you all for being with us tonight. It's kind of a special day. It's a very special birthday for somebody who's pretty amazing."

People followed his eyeline to Ireland, and there were a few catcalls and *woo-hoo*s from the audience. Mara scooted Ireland to the table in the center front of the restaurant. Kal's eyes stayed on her. She wanted to adjust her clothing or her hair.

He smiled, but it was a sad smile. "So I'm going to tell a little story. I hope you'll all bear with me. I had a friend a while back, and we drifted apart. She fell into a bad crowd who made bad choices, and I wasn't there to help her. And then I *couldn't* help her because it was too late. Those choices took her life. I told myself I would never stand by and not do something to help when I was able to ever again. It seemed like an easy promise to make to myself.

"But then, in the name of doing the right thing, I broke a promise to someone else and ended up breaking the something special that I had with that someone. I never meant to hurt her. And I'd do anything to fix it. So this song is for her."

There were a few more catcalls, but then the crowd quieted along with the gentle strum on the guitar.

Kal began to sing.

> *Through the worst day's howling winds*
> *You taught me to howl out loud*
> *To stand up on my tripping feet*
> *Stand above the cruelest crowd*
> *I like it when you laugh*
> *I like it when you don't*
> *I guess I like you . . . however you want to . . .*
>   *be—except alone*
>
> *You are my North Star*
> *I'm anchored to your shore.*
> *You tell me to leave but how can I*
> *Ever sail from your world*
> *When you are everything*
> *Everything. Everything*
> *To me*
>
> *I asked you to be honest*
> *To share the storms you've known*

We'll heal each other's wounds
In each other, we'll find home
I like it when you laugh
I like it when you don't
I'm sayin' I love you . . . however you want to . . .
  be—except alone

You are my North Star
I'm anchored to your shore.
You tell me to leave but how can I
Ever sail from your world
When you are everything
Everything. Everything
To me

Perfectly imperfect me
I'm a wandering soul in tatters.
Stumbling rejection—self-reflection
You're the only thing that matters.
I like it when you laugh
I like it when you don't
I'm howlin' I love you . . . however you want to . . .
  be—except alone

You are my North Star
I'm anchored to your shore.
You tell me to leave but how can I
Ever sail from your world
When you are everything
Everything. Everything
To me

The last chords played and the crowd went crazy. "Happy Birthday, Ireland," Kal said into the mic.

As Kal got down from the stage, the crowd broke out into an impromptu song of "Happy Birthday." Tears streamed down Ireland's face, and she briefly thought how glad she was that she hadn't let Mara put makeup on her.

Kal stood in front of her. "I'm really sorry."

There was no tell. No facial tic revealing a lie. Kal was truly sorry. It was wrong for her to hold him accountable for all the wrongs and lies of her father. He had his reasons for trying to find help. She had been incredibly shortsighted not to see his point of view. "I'm sorry too." She then reached up and hugged him tightly. "Thank you for giving me some time to figure it out."

People in the crowd started a chant of "kiss her, kiss her!"

The tightness that had been in Ireland's chest had finally gone, and she could see Kal clearly, better than she ever had before. She leaned toward him, pulled by his gravity. She tilted her head up. His eyes dropped down to her mouth before locking onto her gaze.

"Seems a shame to disappoint them on my birthday," she said.

Kal barked a laugh at her words. "I would never disagree with that."

Ireland looked up into his beautiful brown eyes and thought how appropriate his lyrics had been. But he was wrong about one thing. She was not his North Star. He was hers.

She tugged lightly on his shirt and pulled him down into a kiss. Not because the crowd wanted her to, but because *she* wanted to.

The world seemed to melt away until there was nothing but the notes of Kal's song ringing in her ears and the warmth of his mouth on hers. She could feel his heart beating a steady rhythm under the palm of her hand on his chest. Everything was going to be okay. She was home.

CHAPTER TWENTY-FOUR
Ireland

Ireland and Mara made it to school early on Monday morning. It was time to go back. They had faced the crowds on Saturday night, and everything had been fine. And sure, there would probably be rumors and gossip in the halls, but it would be okay because they had each other's support.

They had to arrive early because the mural still needed to be finished, and it was important to get it done. The other members of the art club had worked on it a lot over the week prior while Mara and Ireland had been away, but they hadn't finished. Ireland was secretly glad it had taken them longer than they had thought because it meant she got to be part of completing the project she had helped to start.

As Ireland's eyes trailed over the various images and words that made up the school mural, she felt all the ways it showed the individuality of each student while also showing how they all fit together.

Asha, Cooper, Sophie, Julianna, Charisma, and, of course, Kal and Mara were all there. They each had their sections to work on. With paintbrushes in hand, they unified the individual images into one cohesive piece. Mr. Wasden was there as well, guiding them in the ways that they could smooth the images together so that it all worked.

When they were done, they invited the principal to come and see. She stood in front of the mural for a long time. Ireland hoped that the principal could see the mural the way she did: as a collaboration that bound the students together.

"Well, Mr. Wasden. It's an ambitious project, but you and your students managed to pull it off beautifully. I think we should go ahead and keep it."

The art club cheered and clapped and high-fived one another. They gathered up all the supplies and put them away. Ireland went to Janice to borrow some of the cleaning supplies to make sure that the space was perfect. She didn't want Janice to have to clean up after them. With all of the art club working together, the cleanup went by fast enough that they would be a few minutes early for their first class.

Kal took Ireland's hand in his own and they walked to class together. Ireland let out a contented sigh.

"Happy?" Kal asked.

"I really am." *I really am*, she repeated in her head. Because Ireland realized she had been right on that cold night alone in her bathroom.

Being a homeless teenager had not been the worst thing that could happen. That was one of the top-ten truths Ireland Raine had told herself because it had led her to this moment, when she was safe and she was warm and she was loved.

Acknowledgments

Confession: High school was not my favorite. With the exceptions of my handful of amazing best friends, the boy I dated who grew up to be the man I married, and the rare, super-excellent teacher every now and again, I dreaded almost every minute of my high school career. I had a target on my back when it came to a few of the most-popular girls. I don't know why, because I was quiet and tried hard to mind my own business and stay out of everyone's way. But for whatever reason, those girls hated me. I can still recall the flames of humiliation from their torture. Had there been cell phones and TikTok back then, the videos of them bullying me likely would have gone viral.

So, if high school is not your favorite either, it's okay. You are not alone. The people who care about you are the ones who matter in the grand scheme of things and the ones who don't . . . don't matter at all.

If you read the above, you likely noticed that the boy I dated grew up to be the man I married. Some high school romances really are the real deal. This book would not be possible without my high school romance, my first kiss, and my first love: Scott

Wright, who supports my every dream and who makes me laugh as often as he makes me roll my eyes. Thanks for holding my hand through the good and the bad. I love you more than Juliet loves Romeo, than Bella loves Edward, than Elizabeth loves Mr. Darcy. What I'm trying to say is I love you *harifrån till evigheten. Du är min alltid.*

To my kids and grandkids: I love our family group chats with the gifs, memes, and jokes. You all make me so proud. I know I've always had a career, but you people are, hands down, my greatest accomplishment. You are my joy.

Heidi Gordon, from the moment you asked me to go to lunch with you to discuss a career with Shadow Mountain, you have been someone I can count on—not just as my product manager, but as my friend. I am so grateful for that encounter and for you. This book is all because of you and your mind and your vision. And yeah, I changed it a lot from that first conversation, but *you* are its creator.

Lisa Mangum, my editor and dear friend: I so appreciate that you and Maddie Senator help me be a better writer, thank you! And Lisa, thanks for being willing to do the 360 photo booth with me when I was feeling insecure about doing it on my own. And for everyone at Shadow Mountain who put so much of your hearts into my projects, I appreciate you all so much! Special shout-out to Halle Ballingham for her work on this amazing cover, and to Karl-Erik Bennion for his artistic additions. They made the cover something that shines.

Heather Moore, you are my favorite first reader. I love the little smiley faces and great insights you leave when you help me with an edit. You make me more than just a better writer. You make me a better human. Thank you for being my friend. Thank you, Sarah John, for all the brainstorming and workshopping of this story. Both you and Heather are the best road-trip buddies.

I recently spent a weekend with some of my writing friends, and it is a fact that I would not be where I am today without those friends encouraging me and driving me to improve (and let's be honest—for listening to me whine). There is not enough paper and ink to name all the people in the writing community who inspire and uplift me, but you know who you are. Thank you.

I owe a lot to my parents. Hi, Mom and Dad! You did a good job. We all turned out great—even Gary. (Okay, okay, especially Gary.)

Finally, thank you, dear reader. Without you, I would be entirely unnecessary.

Discussion Questions

1. Ireland faces some bullying directly related to her being un-housed. How does Ireland's experience of being unhoused challenge common stereotypes and misconceptions about un-housed youth?

2. Ireland jokes about her housing situation when she's alone, but it's also something she is embarrassed about and doesn't want anyone to know. How does Ireland's secret of being unhoused impact her self-perception and interactions with others, especially Kal? How does she navigate the challenges of being a high school student while living in secret?

3. The mural creates an opportunity for connection between students. In what ways does art serve as a means of expression and communication in the novel, particularly through the school mural and the anonymous messages exchanged by Ireland and Mara?

4. Mara and Ireland don't like each other due to some of their pre-conceived assumptions about each other. In what ways does Ireland's rivalry and then friendship with Mara reflect the novel's broader themes of trust, betrayal, and forgiveness?

5. How does the anonymous exchange of messages on the school mural symbolize the power of connection, empathy, and understanding between individuals, especially in the face of adversity?

6. Let's talk about hard things and explore the theme of resilience. How does Ireland maintain her optimism and hope despite facing numerous challenges and hardships?

7. Discuss the role of community and support systems (or lack thereof) for Ireland as an unhoused teenager. How do societal attitudes and policies contribute to her struggles?

8. Kal is nicknamed "Superman" and is accused of having a "saving-people-complex." How does Kal grow throughout the novel? What motivates his decision to reveal Ireland's secret, and how does this decision affect his relationship with Ireland?

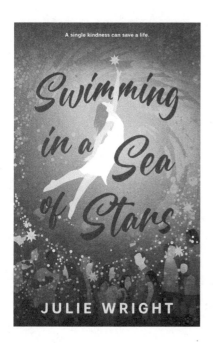